SHIP OF DREAMS

BOOK #2

REBECCA HEFLIN

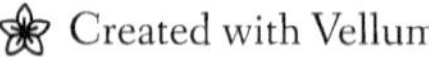 Created with Vellum

ACKNOWLEDGMENTS

To Yvonne,
You know why.

Though this is a re-release of SHIP OF DREAMS, I'd like to, once again, thank my ensemble of beta readers for this book: Lynda, Yvonne, Susan, Paul, and of course, my hubby, Ron. Your feedback is invaluable. And Ron, thanks for correcting my golf mistakes.

I also owe a debt of gratitude to Ryan and Ashely, my very own advertising couple who kept me out of the weeds when it came to all things advertising. Any mistakes in my portrayal of this profession are my own.

To my fashionista friend, Nina, thanks for helping me find the perfect wedding dress for my heroine.

Finally, thanks to my readers. Without you, my stories wouldn't be possible.

QUOTE

The course to true love never did run smooth.

— Shakespeare

CHAPTER ONE

Laura Armstrong strode toward the building housing the New York offices of Imperial Cruise Lines. Her stiletto heels clicked a staccato on the sidewalk as she tested the limits of her snug pencil skirt.

Tapping out a message on her smartphone, her mind five steps ahead, she nearly took a header when the heel of her shoe plunged into a sidewalk seam. The text message all but forgotten, she twisted and turned, unable to dislodge the stubborn heel.

Risking a tear in the cherry-red patent leather of her sky-high Louboutin ankle-straps—the ones with the plunging vamp revealing her sexy toe cleavage—wasn't an option. But between the ankle-strap and her figure-hugging skirt, she couldn't slip out of the shoe, nor could she bend over and unfasten it either.

Perfect. She'd be late for her meeting with Imperial's CEO.

Daddy Dearest thought Giddings-Rose couldn't handle an account the size of Imperial. Check that. He thought she couldn't win an account the size of Imperial.

Determined to prove her father wrong, she'd get the account and the corner office. That was, if she could pry her heel out of the sidewalk.

Bustling New Yorkers in suits and skirts just stepped around her, dodging her like an out-of-place trashcan. "Well, sh—"

"Hold still, sugar, or you'll break the heel."

The masculine voice called to mind the mellow sweetness of the fine Kentucky bourbon she'd once sipped at the Derby. Rich and mellifluous, with a hint of Southern graciousness. Even so, there was no denying the authoritative tone. "And that would be a damn shame." The hand that wrapped around her ankle from behind was broad and masculine, but well-manicured, topped with an elegant Cartier watch.

Not her type. She preferred her men with a little more grit than polish. So why did tantalizing warmth spread up her leg?

With adept fingers, he unbuckled the ankle strap and lifted her foot from the still-lodged shoe. Having no other choice to avoid either resting her bare foot on the filthy Manhattan sidewalk or the humiliation of falling on her face, she reached back and grabbed his shoulder.

Hmm. No padding there. Nothing but muscle beneath that expensive tropical-weight wool suit. She caught a glimpse of charcoal-gray fabric, dark hair, and Italian shoes in rich mahogany leather.

But she'd yet to lay eyes on her rescuer's face.

Nathan Maxwell took advantage of the up-close and personal view. Trim ankles met shapely, muscular calves, and judging from the fit of her skirt, a firm derriere topped off those swimsuit-model legs. Beneath his touch, soft skin beckoned further exploration. Long, honey-blond hair hung almost to her waist in a sleek ponytail. The fragrance of her haute couture perfume drifted over him, reminding him of magnolia-scented summer nights.

Focusing on the task at hand, he gently pried the heel from the sidewalk seam and examined it. "No harm done." He grasped her ankle and settled her foot back into the shoe and fastened the strap, but not before noticing the firecracker red nail polish. He laughed. "Here you go, Cinderella."

The warmth of his laugh slid over her, knocking her a little off balance even though she'd placed her foot firmly back on the ground. "Thank you, uh . . ." She turned and looked up into golden-brown eyes the color of that same sweet Kentucky bourbon.

"Nathan, Nathan Maxwell. My pleasure, ma'am." He flashed a devastating grin, igniting gilded sparks in his eyes.

There was that southern drawl again—subtle, like the peach undertones of a fine pinot gris. "You're not from around here, are you?" she asked.

Her sardonic smile weakened Nathan's knees more than any toothy grin ever did. "My accent give me away?"

"No, your courtesy."

Nathan chuckled. "My grandmother would have expected nothing less." The woman's eyes, cool blue like the May sky overhead, captured his and held. No shrinking violet, this one, he mused. A full, determined mouth painted to match the red of her toenails set off an arresting face with high cheekbones, a stubborn chin, and aquiline nose.

"Well, thank you, Nathan." Maybe she should add suave, polished men with a hint of Rhett Butler to her menu, Laura thought. Her phone, all but forgotten in her hand, buzzed. "I, uh, I've got to go. Thanks again, Nathan

Maxwell." Something about the way his name rolled off her tongue . . .

"This is Laura," she said into her phone as she walked away.

Nathan watched as she strode down the sidewalk, hips swaying to some inherent rhythm. "Come on, Laura, glance back." She turned and gave him what he wanted, another glimpse of that bold, beautiful face.

"It's going to be a great day." Glancing at his watch, satisfied with the outcome of the errand that brought him to this part of Manhattan in the first place, he hailed a cab back to his office.

———

Giving herself a mental snap-out-of-it slap to shake the charming Rhett Butler from her thoughts and focus on the goal, Laura briefed Katie, the head of the Giddings-Rose research team, on her latest project.

"I'm going to need the demographics on Imperial Cruise Lines, and its three closest competitors, ASAP."

"We're going after Imperial? What happened to Kendall-Monroe?"

"Fired. And use your street team to find out the inside scoop on Kendall-Monroe and Hawk Media. I'm on my way to meet with the CEO of Imperial now."

"Damn, woman, you work fast."

"Jackson Jefferies is a long-time friend of the family, so getting a sit down was easy. Convincing him to listen to someone besides my father is a different story."

Jackson Jeffries was the CEO of the cruise line, one of her father's closest friends . . . and one of her father's best customers. Her family's shipbuilding business built Imperial's liners, and Jackson relied heavily on her father's counsel.

While at her best friend's wedding over the weekend, Laura's father had received an email from Jackson saying they'd fired their advertising agency. Since her irksome father had already given a competitor agency a heads-up that Imperial was in the market, time was of the essence.

"If anyone can convince him, it's you. You could sell moonshine to a teetotaler."

"Thanks. I think. Anyway, wish me luck."

"Good luck. And call me when you're done."

Laura stashed her phone and entered the cool two-story lobby, walking directly to the security desk. After signing in, she took the elevators to the top floor for one of the most important meetings of her career.

A full-service advertising agency, Giddings-Rose had made a name for itself creating ad campaigns for traditional Fortune 500 companies, including insurance companies, department stores, banks, airlines, and manufacturers. But Laura's goal was to drag Giddings-Rose kicking and screaming into the twenty-first century, with accounts who wanted rich media campaigns, digital brand development, interactive marketing and communications strategy, and pay-per-click campaign management. The future of advertising.

When she'd first approached Curt, the agency's VP of Business Development, about Imperial and its needs he'd been skeptical, but the agency couldn't count a cruise line among its accounts, and having one would look good in its portfolio. And on his resume.

"What do you want, Laura?" Curt had asked.

She'd used her tough-minded skills on him. "I *want* your

job, but I bring you Imperial, I'll take the VP of Client Management that's coming open."

"You bring me Imperial, and we'll talk about it."

"No." She approached his desk. "I've reeled in some big fish for this agency. It's time I reaped the rewards of all that hard work. Dammit, Curt, you know I deserve it."

Curt held her gaze. "I know. Look, I'll go to bat for you, but I can't promise anything."

"That's all I'm asking. Thanks, Curt."

The elevator doors opened on the lobby of Imperial Cruise Lines, bringing Laura back to the present. She took a deep breath and stepped onto the polished marble floor with all the determination of a gladiator stepping into the Roman Colosseum. "Showtime."

———

Nathan sat down at his desk, as his assistant followed him in with phone messages and meeting requests. He'd only been at Hawk Media a week and he already had a full schedule.

"Mr. McCutcheon would like to see you when you get a moment, and I need you to sign these forms for your corporate credit card." Cassie placed the stack of messages on the desk and handed him the forms.

"Thanks, Cassie. This credit card can't come soon enough. I need you to book a trip for me. Here's all the information." Nathan handed her a brochure with the ship circled. He didn't care what itinerary, as long as he got on that ship. He'd already completed the company's travel profile so Cassie would know his preferences. "And I need it booked first thing."

Cassie took the brochure, lifting a brow. "Is this business or pleasure?"

"Oh, this is business, but who says they're mutually exclusive?" He gave her a wink as he rounded his desk.

The corridors of Hawk Media were hushed, the plush carpeting lending a soft touch to the otherwise glass and brushed chrome ultra-modern office space. The account executives whose offices lined the halls were hard at work, studying spreadsheets, talking on phones, tapping out emails, or meeting with members of their teams. A group stood in front of an oversized digital white board in what served as the agency's idea space, throwing suggestions up on the board.

The nimble mid-size company had only been around a little over ten years, but they were making a splash in the ad biz, especially after they'd snatched the Kensington hotel chain right out from under Concept Advertising.

They'd done the same thing with him.

Hawk Media had wooed his biggest account away from him, but while the CEO preferred the New York-based agency's philosophy, he'd told Hawk that Nathan was part of the package. So after almost ten years with the same boutique agency in Atlanta, first as an account coordinator, before working his way up to senior account executive, Hawk had come calling. And Nathan had listened. In the immortal words of Don Corleone, "They'd made him an offer he couldn't refuse."

Though it broke his heart to leave behind his Buckhead home and the proximity to his sister, the siren song of the Big Apple couldn't be ignored, and the position, Vice President of Business Development, the salary, and the bonuses were too good to pass up. Especially now when he needed the money.

He'd make a name for himself in the big city. Not bad for a boy from the hills of North Georgia who'd once been told he'd never be more than a whore's bastard.

First order of business—get the Imperial Cruise Lines account.

"You needed to see me?"

Hawk glanced up from his sleek computer. "Yes. Have a seat."

At only forty-six, Hawk McCutcheon was on a high-speed trajectory to success. His blond locks lent him a devil-may-care surfer look, but those who judged the book by its cover did so at their own peril. A former All-American quarterback, he played by the rules, but that didn't mean he didn't play a tough game. And while he had an easy smile and a generous nature, he expected one-hundred-ten-percent from his employees.

Family photos ranged the credenza behind his immaculate Lucite desk, including one of him and his father, U.S. Senator Mitchell McCutcheon, at the President's inauguration ball. Star-studded lifestyle notwithstanding, according to his employees, Hawk was a tried and true family man.

"Where are we on Imperial Cruise Lines?" Hawk eyed him over a pair of reading glasses.

"Cassie's booking my trip as we speak—on the *Nave dei Sogni*—the first availability. Research team is pulling demographics, financials, and current marketing collateral, and the same information on Imperial's three closest competitors. Word on the street is Imperial is seeking to lower its age demographic, attract younger, more dynamic clientele, with lots of sports and entertainment dollars to spend. And they're building a smaller liner with an eye toward uncompromising quality and an even higher staff-to-guest ratio to do it.

"We already have the data on the spending habits of this demographic," Nathan continued, "we just need to do some number crunching. Imperial is looking for interactive marketing services for the digital space. They fired Kendall-Monroe because the agency's ideas were . . . 'antediluvian,' to use the Junior Jeffries' term.

"Well, we'll deliver fresh, innovative ideas that will blow any competition out of the water. Pun intended," Hawk finished with a grin. His expression grew determined as he tapped the desk with his finger, "I want this account and you're just the man to get it for me."

———

Jackson's assistant escorted Laura into a modest-sized, but well-appointed office. Behind the mahogany desk sat a man, that although her father's contemporary, appeared years younger. His thick pewter and silver hair, tanned, clean-shaven face, and ready smile gave Jackson Jeffries the appearance of a well-aged movie star.

He rose as she approached his desk, his gray eyes alight with approval as he appraised her. "Little Laura Armstrong has grown into a beautiful, poised young lady. How did that happen? Last I saw you, you were headed off to college."

She smiled at the compliment. "That was a decade ago."

"Has it been that long?" He indicated a group of chairs around a beautifully-restored leather steamer trunk that served as a coffee table. Models of Imperial's ships, old and new, ranged the office on their own wood pedestals, down-lighting illuminating every detail. Photos of dignitaries from around the world covered the walls.

It was a comfortable office. A well-lived-in office. Not the showplace she'd expected from the CEO of one of the world's most prestigious ultra-luxury cruise lines. But then again, she had memories of Jackson as a kind, unassuming man. One who actually loved his wife and children and didn't put the importance of the bottom line ahead of his family.

"And now you're with an advertising agency, and you'd like to talk to me about Imperial's business." He leaned forward, propping his elbows on his knees.

"Yes." Despite his humble demeanor, he always could cut to the chase.

"All right. I'm game. Tell me about your agency."

Before she could start her pitch, the office door opened and a tall, good-looking younger version of Jackson entered the room. Same thick hair, but light brown with hints of premature gray at the temples, same gray eyes, same ready smile. The apple didn't fall far from the tree.

She remembered Jackson Junior, or Jack, from dinners at the country club, golf outings, parties at her parents' house, and high school. She'd tried her sixteen-year-old girl's wiles on him. Four years older, he hadn't been impressed, having eyes only for Miss New York and his girlfriend at the time, Stephanie Smallwood. They'd married after college, only to get divorced five years later.

"Jack, you remember Milt's daughter, Laura."

"Yes." His eyes lit up. "Of course."

"Laura was about to tell me a little about her agency–"

"Giddings-Rose," she supplied.

"Giddings-Rose?" Jack interjected. "Laura, I should tell you, we aren't looking for a traditional Madison Avenue agency. We already fired Kendall-Moore. We want to move into the digital age, freshen our brand and broaden our consumer base, with a focus on a younger demographic."

"You're speaking my language," Laura said with a grin.

Jackson beamed at his son. "Jack is our Vice President of Customer Relations and he's been pushing for Imperial to enter the age of social media." He chuckled. "What I know about social media could fit in a thimble."

Laura jumped in with both feet. "Imperial has catered to the older wealthy client, but with that clientele dying off, the line needs to refocus its brand on a younger demographic, people my age, with copious amounts of discretionary income."

Jackson Senior and Junior eyed one another.

Jackson spoke first. "We had that in mind when we designed the newest ship—"

"The *Nave dei Sogni*," Laura interjected.

"That's right," Jackson said, "and its itineraries, shore excursions and onboard activities, but we haven't been able to reach that client. Now we're building a new, smaller four-hundred-fifty passenger liner—the ultimate boutique ship—"

Jack interrupted, "—which will offer unstructured cruises that give passengers the feel that they are truly on a personal yacht. This won't be your grandparents' cruise. Most passengers on the *Sogni* have been our usual clientele, perplexed by the offerings. The only people your age we get on the ship are there because it's their parents' or grandparents' anniversary or birthday."

"Forget what you think you know about Giddings-Rose," Laura started her pitch. "We have the finest creative team in the business, with two Webbys, five ADDYs, one Mosaic, and fifty years of experience combined, the media buying power of the large agency we are, but with the digital savvy of an interactive agency. We give you the best of both worlds. Strategic planning, web design and development, search engine marketing, digital lead generation, digital brand development, rich media campaigns, interactive marketing and communications strategy, data mining, and ROI assessment." She took a breath.

"You don't have a cruise line in your client roster," Jack pointed out.

"No, we don't, but we do have an international airline and a five-star hotel chain on our books, plus one of the world's top travel companies, so we have experience in the high-end travel and hospitality industry."

Jackson glanced at his son and nodded. "Okay. We'll give Giddings-Rose a shot."

"But your initial research and creative is on spec," Jack added. "We'll expect your pitch the end of July, but we'll have a pre-pitch meeting with both agencies before that. We'll be in touch to set that up."

Laura stuck her hand out to Jackson. "Thank you."

"It's a pleasure to see you again." Jackson covered their clasped hands with his other hand. "You truly have grown into a beautiful woman."

"Thank you, Jackson."

"I'll walk you out." Jack guided Laura through the door. "How did we not know you worked for an ad agency?"

She raised an eyebrow. "Have you met my father?"

Jack laughed. "Right. Then how did you find out we were looking?"

"My father blurted it out, forgetting his daughter was in the business." If he even knew in the first place.

"Maybe that's a good thing. A little competition never hurt anyone, and Imperial can only benefit."

They'd arrived at the elevators. "My father was right," Jack said, his face earnest.

"About what?" Laura turned to face him.

"That you've grown into a beautiful woman."

Alrighty then. "Flattery will get you everywhere, Jack, but I think I'm the one who should be sucking up to you."

"Then you can start sucking up by having dinner with me."

She tilted her head as the elevator dinged. "Perhaps." She stepped into the elevator and turned around. Just before the doors closed, she said, "Call me."

CHAPTER TWO

L ater that same day, Nathan sat at the head of the conference room table surrounded by representatives from the various departments. Imperial wasn't the only account on his plate.

Hawk Media began as an interactive agency, but over the last five years had grown into a more agile version of a full-service agency, complete with creative and production departments, strategic market planning, and media buying. But digital and social media still remained at the core of Hawk's services.

Today's meeting involved a tech giant ready to roll out its latest technology in just eight months, which put Hawk Media under the gun to plan and implement the campaign for its launch two months earlier in order to stimulate antici-pation in their users and users-to-be.

An existing account, the agency had gigabytes of analytics on the company, so it was a matter of defining the message, creating the collateral and the print and digital ads, and buying the media.

Nathan needed to get his head in the game, but his

mind kept drifting to that morning's sidewalk encounter. Who was she? What did she do? Where did she live? Was she single? Married? Maybe she was a lesbian. He frowned at either possibility.

"Nathan? Did you have an issue with the latest timeline?"

He glanced up to see Pramod standing in front of the digital white board, a perplexed look on his face. "Hmm? Oh. No. It's fine, why?"

"You had a frown on your face."

Chagrin washed over him. "Oh. It's nothing. Sorry. Please continue."

"Right."

Get it together, Nathan. Hawk Media didn't hire you to daydream about women. Well, not women, but one woman in particular. One woman who'd left a definite impression after such a brief encounter.

———

"Talk to me," Laura said as soon as Katie answered the phone.

"First, how'd it go?"

"I wouldn't be asking for numbers if I didn't need them."

"Hot damn."

"And I think I might have a date with Jackson Junior."

"No shit?" Katie laughed. "I so want to be you."

"So, talk numbers to me, baby." Laura dodged harried pedestrians, as she listened to Katie's rundown on Imperial Cruise Lines.

"The average income of the cruise line's customers is five hundred K. Average age is between forty-five and sixty-five, so you're about fifteen years early to the party, which is good, since word is that's the demographic they're looking to entice."

"That's what Jackson said. Perfect," Laura interjected.

"I've been poking around on their website, and boy, Imperial doesn't pull any punches when it comes to pampering its guests with all-suite, all-veranda staterooms, five-star dining, a spa that puts Guerlain to shame—not that I've been there mind you, but I've drooled over pictures—staterooms that offer elegant furnishings, Bang & Olufson sound systems, fresh flowers daily, and Egyptian cotton linens. But they really need to update to responsive formatting for their website."

Laura flipped through the rather pedestrian, traditional brochure she'd picked up, as she walked along East Seventy-Sixth Street toward her office building. Ignoring the need for updated collateral, she skimmed the contents. She knew Imperial catered to those with discerning tastes and the money to appease those tastes, but she didn't expect to be so . . . wowed by the line's luxurious offerings. After all, she'd stayed in her fair share of five-star hotels and resorts around the world.

Turning down Madison Avenue, she told herself to look away from the Louboutin store window. *Since when did I ever do what I was told?*

"Holy crap! You should see this penthouse stateroom," Katie continued. "The bathroom is bigger than my apartment. The ship is like a floating Four Seasons. No, it's like a floating Four Seasons on crack."

At Laura's silence, Katie prodded, "Are you listening to me, or are you standing in front of the Louboutin window drooling?"

"No. Okay, yes. But they have this pair of hot pink satin pumps. And I swear they're calling my name."

"You and your shoes. Focus, Imelda."

"Right. I have enough shoes anyway. Said no one. Ever." If there was one thing that could distract her, it was shoes, of the über expensive variety. Well, that and a hot man—preferably one with an accent. "Okay. I'm back." With one last glance at the delicious window display, she refocused her attention. "What else you got?"

"Two of their ships, the *Sogni D'oro* and the *Fantasia*, carry approximately fifteen hundred passengers, but their newest addition to the fleet is a thousand-passenger ultra-luxury liner they've christened *Nave dei Sogni*."

"Right. *Ship of Dreams*," Laura muttered to herself. "That's the one I want." Fitting. "Ask Sanjita to make the arrangements—the earliest date possible. And I want the penthouse."

"But—"

"I'll personally make up the difference in cost. No one will ever suspect an occupant of the penthouse is an account executive. Let me know if I need to pull a few strings with Jackson."

"Damn, Laura. I repeat, I want to be you," Katie huffed out.

"Not if I don't get this account, so have Sanjita get me on that ship. ASAP."

———

"How's the honeymoon?" Laura set aside the spreadsheets Katie had created on Imperial, and took a few minutes to prop up her feet, and catch up with the new Mrs. Darcy Butler Ryan, her newlywed best friend.

A half-eaten salad sat on her desk, long abandoned in her analysis of the numbers.

"Oh, Laura, it's so romantic. Long walks on the beach, candlelight dinners, breakfast in bed." Darcy sighed. "It's perfect."

Laura rolled her eyes at Darcy's effusive, dreamy description, but she couldn't be happier for her. After years of searching for the perfect man, Darcy finally found him right under her nose—in the form of her best guy-friend, Josh Ryan.

Now they were spending two weeks at the Four Seasons in Nevis. "And how is the ambulance chaser? Missing the sound of sirens yet?" She couldn't resist, even though she knew Josh didn't practice personal injury law. She and Josh had a long-running battle over who could deliver the sharpest jab.

"Are you two going to poke at one another until we're old and gray? Besides, he's a mediator now, not a lawyer."

"Just because he's your husband doesn't mean I can't use him for target practice. And once a shyster, always a shyster. But on to more important things. How's the sex?"

"Laura Danforth Armstrong, I am not going to discuss my *married* sex life with you. It's too personal."

Laura winced at the use of her middle name—her mother's maiden name. "Can't blame a girl for trying." She accepted a note from Sanjita, glanced at it, and nodded in response. "Come on, throw me a bone. I've hit a dry spell."

"What, no hot new guy with a sexy accent?"

Laura had an affinity for men with foreign accents. Darcy once accused her of hanging out at the U.N. to pick up guys. She thought about Jack Jeffries, but quickly moved on to her knight-in-tropical-weight-wool. Tall, good-looking Nathan.

He had a sexy accent—a Southern one. And a devilish grin. "No, and I won't have time in the weeks ahead, anyway. Which reminds me, I won't be home when you get back so you'll have to save the vacation slide show for later."

"Why, what's up?"

"Remember that cruise line shopping for an ad agency? Well, I'm going after it, and I leave that week for a ten-day Mediterranean cruise."

"You have such a tough life."

Laura laughed. "Said the pot to the kettle. Let's see, two weeks in Nevis this month, followed by two weeks in Napa and Sonoma after you return." Laura and Josh had thrown aside their rivalry to surprise Darcy with a two-week trip for her thirtieth birthday. A best-selling romance author, Darcy's next series was set in California Wine Country. They thought the trip would jumpstart the inspiration. And, at the time, give Darcy a much-needed break from her all-out pursuit of Mr. Right.

"Lots of men with accents on that trip."

"Yes, but most will be old enough to be my grandfather."

"Well, don't injure yourself playing shuffleboard in hooker heels."

"I'll try not to. Gotta run. I've got some work to finish up, and my personal shopper from Neiman's called. I see a new bikini and maybe a slinky new dress or two in my future."

"I repeat, you have such a tough life."

———

Drawing the tie from his neck, Nathan walked through the door of Hawk Media's corporate Upper East Side apartment and dropped his briefcase on the floor beside the foyer table.

Boxes still stood, waiting to be unpacked. He'd had no time to settle in, so far unpacking only the essentials. Since the apartment was furnished, his own furnishings were in storage until he could find a place to buy.

Something with a view, he thought, or maybe something with a tidy yard. Of course, he'd pay twice as much in New York for a place half the size of his home in Atlanta. But the farm came first.

The boxes would have to wait a little longer. His days would be long until he left for the cruise in two weeks. And after he returned, who knew when he'd get around to them. Grabbing a glass from the cabinet, he opened the bottle of scotch he'd managed to unearth last night and poured two fingers. Toasting himself, he let the honeyed warmth glide down his throat.

And, leaning against the counter, thought again of Laura.

For the life of him, he couldn't figure out why he didn't ask for her number. Or at least her last name. Oh yeah, because he wasn't after women. He was after a certain cruise line account. Not, he thought, that she would have given him her information even if he'd asked for it.

Funny, as a leg man, he'd have thought those long sexy legs of hers would have been the main feature he'd remember about her. Especially since he'd had his hand wrapped around one of those legs.

But it wasn't the first thing that came to mind when he thought of Laura. It was her eyes. Cool and deep like a mountain lake. Then there was that mouth. Full lips, a half smile that formed a hint of a dimple at the very corner. A very kissable mouth, that.

Scrubbing his hand through his hair, he reminded himself he had no time to fantasize about what else that enticing mouth could do. Odds were, in a city this big, he'd never see her again anyway.

Swallowing the rest of the scotch, he retrieved his briefcase for the spreadsheets he'd be up half the night poring over.

———

Fishing the last shrimp from her Pad Thai, Laura popped it in her mouth before resuming her draft of the creative brief for a clothing line by a hot new designer. The BoHo clothes didn't suit Laura's taste level, but that didn't mean she couldn't work up a kick-ass creative brief.

In the hush of the office—everyone else having left a couple of hours earlier—Adele sang softly from the computer about turning tables. Another hour, two at the most, and she'd have it finished. Then she could head home for her hot date . . . with a Brad Pitt movie on Netflix.

She jumped at the knock on her door and coughed as she almost swallowed the lump of partially-chewed crustacean. "Jesus, Curt, you scared me. I thought I was the only one left."

He smothered a chuckle. "Sorry about that. I saw a light on and came to investigate." He approached her desk and slumped into a chair. "Why are you still here?"

"I'm finalizing the creative brief for the Kim Sun Lee account."

"I didn't think the team needed that for another two weeks yet."

Laura shrugged. "No sense in waiting when I can get it done now."

He looked around her office, then out the window at the dimming summer light. "No, why are you still here?" He glanced at his watch. "It's almost eight-thirty on a Friday night." He eyed the spreadsheets, sketches, and notes piled on her desk alongside the takeout boxes. The half-finished bottle of water. The diet soda can. "Don't you have a home?"

"I could ask you the same thing," she pointed out as her fingers continued to fly over the keys, glancing up in time to see his soft, sad smile that said *touché*.

"Shelby's visiting her sister in Maine, and the kids are at a sleepover. I thought I'd catch up on a few things."

"Same here. Since I'm leaving in a couple of weeks, I want everything in order before then." That, and her parents were in Manhattan and had asked her to join them for dinner. Well, her *mother* had asked her to join them, anyway. So she'd needed an excuse. To hide.

Hiding. *That's* what she was actually doing. Hiding from her parents. Just like she'd done when she was a teenager. Only then she'd done her hiding at Darcy's.

"Come on." He picked up a container and, looking in it to find it empty, tossed it into the trash. "Let's go. I'll buy you a drink, then see you home."

"Curt, you don't have to do that."

"I know I don't. Let's go. That's an order. Besides, I have something to talk to you about."

Laura hesitated a moment, wondering what he needed to speak with her about. "All right." Saving her work, she clicked off her computer and grabbed her purse and tote bag.

———

"So what is it you need to talk with me about?" Laura asked, as she took a seat at a table in a trendy little bar on East Seventy-Sixth Street, not far from Giddings-Rose.

"Let's order first," Curt said, as the waitress approached their table.

"Come on, Curt, you're killing me here." Getting nothing else from him, she relented and ordered a Sonoma Cab. She wanted something stronger, but decided against it, in case the topic turned serious.

Curt ordered a scotch, neat, and the waitress left to get their drinks.

Laura leaned across the table. "Are you going to keep me in suspense all night?"

"I don't know. I might. It's not often I see the unflappable Laura Armstrong squirm. It's kinda fun." His face bore a mischievous expression.

"Fine." She folded her arms and gazed out the window at the pedestrians. The only telltale sign of her anxiety the bouncing of her leg beneath the table.

Curt chuckled.

The waitress delivered their drinks, and after taking a sip of his scotch, he spoke. "You asked me to talk to Duncan about a vice president position for you."

She paused a moment, with the wineglass halfway between the table and her mouth, before regaining her composure long enough to take a sip of her wine. She nonchalantly reached under the table and placed her other hand on her still-bouncing leg. Duncan Giddings was the agency's CEO, and the third generation Giddings to run the agency.

"As you know, Dave is retiring in August, and we'll need to fill the opening. Also as you know, Giddings-Rose likes to promote from within."

Laura held back a groan. Curt could be rather long-winded and often circled his point like a plane circling LaGuardia Airport. There was one other candidate whom she thought had a shot at the position, Rusty Maltby.

He'd been with the firm two years longer than she and he'd recently scored an international cosmetics line. But he'd also gotten drunk at the last holiday office party and made a pass at Duncan's trophy wife. *Woops*. The only reason he didn't get canned was because he didn't know the woman was the latest in a long line of Mrs. Giddings.

"I met with Duncan this morning. It was a good meeting . . ."

As Curt waxed on about the various topics of discussion, Laura's frustration grew. Just when she'd begun to think there was no point to the story even remotely connected to her, if any such point existed at all, he said, "So, if you bring in the Imperial account, the job is yours for the taking."

"Wait. What?"

"The job. It's yours if you bring us Imperial."

Her leg started bouncing again. Her poker face firmly in place, she nodded, while inside she was doing a fist-pump. "Thank you, Curt. I appreciate you going to bat for me. I won't let you down."

With the pitch set for the end of July, she could be a vice president—the next step in Laura's Life Plan (a.k.a. The LLP) of becoming one of the most powerful women in advertising—by her sixth anniversary with Giddings-Rose.

And not long after her thirtieth birthday, which would make her the youngest VP at the agency.

Not bad for, in her father's words, a monumental failure. Not bad at all.

Take that, Daddy Dearest.

CHAPTER THREE

The past two weeks had flown by, and Laura's last day in the office was packed with meetings. First, a meeting with the research team to finalize the research plan for the cruise, followed by a briefing with the creative team for another client, an up-and-coming beverage company targeting the young and health-conscious, then a meeting to review the preliminary art and copy for a high-end jewelry store chain.

First up, Imperial. With some key members of the research, social media, and brand planning and development teams gathered around the table, Laura opened the Imperial account meeting. "What have we got?"

Havi, the social media guru, tossed out, "Lack of social media presence. What's there is dying on the vine without a communications plan and a staff dedicated to monitoring its content. They need to take control of the message to communicate with clients and potential clients, use it to distribute information, connect with customers with real-time updates and responses to questions. As we all know"— Havi indicated all the thirty-somethings sitting around the conference table—"Millenials, their target demographic, tweet. A lot."

"This is the primary reason Imperial can't reach their target demographic," Celeste added. "But also because Imperial's brand is dated. When the target audience looks at Imperial, they see their grandparents' cruise line. It's going to take more than adding a new ship and more adventurous itineraries. Odds are their typical passenger is confused by the line's latest offerings."

"So brand confusion is an issue," Laura muttered as she entered notes into her iPad. "Since they don't want to throw the Baby Boomers out with the bathwater, a new line with fresh branding could work."

"But the current brand could use a facelift," Celeste continued. "Even if they don't want to ditch their current market, they are getting older, and there will be others, like Gen X-ers, to take their place in the line of succession. Targets that still want what Imperial has to offer. Only fresher."

"All right." Laura looked up at the group. "What's the plan?"

———

Nathan punched in the security code to his apartment building, then fumbled for the key to his door. What a day, and he still had to pack for the cruise. *Check that.* First he'd have to *unpack* some boxes before he could *pack* his suitcase for the cruise. So far he'd only unearthed his business suits and his work-out clothes. God only knew what boxes held his jeans and other casual wear.

"Mr. Maxwell, I have a package for you." The building's security guard pulled a box out from behind the desk. "You'll need to sign for it."

"Thanks, Omar." Glancing at the mailing label, he saw his sister's address.

"Do you need help carrying it up?" Omar asked, as Nathan balanced the box, his briefcase, the bag of toiletries he'd just picked up from the local Duane Reade, and his other mail.

"No, I've got it. Have a good night."

Nathan had a general idea what the box contained and he wasn't sure he was ready to deal with the memories.

Setting the package on top of a stack of unopened boxes, he flipped on the lights and headed for the kitchen. If he recalled, there was a box of Chinese takeout left over from the night before.

As he shoveled a forkful in his mouth, he thumbed through his mail. "Mmm, mm. Nothing like cold beef lo mein," he muttered to himself. "Damn, I really need to eat better."

Not that he didn't know how to cook. His grandmother had been an excellent cook, and she'd taught him how to make a kick-ass pot of greens, some flaky biscuits or savory cornbread, even his favorite—pecan pie—but who had time for that?

Oh well. Soon he'd be eating like a king, if the five-star reviews of Imperial's cuisine held true.

Seeing nothing of interest in the mail, he moved into the living room, taking his cold, one-star meal-in-a-carton with him, and stared at the box, considering. If he didn't open it before he left and acknowledge its receipt, his sister would pester him the whole cruise.

Setting aside his *ersatz* dinner, he reached into his pocket and took out the bone-handled pocketknife his grandmother had given him for his sixteenth birthday. A gift he knew she'd splurged on. Slicing through the tape, he lifted the lid. And memories flooded his brain.

On top was the battered copy of *To Kill a Mockingbird* his grandmother had made him read. He'd groused and complained, but it wasn't long before he couldn't put it down. And he'd read it dozens of times since then.

He pulled an envelope written in his sister's hand out of the book and opened it.

Dear Nathan,

I went through Gram's things and enclosed the items I thought you'd want. I think she kept everything from the time we moved in with her until the day she died. Every drawing, every report card, every letter we ever wrote to her. She even had the local newspaper clippings about the 4-H ribbons I'd won. God, I miss her.

Yeah, he did too. He rubbed a hand over the ache in his chest that never went away.

By the way, the developer called again. He's pushing hard. And the bank has called several times. We need to move on this soon.

I miss you. Hope the Big Apple is everything you dreamed. I'll be up to visit as soon as I can.

Hugs,

Amanda

Yeah, right. Like she had time to visit New York.

He hated leaving his sister to deal with an aggressive mortgage lender, and an even more aggressive developer. She had a heavy enough burden trying to keep the farm going, without dealing with a hostile mortgage lender, avaricious developers, and pushy real estate agents. The house needed a new roof to boot, but that would have to wait until they'd taken care of the mortgages.

Both he and his sister had been shocked to learn their grandmother had mortgaged the farm to the hilt. A farm that had been in her family for generations. She'd used the money to send him and Amanda to college. Money she'd said she'd saved for just such an expense.

He closed his eyes, the pain of her sacrifice overwhelming him. She would have known she'd never be able to repay the mortgages. Her life insurance had been barely enough to cover her medical bills and funeral costs.

Well, he'd be damned if he'd let some greedy land developer keen to build a neighborhood of McMansions for a bunch of country wannabes put his family's land on the chopping block.

The bonus he'd receive upon closing the Imperial account would just cover the two mortgages. And close the Imperial account he would. He and Amanda just needed to hold the bank and the developer at bay until then.

Setting aside his sister's note, he reached into the box for a bundle of letters tied with string. Letters he'd written his grandmother from college.

Seeing a large manila envelope, he opened it, and found a stack of photos. On top, a photo from his high school graduation, his grandmother beaming by his side, and beneath that his official college graduation photo, the one she'd kept on the fireplace mantel.

His aching heart climbed to his throat when he came upon the photo of his mother. He held it under the light. She must have been eighteen at the time, right before she'd gotten pregnant with him.

She'd been a beauty. Raven hair, warm, brown eyes, brilliant smile. So young, her life ahead filled with unlimited possibilities. But she'd made some bad choices, and ashamed by those choices, and their consequences, she'd become estranged from her own mother.

He looked back at his graduation photos. He'd seen the same gleam, the same energy in his own eyes, as he saw in his mother's. He could hear his grandmother's frequent admonition, "Always do the right thing, no matter how hard it is."

And, dammit, he'd made the right choices, even when they were hard. Sighing, he put the photos back in the envelope. His unplanned trip down memory lane had left him drained. The unpacking and packing would wait until tomorrow.

———

On top of everything else she had to do before she left for the cruise, Laura had the bright idea to welcome Darcy and Josh home with a small surprise party. What *had* she been thinking?

So on Friday evening, she called Darcy's house phone, hoping Millie was there to let the caterers in. "Ryan residence."

"Did they promote you to housekeeper?"

"Cruella, is that you?"

"Funny." Laura beeped at the taxi in front of her as soon as the light turned green. "I'm on my way."

"Thanks for the warning."

"Did you let the caterers in?"

Millie released a long-suffering sigh. "No. I left them

standing on the stoop with trays of food in their hands. Of course I let them in."

"Don't mess with me, Millie. You know I can take you."

"Maybe, but I'd still be smarter than you."

Laura practically heard the smirk through the phone, but chose to ignore Millie's dig. "Did Mark and Chris get the banner hung?"

"Yes, your ladyship."

"Champagne chilling?"

"Yes, Your Ladyship. And I polished the silver, scrubbed the floors, cleaned the windows—"

"Okay, I get it." Laura rolled her eyes. "Thanks for taking care of everything."

"You're welcome."

"I'll be there shortly, if this—" she blew her horn again "—police car would get out of my way."

"You're blowing your horn at a policeman?"

"Well, he's in the way."

"God forbid. Goodbye, Cruella."

Laura had ordered trays of tapas for the guests, and an elegant dinner for Darcy and Josh to enjoy after everyone left. They'd been traveling most of the day and would be exhausted, so Laura thought she'd extend the honeymoon by one more evening with a romantic dinner for two—after the initial surprise. She'd also arranged to have staple food items in the kitchen so that they could spend a leisurely morning in bed.

Finding a parking space around the corner from Darcy's —and now Josh's—Park Slope brownstone, Laura pulled her red Fiat 500 into it, and reaching across the seat grabbed the bouquet of white roses her assistant had ordered for the occasion. She glanced at her watch. She'd made it by the skin of her teeth.

Letting herself in with her key, she called out, "I'm here."

"I'll alert the media," Millie said as she stepped out of the living room. Dressed from head-to-toe in her usual dingy brown, Millie looked every bit the unkind 'Mousey Millie' nickname Mark and Chris had given her. From her Marian-the-Librarian bun to her sensible shoes, and everything in-between, Millie was a study in browns.

"The cast of *The Grapes of Wrath* called. They want their wardrobe back."

Millie glanced down at her clothes, her brow furrowed. "What? What's wrong with what I'm wearing?"

In direct contradiction to her appearance, Millie had this voice. A voice that called to mind a dimly lit boudoir, the sensual strains of Ravel's "Boléro," and red lace lingerie. *Pfft.* Listen to me, Laura thought, I'm starting to sound like one of Darcy's steamy romance novels.

"One of these days, Millie. So help me, one of these days," Laura said, referencing her multiple threats to stage a What-Not-To-Wear intervention. "Where's everyone else?"

"In the kitchen."

"Put these in water." Laura handed the bouquet to Millie.

"Yes, Your Ladyship."

After giving the living room a quick once-over and seeing the trays of food were properly displayed, the champagne nestled in the ice bucket, and the 'Welcome Home' banner hanging over the fireplace, Laura made her way to the back of the townhouse, hearing the low hum of voices. All of Darcy's and Josh's closest friends and family were there. Mark, Chris, and Martin from Josh's office, along with Martin's wife, Cindy, spoke with Darcy's parents, Jeff and Vanessa.

Darcy's sister and brother-in-law, Anne and Matt, laughed at something Darcy's literary agent and godmother, Gloria, had said. Judging from the highball glass in her hand, Gloria had already tapped into the Bombay Sapphire gin Darcy kept in the liquor cabinet especially for her, while Darcy's editor, Elise, sipped from a glass of wine.

She'd made sure Kelly and Daniel were there as well. Hero-lawyer Josh saved Kelly's home from foreclosure, and became an unofficial big brother to her son, Daniel, in the process. Not that Laura would ever call Josh a hero to his face. Even if that's what he was.

Whispering in the corner were Brandon, Darcy's brother, and his long-time partner, David.

Darcy's mom, Vanessa, a Jane Austen scholar at Barnard College, had named all her children after her favorite Austen characters. Darcy Elizabeth, Frederick Brandon, and Anne Elinor.

"Laura!" Jeff greeted her as she walked in. "How's the world of advertising?" He walked over and, wrapping his arm around her shoulders, pressed a kiss to her cheek.

Darcy's father had been more a father to her than her own. His support and encouragement, along with the occasional kick in the ass, kept her on the right track. And Darcy's mother offered the love and warmth her own mother never did. Vanessa drew her in for a hug. "You're so thoughtful to do this for Darcy and Josh."

Laura brushed it off. "It's nothing. Let's move into the living room. They should be home any time now."

As soon as everyone crowded into the living room, Laura glanced out the bay window to see the car pull up out front. "Shh. They're here." The driver gathered the luggage from the trunk and carried it to the stoop. With a rattle of keys, the front door banged open amongst giggles and the unmistakable sound of smooching. Laura rolled her eyes and lifted a hand to hold the snickers and cries of surprise at bay.

Josh stepped into the foyer, Darcy still in his arms after carrying her over the threshold, their lips locked, unaware of their audience.

Laura spoke up. "Oh, give it a rest. Now you're just rubbing it in."

Josh spun around with a stunned Darcy, as everyone yelled, "Surprise!"

———

Josh set Darcy on her feet before sharing some high-fives and fist-bumps with his buddies, Daniel among them. "Daniel! What's up, dude? Besides growing, like, five inches since we've been gone." Josh turned to Kelly. "You must have been feeding him nothing but your parents' steaks." Kelly's parents owned a butcher shop in Harlem.

Darcy grabbed Laura for a hug, then drew back. "You said you weren't going to be in the country."

"A little fib." Laura made as if she studied her nails.

"Aren't you going on the cruise?"

"Yes. I leave Sunday, so the slide show will still have to wait."

"You're such a little sneak." Darcy glanced around the room. "Did you do this?"

"Pfft. We all did," Laura indicated the others in the room.

"Mom! Dad!" Darcy rushed her parents, hugging and kissing them, before moving on to the rest of the welcoming committee.

"Welcome home." Gloria patted her cheek. "You're out of gin."

"I missed you too, Gloria," Darcy said as she teared up. "And Millie!" She hauled a stiff Millie in for a hug.

Laura shook her head. Darcy knew full well Millie didn't like displays of affection, especially public ones. Laura turned and greeted Josh in her usual manner, "Voldemort."

"Bellatrix."

"What's the difference between a porcupine and a Mercedes-Benz full of lawyers?" Laura asked.

"The porcupine has pricks on the outside."

"Damn. They really need to come up with some new lawyer jokes."

"They, who?" Josh's brow furrowed in confusion.

"The lawyer-joke-maker-uppers." She waved her hand in the air, indicating the ephemeral individuals who did such things.

"Thanks for the welcome home party." Josh leaned down and kissed Laura's cheek.

She nudged him away. "Don't go all mushy on me. Marriage to my best friend turning you into a wussy?"

Josh laughed before making his way through the crowded living room.

"Who's turning into a wussy?" Gloria asked in her gravel against glass voice, as she selected a beef tenderloin crostini from one of the trays.

"Josh." Laura followed suit and picked up a crostini, smirking as she glanced at Josh's retreating back.

"I suppose love does that to you. Something you would know nothing about," Gloria said around a bite of meat and pesto.

"And you do?"

"More than you, which I realize isn't saying much."

"Love will never make me mushy." If she ever found love, which she doubted. She watched as Josh placed a kiss on Darcy's forehead. Not that kind of love, anyway.

What was she talking about? Nowhere in Laura's Life Plan was there a man. Not a one. At least not a permanent one.

"Careful there, Queen of the Booty Calls. Never say never." Gloria stuffed the olive from her dirty martini in her mouth. "When do you leave for your cruise?"

Laura narrowed her eyes. "How did you know about my cruise?"

Gloria lifted a shoulder, her short-cropped bright red hair standing out in spiky tufts around her head. "Darcy must have said something."

Hmm. "I leave Sunday, why?"

"No reason." Gloria breezed off in Vanessa's direction.

What was that woman up to? Laura wondered. She had known Gloria for as long as she'd known Darcy. Gloria was a significant part of Darcy's life, as both her godmother and her literary agent. But there was something about her that Laura couldn't put her finger on. She always seemed to *know* things, as if she had a direct line into your life. "Pfft." Laura glanced at the drink in her hand. "Must be the champagne."

———

Jeff and Vanessa said their goodbyes. "Laura, we'll give you a ride home, so you don't have to pay for a taxi," Jeff offered.

"Thanks, but I drove."

"Enjoy your cruise, then!" Vanessa said just as they closed the front door behind them.

Laura and Gloria were the only ones left. Gloria polished off the last of her drink. Her fourth—after sending Chris, or was it Mark?, out to get more gin.

"Thank you for everything!" Darcy's eyes sparkled as she hugged Laura. "You're awesome."

"Just call me Your Awesomeness. Don't forget your dinner in the oven."

"Have fun on your cruise. You're sure to meet some hunky guys with accents to while away the hours with."

"What I'll be whiling away the hours with is research. This is business, remember? I'm not going to let anything get in the way of getting this account." Especially a man. Accent or no.

"Laura." Darcy took her hands and looked her straight in the eye. "I hope you get this account because you want it so badly and because you deserve it, but you don't have to prove anything. You're already a huge success. And nothing is going to change that."

"Who said I was trying to prove anything? It's just the natural progression of my career."

"Right." Darcy sighed. "Laura's Life Plan."

"Yep, the LLP."

A slightly inebriated Gloria joined them in the foyer. "Come on, old woman, I'll drive you home," Laura said, as she opened the front door. "Bye, Dracula," Laura called to Josh.

"See ya, Elphaba," he yelled back from the kitchen.

Gloria tottered along beside Laura, weaving a bit. "Careful, there," Gloria slurred. "Don't get those hooker heels stuck in a sidewalk seam."

Laura shot Gloria a narrow look. *WTF?* "How'd you know about that?"

"Know about what?"

"Oh, never mind." Must be the excitement over her upcoming departure. 'It'd made her loopy. Of course Gloria wouldn't know about her Nathan encounter.

CHAPTER FOUR

"What the hell do you mean you're taking a cruise?"

Well, that got her father's attention, Laura thought, as she pushed the pear tart—prepared by the latest in a long line of cooks—around on her plate.

"Yes, dear," her mother, Cherise of the Perfect Hair, chimed in. "Why would you take a vacation now? You'll miss your grandmother's eightieth birthday."

Laura knew her grandmother would be none too pleased that she wouldn't be there to worship at her feet. As the family matriarch, her paternal grandmother ruled over the family like Lady Catherine de Bourgh over Rosings Park. You couldn't hang out with the Butler family and not learn a thing or two about Jane Austen.

Laura's slacker brother, Neil, sat across from her, his face wearing a smug look she'd like to erase. With a pumice stone.

Family dinners were such a joy, and this one was no exception. What a way to spend a perfectly good Saturday evening.

"It's for business. And I can't put it off. Time is of the

essence." She eyed her father. "Thanks to Milt telling Hawk Media about the account."

"What do you mean? Are you going after Imperial?" Her father's mulish face took on a purple hue.

Laura lifted her chin as her leg began bouncing of its own volition. "Yes, and I'm going to get it, too." She winced at the petulant sound of her own voice. So much like a little girl's voice. A little girl who had craved her father's attention but had never gotten it.

"I won't help you. Don't expect to throw around the Great Lakes Shipyard name."

Laura's spine stiffened. "I don't want or need your help."

"Besides, I told McCutcheon about that account. Just leave it alone." He drank from his highball glass—his standard twelve-year-old single-malt scotch.

Her father might be used to getting what he wanted using that tone, but not this time. She narrowed her eyes at her father. "What's in it for you? What will you get out of McCutcheon if his son gets the Imperial account?" As a U.S. Senator who headed up the Armed Services Committee, McCutcheon's actions could greatly impact her father's business, specifically the military division.

Her father had the grace to look uncomfortable. "You wouldn't understand men's deals."

"Tell me, does Neil understand 'men's deals'?" She glanced over at her brother. "Since he *is* the VP of Ethics and Compliance. Or whatever title you created for him," she muttered. That wiped the smile off Neil's face. Daddy Dearest created the position for her brother, since every other job he'd held was beyond his abilities. In this position, Neil essentially did whatever his father told him to.

"Now, dear"—Her mother placed her hand over Laura's

—"don't upset your father. He works hard. And must sometimes rely on the good will of friends."

"Cherise," her father warned with a shake of his head.

"You can put off your little cruise a week," Cherise continued. "See your grandmother on her birthday, then if you must take a cruise, the Liphams have a wonderful yacht. If they're not using it, I'm sure you could take it wherever you'd like."

"Mother, the cruise is for business, it can't wait a week, and I'm not going after the Liphams' account, I'm going after Imperial's." She placed her napkin beside her uneaten dessert. "Please give my best to Grandmother. I have to go home and pack. Goodnight."

Outside her family's Westchester estate, she took her first full breath since arriving two hours before. She climbed into her car, cranked up Coldplay, and tried to leave the stress behind. This cruise might be business, but ten days half a world away from her family was a vacation, no matter how you looked at it.

———

The drive home relieved some of the tension, but Laura couldn't have been happier to walk into her apartment an hour later. "Ahh. Solitude." Dropping her keys onto the ebony console table in the foyer, her first stop, the kitchen, for a little something to complete the relaxation process.

Picking up the remote on the way to the kitchen, she turned on some music, then poured a glass of port while Natasha Bedingfield sang about reaching for something in the distance. She took a sip of the port and let its honeyed warmth wash away the remaining stress.

Walking over to the wall of windows that formed the exterior corner of her dining and living room, she stared out at the lights of the city beyond and took a deep breath.

Contrary to what most people thought of Laura Armstrong, bad-ass advertising executive, she needed the peace and solitude of her home to recharge. She worked hard and played harder. No question about that. But even she needed quiet time. Time with no one who dictated to her. No one who expected anything of her. No one who criticized her. Or even worse, openly ignored her.

Wandering aimlessly around the Fifth Avenue penthouse apartment she'd purchased recently with the inheritance from her paternal grandfather, she knew she'd made a wise investment.

Chic yet serene, with fantastic views of Central Park and the Upper East Side, the apartment's scheme conveyed an understated elegance. Decorated in whites and creams, with black accents like the gleaming granite countertops and built-in bookcases, and touched with splashes of aqua, coral, and pale yellow, the apartment served as an oasis from the insanity that often defined her life.

She couldn't imagine living anywhere else. Not too far from the vibrant Manhattan nightlife she loved, but removed enough to offer the respite she needed. Here, lately, she needed more respite and less nightlife. She sighed. "I must be getting old. Before you know it I'll be going to bed with the sun."

Pressing a thumb to her right eye where a headache threatened to erupt, she tried in vain to dismiss the evening at her parents'. What the hell did she expect? To one day walk in and find a Norman Rockwell family? Things weren't going to change, so why did she always come away disillusioned?

Natasha's soulful voice poured from the sound system. Laura often felt as if *she* were reaching for something in the distance. Something she couldn't define.

Growing up, she'd received little attention from her father. More indifference than outright disregard. The only attention her mother had given her was to criticize her appearance, her behavior, and her interests. While Laura liked all things fashion, she also acted the tomboy, playing sports like basketball and volleyball, where her height offered an advantage. Her mother hated that her daughter took up sports, but couldn't be bothered enough to put a stop to it.

She'd dutifully attended finishing school to learn good posture, how to make polite conversation, which fork to use when, and the art of thank-you notes. Complain though she did about those courses, the skills she learned served her well in her professional life. Score one for her mother.

Beginning with the first generation Armstrong shipbuilder, there had been a male heir to the Armstrong dynasty. Even so, being the firstborn, Laura just knew she would one day take over the family business. She used to pretend she was a shipbuilding magnate following in her father's footsteps. She worked hard to be the very best at everything so she'd be smart enough to handle the business and make her father proud.

When her baby brother came along, "heir to the Armstrong dynasty," her father's indifference turned to complete disregard, as he essentially forgot her existence. From that point on, her brother could do no wrong in her father's eyes.

Where Laura worked hard, her brother slacked off. Even when his grades fell far below hers at the same age, her father offered excuses. *He's smarter than his teachers.*

He just needs more stimulation. Or her favorite, *He's got his eye on the Armstrong business and can't be bothered with mundane schoolwork.*

As for her mother, well, Cherise was too busy with committees, bridge club, hair and nail appointments, and society dinners and gatherings, to help much with the kids. She may have given birth to them, and the jury was still out on that—she couldn't see her mother willingly participating in such a messy, painful process—but other than making sure Laura was polished and educated so she could find and marry the appropriate man, she had no other role in the upbringing of her children.

Having no idea what to do with a boy, Cherise left Neil's upbringing to his father. Big mistake.

Her father's disregard turned to unmitigated disdain when at the tender age of twelve she failed on a monumental, and very public, level. While many witnessed her epic failure, no one, not even Darcy, knew the words her father spoke later that evening. And no one ever would.

After that, she lost all hope of ever gaining her father's love and affection, much less his respect.

But she never gave up on being the best she could be. Where she'd once worked hard hoping to gain her father's attention, if not his love, she now did it for herself alone. She discovered a love of winning, and she loved the praise that came with it, even if it didn't come from her parents.

Left to her own devices most of the time, Laura developed a resourcefulness and independence. Science project: she developed her hypothesis, did her research, gathered her supplies, and completed the project, earning high marks. College applications: she wrote her essays, completed her forms, mailed them, fielded any interviews, and arranged for her apartment when she was accepted.

After being independent for so long, she had no desire to hitch her star to anyone else's wagon, much less a man's. Besides, why do that, when she knew she could succeed on her own?

Laura's paternal grandmother, Octavia Spencer Armstrong, reigned over her family like a third-world dictator, especially after her husband died. Laura's paternal grandfather, Parker, had been kind to her during his lifetime. Not overly effusive, but at least he'd paid attention to her. Upon his death when she was only sixteen, he'd left her and her brother substantial trust funds.

She took control of that fund four years ago at age twenty-five. The money gave her financial independence, so even if her grandmother followed through with her many threats to disinherit her, she'd be secure. She managed her trust fund investments with the same attention to detail as she managed her client accounts.

Given her financial resources, it was fair to say she didn't work hard for the money. She worked for the satisfaction of a job done well. She loved the hunt for new accounts, the adrenaline rush, the challenge, and finally, the kill when the agency scored the account. The diversity of the work didn't hurt.

Laura knew she couldn't completely escape from her family's influence and DNA. She'd learned her haughty stare and overbearing manner from her grandmother, but she liked to think she only dispensed them when they were well-deserved. She'd inherited her father's workaholic tendencies, her mother's glorious mane of hair and blue eyes, and her grandfather's determination.

It was this determination that often made her and her grandmother butt heads. Her grandmother deplored her 'loose' lifestyle, and while her grandmother was outspoken, she found it unflattering in her only granddaughter.

Laura sighed as her aimless wandering took her to her favorite room, the solarium just off her bedroom that connected with the garden terrace, which thanks to her skillful gardener, bloomed in a riot of color and texture.

She collapsed into an upholstered chaise and drained the last of her port. She'd succeeded in everything she set her mind to. Except gaining her father's love and affection.

She glanced at a photo of herself with Darcy's family. Laura found solace in them. Their support was a balm to her soul, but could never be a substitute for that of her parents.

She and Darcy met in kindergarten and stayed together until they each went to college, Laura in Chicago at North-western—to get away from her family—and Darcy in New York at Columbia—to stay near her family.

"Enough of the pity party." She glanced down at her empty glass. "I've got some packing to do. Look out Mediterranean! Here comes Laura 'Bad-Ass' Armstrong."

CHAPTER FIVE

The *Nave dei Sogni* lived up to its name, from its hip Art Deco décor to its luxurious appointments. With a style reminiscent of the great ocean liners of the 1930s, the public areas of the ship boasted unapologetic glamour. Deco-Page, the elegant lounge, where she sipped her vodka martini from etched glass, could have come straight out of a classic Hollywood movie.

From its high-gloss black walls and cream trim, which lent a tuxedo effect, to its Murano glass chandelier and mirrored accents, the room begged for Fred and Ginger to come waltzing in.

While she appreciated the grandeur and sophistication of the décor, she thought something more casual yet refined would appeal to the target demographic better. Like her penthouse stateroom, which offered a soothing respite from the rich colors, bold geometric shapes, and distinctive drama and elegance of the rest of the ship.

Decorated with a muted palette of creams and browns, dark woods, and an eclectic collection of furniture and accessories, complete with a sunburst motif, the stateroom offered polished luxury without ostentation. And Katie had been right. The bathroom *was* bigger than many New York City apartments, with a huge white marble soaker tub alongside a picture window.

With job perks like this, who needed vacations?

After her arrival in Barcelona the evening before, she'd had a little time in the morning to explore the two-thousand-year-old city before boarding the ship. She'd walked along La Rambla, a favorite destination of tourists. The tree-lined street had been crowded with people where languages and accents from all over the world blended with local Catalan.

The Mercat de Sant Josep, or simply La Bouqeria, with its almost endless stalls of fruits, vegetables, cheeses, meats, and herbs, tantalized her senses with the astonishing array of colors and aromas, and whetted her appetite for the five-star cuisine of Imperial's world-renowned chefs.

A short nap, hot shower, and quick email check in her luxurious stateroom had refreshed and revived. Before heading to Deco-Page she'd taken a selfie standing on her balcony and sent it off to Darcy with a text with the trite expression, 'wish you were here.'

From her perch at the bar, Laura eyed the other passengers, most of whom were much older than she. Except for the bleach-blond with the impressive girls squeezed into a black and gold lamé dress. She'd seen her earlier as she'd boarded the ship, on the arm of a man who looked old enough to be her great-grandfather. If he made it through the cruise alive, it'd be a miracle.

She also spied a tall, attractive, middle-aged man with wire-rimmed glasses and a wedding ring, chatting up a couple from California whom she'd met in her hotel in

Barcelona. He, an author and motivational speaker; she, a jewelry designer.

Other than that, the cruise didn't promise much hope for excitement, but since she'd be working, it was just as well. She offered a pleasant smile to a gentleman with a bad comb-over and received a glare from his diamond-studded wife. *Sheesh. Don't get your support hose in a twist, madame. Just trying to be friendly.* As if she would go after her portly, pasty-faced husband.

Laura turned back to the bar and signaled the bartender for another martini. Italian. The bartender, not the martini. At least she could enjoy the view, she thought, as Sexy Sergio expertly mixed her drink. And what a view it was. Jet-black hair thick with waves, the strong facial features of his Greek and Roman ancestors covered now with a five o'clock shadow, full mouth. Sergio turned to grab a bottle off the mirrored shelf behind the bar. A nice tight ass. And, of course, an Italian accent. What more could a girl wish for?

———

Adjusting his tie, Nathan stepped into the lounge, and surveyed the crowd, mentally tallying the age ranges of the clientele. It looked like an AARP-convention.

He halted his survey. "Well, I'll be," Nathan muttered to himself. If it isn't Laura with the kissable mouth. What the hell were the odds? As he stood rooted to the spot, she swung those luscious legs around, crossed one over the other, slow and seductive, attracting the attention of just about every male in the room, and some females, too, before turning back to the bartender.

The black dress she wore opened down the back almost to her tailbone, offering a delectable view of smooth skin.

Her hair, which she wore in the same sleek tail as before, draped over her shoulder, and jet-black earrings dangled from her ears. He'd like to pull that band from her hair and spread it around her shoulders, run his fingers through it. On her feet, hot pink stiletto pumps screamed 'sex-me-up.' *Hellfire and damnation.*

Giving himself a mental shake, he reminded himself this was a business trip. He started to walk in the opposite direction, then recalled what he'd told Cassie about work and pleasure not being mutually exclusive, and changed course. He could at least buy a beautiful woman a drink. After all, it was the gentlemanly thing to do. He approached the bar just as she reached for her drink.

"Put it on my tab."

———

Laura recognized the bourbon-infused voice without the need to see its owner, but that didn't diminish the surprise over its owner's presence onboard a ship churning through the Mediterranean Sea. Covering her astonishment, she slowly turned to face Nathan. "Well, if it isn't the Southern Prince Charming. Rescue any more damsels-in-distress lately?"

"Does the woman who got lost on her way to the dining room count?" His eyes lit on her face, all warm and obliging.

Her imagination hadn't run away with her. He stood behind her barstool, looking as handsome and polished as she remembered him from their brief encounter. This time she also got a whiff of his spicy cologne.

She glanced back at Sexy Sergio. There was something a little dangerous about Sergio. She could see it in the eyes, around the stubborn mouth. More her type than the man who stood behind her. And yet, when she'd heard that voice, her insides had gone a little gooey.

"Sir?" Sergio of the Dangerous Eyes asked.

"I'll have what she's having."

"Thank you for the drink–even if the cruise is all-inclusive." She raised the glass to her lips, took a sip. "I pictured you as a scotch man."

"I like my Macallan as much as the next person, but when you're surrounded by this much glamour"—he swept his hand around the room, ending with her, as his gaze traveled the length of her—"it only seems fitting to have a martini." The passenger next to Laura vacated the bar stool, so Nathan claimed it. "I must admit I'm surprised to hear you pictured me at anything."

"Well, Nathan, you are a fine specimen of a man." Black suit, blue shirt, Hermès red and blue silk tie. All on a six-foot-two-inch athletic frame. Oh yes, he was one fine specimen. Too bad he didn't have the rough-around-the-edges image she preferred.

He flashed her a grin, acknowledging her compliment.

"It'd be a cold fish who didn't picture you at . . . something." She plucked the olive from her drink, popped it into her mouth, and chewed thoughtfully as she eyed him. "This is quite the coincidence." Laura pointed between the two of them. "I suppose I should say something about a small world. After all, we met only once and briefly, in Manhattan, and here we are four thousand miles away on the same ship for ten days."

"Considering we met outside the cruise lines' offices, perhaps not such a coincidence."

She tilted her head. "I suppose."

"Are you traveling alone?" Nathan asked.

"Yes. You?"

"Yes."

Laura had already developed her story. Using her middle name, she was Laura Danforth, bored trust-fund baby, taking a short vacation from the exhausting round of galas, theater performances, and multi-million dollar fundraisers after her parents had to back out of the cruise they'd already booked.

"Since we're both alone on what appears to be primarily a, er, 'silvered-hair couples' cruise, may I escort you to dinner?"

She considered Nathan and his offer for a moment. A quick glance at this left hand revealed no ring. "You're not married, are you? Because I don't play with married men."

"No, I'm not married or otherwise committed. I don't even have a goldfish."

Laughing, Laura thought, Why not have a little fun? Who needed rough edges when the man looked like Nathan. "Then how can I turn down such a genteel offer? Your grandmother would be so proud."

———

S ince she and Nathan were both traveling alone, neither one had made dining reservations, but rather chose to eat in the main dining room. Imperial's boast of five-star dining didn't disappoint. The service was impeccable, and the food as pleasing to the palate and the eye as that found in any top New York restaurant.

They'd been seated with two other couples, an American investment banker and his plastic-surgeon wife who looked like she'd had one too many of her own procedures, and an Italian politician and a woman he introduced as his mistress. Laura had to bite her tongue to keep from asking where the wife was. Shopping in Milan, perhaps, or home with their precocious brood?

The banker introduced himself as Gordon Vogler, and his wife as Veronica. Veronica Vogler the Vampire—lovely alliteration, that—her plasticized skin lending her the well-preserved appearance of those mythical bloodsuckers. The politician, Franco Abruzzo, glad-handed everyone at the table as if they could all vote for him in the next election.

The mistress, Natalia Brusca, had that sexy, tousled, heavy-lidded Sophia Loren look. The politician, however, sported a bad toupee and a paunch. What could she see in him? Laura wondered. She mentally snorted. Other than money, judging from the carat-weight of the diamond pendant around her neck. And perhaps power.

"So, Mr. Maxwell, what is it that you do?" Gordon asked.

"Nathan, please," Nathan responded, wiping his mouth with his white linen napkin, before placing it back in his lap. Taking a sip of his wine, he cut a glance at Laura and the other table companions. "I'm in corporate relations. Nothing as interesting as banking or politics, I'm afraid."

"And you, Ms. Danforth?"

"Please, call me Laura." She waved her hand in the air, "Nothing as interesting as corporate relations, banking, or politics." Here was the opportunity to try out her story, sticking as closely to the truth as possible, without giving away her clandestine purpose. "Right now I'm taking some time away." Not a total lie. She was taking some time away —from her dysfunctional family.

"I'm a—how you say?—exotic dancer," Natalia piped up in tortured English. She reached out for Franco's hand, patting it. "We met when Franco, er, view my *interpretazione* of *Swan Lake*, right, *cucciolo*?"

Oh no, she did not. Did she just call him puppy? Laura covered her mouth with her napkin to cover the snort that almost escaped. *Swan Lake? Alrighty then.*

Nathan shot her a glance, eyebrows raised.

Instead of being embarrassed by her revelation, Franco beamed with pride.

An awkward silence fell over the table.

"Do you take cruises often?" Nathan tossed out.

Anxious to fill the void, Veronica the Vampire said, "Gordon and I take two or three cruises a year, always with Imperial."

"I've taken numerous cruises, some with my wife, some with my mistresses," Pauncho Villa interjected.

Everyone turned to Franco, bug-eyed, requiring Laura to cover a laugh with both a cough and her napkin.

Mistres*ses. Plural? My, my. Maybe there was more to Pauncho than meets the eye.*

"This is my first cruise," Nathan said, making it Laura's turn to look at him bug-eyed.

"What do you recommend for the first-time cruise experience?" he continued.

As their table companions began giving cruise advice, Laura took a moment to observe Nathan. He spoke with a lazy Southern drawl, but had the polish of education. He dressed with the urbanity of the wealthy, but hadn't taken a cruise until now. A perplexing mix of disparate qualities.

Gordon began speaking specifically of Imperial and what they had to offer, regaining Laura's attention. *Perfect.* Nathan had presented an opportunity to pick the brains of Imperial passengers, and she'd zoned out.

"We appreciate the level of service we receive on an Imperial ship," Veronica said. "I never have to lift a finger. The staff seem to anticipate my every need, even before I know I need it." She could barely crack a smile what with all the collagen and Botox in her lips.

"And they're very discreet," Franco added with a wink.

"Er, yes, I'm sure discretion is their middle name." Laura glanced at Nathan, whose eyes twinkled in response.

———

An after-dinner walk on the deck gave Laura the chance to check out the ship's outdoor amenities. She and Nathan strolled along the lido deck toward the pool, deserted this time of night. Laura shivered when they rounded a corner and walked straight into a brisk wind off the water.

Nathan spun her toward him and ran his hands up and down her bare arms. "You're cold. We should go in."

Laura looked up into his golden-brown eyes, then glanced down at his lips. *Go for it.* "I can think of another way to warm up."

Nathan chuckled. "My grandmother warned me about girls like you." His hands rested on her shoulders as he leaned down, bringing that tantalizing mouth closer to hers.

"Oh yeah? What did she say?" Laura raised her mouth to his, her eyes still on his lips.

"'Nathan,' she said, 'there will be women out there, fast women, that will want to take the lead. Don't let them.'" He came closer still, his breath soft on her face.

"And what did you say?" Laura's breath caught and her heart did a little two-step. She'd never been so wrapped up in the anticipation of a kiss before. The usual guys she'd, *er,* dated, if that was the word, just dove right in, taking what they wanted. More the instant-gratification type herself, so did she.

This expectation, this breathlessness, was new to her, and not unwelcome. She licked her lips as her gaze focused on his mouth, a breath away from hers.

"I said, 'Nathan'—I wouldn't have said it to my grandmother, you see"—the corner of that delicious mouth lifted—"so I said it to myself." His grin faded as he stepped into her, stopping just shy of a kiss. "'Sometimes it's nice to be led.'"

Laura took that as her cue. She grazed his lips with hers, and, taking a page from his playbook, didn't dive immediately into the deep end, but rather glided gently into the shallows.

As his hands skimmed the column of her neck to cup her face, a breathy moan escaped her. She gripped the lapels of his suit, pulling him into her as he changed the direction of his mouth before taking the reins. His tongue parted her lips, deepening the kiss, and sending her pulse into overdrive.

Tongues tangled and danced, breathy moans filled the air, teeth nibbled and nipped, as her hands slid up his chest and into his hair, fingers combing and tousling. His spicy cologne filled her senses, the heat pouring off his firm body, even as his hands slid along her ribs to her waist tugging her hips against him.

She loved kissing, but it had always been the hors d'oeuvres, not the entree. This kiss was the hors d'oeuvres, the entree, and the dessert, all rolled into one tasty meal. One she didn't want to end.

Nathan retreated, leaned in for another taste, then retreated again. "Well, I don't know about you, but I'm warmed up." He pressed his forehead to hers.

She was more than warmed up. She was revved up. Maybe this cruise offered more than a career opportunity. A shipboard fling—complete with a built-in end date—might be fun. Something new.

———

Nathan returned to his cabin around one a.m. smelling of Laura's perfume, and tasting her lips, jet-lagged and bone-tired, but also wired. After that soul-searing kiss on the lido deck he'd put a little distance between them and sought out more public entertainment in the form of the ship's glitzy nightclub. There hadn't been too many couples on the dance floor, and those that were there were grooving to Lady Gaga with moves from another era. But what the hell, they were having fun.

Laura had put those long, sexy legs to work on the floor, giving Nathan a run for his money. He liked to think he could hold his own, but she'd smoked him with her moves. Moves that could have given any one of the septuagenarians on the boat a heart attack.

They'd shared another steamy kiss in the elevator to her stateroom deck, where he'd said goodnight, notwithstanding the disappointed look on her beautiful face. He was tired, and he knew she had to be tired as well. They'd never have done justice to the sex they both wanted to have.

Peeling off his sweaty shirt, having discarded the jacket and tie long ago, he stepped into the bathroom for a quick shower before collapsing into bed. Alone.

He stood beneath the shower's spray. The heat of the water washed away the energy buzz he had going, and turned his body to mush. Dog-tired, he shut off the water and grabbed a fluffy towel from the rack.

Laura offered the potential for a hot little interlude. With her mouth pressed to his, fingers entwined in his hair, he had to remind himself he was here on a reconnaissance mission, not a vacation. Spending too much time with her could take time away from interacting with other passengers. Time away from his subtle interrogation techniques on the crew.

He toweled his hair then slung the towel over the rack. His mind made up, he crawled into bed and drew the covers up.

His grandmother would be ashamed at his ungentlemanly behavior, but tomorrow, Laura Danforth would be on her own.

CHAPTER SIX

Early the next morning, Nathan walked into the state-of-the-art fitness center intending to get a workout in before heading out on the shore excursion into Marseille later in the morning. He'd had a fitful night, with dreams about the beautiful Laura Danforth, in a variety of states of undress, tormenting him with that luscious mouth. He'd finally woken in a pool of sweat.

And there, on the treadmill, running like a gazelle, was the object of his desire. Tight running pants, skimpy tank top. He groaned. He thought a workout would clear his head, now here he was again fantasizing about Laura.

Women weren't usually a distraction for him. Not that he didn't like women. He did. A lot, in fact. He liked how they smelled, the way they walked, how they tasted. And he liked romancing them with flowers, fine wine and candlelit dinners, but he'd never had a problem keeping his eye on the ball. Until now.

He nodded a greeting at the older gentleman working out on the Cybex machine, performing an inept shoulder press.

Nathan chose the elliptical trainers on the opposite wall. He'd miss the view of the port, but at least he would work up a sweat in something other than erotic dreams. Punching in his preferences, he started his workout, and avoiding Laura's reflection in the mirrored wall in front of him, focused on the available equipment in the center, considering how to use the amenities to his advantage in an ad campaign.

"Hi."

He nearly lost his rhythm when he turned to see a sweaty, heavy-breathing Laura standing next to his machine. "Morning."

She wiped the sweat from her face and neck with a towel. "Thanks for last night. I had a great time."

Nathan glanced over at the man on the Cybex machine who'd abandoned his awkward exercise to listen.

"My pleasure."

"You've got some pretty amazing moves." Laura flashed a flirtatious grin.

Mr. Cybex's eyebrows winged up, as he made no pretense to cover his eavesdropping.

Feeling wicked, Nathan leaned down from his position on the elliptical. "Sugar, you've got some pretty amazing moves of your own. And those legs—what you can do with those legs—well, it ought to be illegal."

"It is. In some countries." She flung the towel over her shoulder and sashayed over to the yoga mats as both men watched, mouths hanging open.

Nathan snapped his jaws closed and tried in vain to concentrate on the circular motion of the foot pedals. Off to his left, Laura laid down on a mat, stretched, then rolled up and over her legs, grabbing her feet and folding herself in two. After holding this position for a few breaths, she opened her legs into a straddle and, lengthening her torso between them, pressed her chest to the floor.

Nathan's mouth went dry, and judging from the look on Mr. Cybex's face, he might have to perform CPR any minute. *Sweet Jesus.* He'd hit the twenty-minute mark and had hoped for at least thirty, but his libido couldn't take much more. He reduced the elliptical's speed, then stepped off, before wiping sweat and the lustful expression from his face with a towel.

He turned in Laura's direction and paused in indecision. Mr. Cybex quirked a brow, and then nodded toward her, a look of encouragement on his weathered face.

Taking his wordless advice, Nathan went over and stood next to Laura just as she lifted into a yoga move, something to do with a dog looking downward, he recalled from a former girlfriend's workouts, her derriere to the ceiling. Nathan almost swallowed his tongue. "Ahem."

She shifted into another yoga position, something about a snake. "Yes?"

Squatting next to her, he asked, "Are you going on a shore excursion?"

She lifted back into the dog position. His gaze traveled up her long legs.

"Yes. You?"

Dammit, woman! Focus, Nathan. "Yes. Would you like to go together?"

She shifted into a plank and turned her head, her face glistening from the exertion. And damned if that wasn't sexy. "Sure."

Nathan stood and stepped back before he did something to shock Mr. Cybex into that heart attack. "Great. Meet me on the lido deck in an hour."

She moved to a side plank, right arm lifted in the air, "See you then."

Leaving the fitness center, Nathan couldn't remember a more sexually frustrating workout. Mr. Cybex gave him a thumbs-up as he tossed his towel in the hamper and headed for a cold shower. So much for leaving Laura Danforth to her own devices.

Laura finished drying her hair and pulled it back in a thick braid slung over her right shoulder. She slipped into a pair of white snug-fitting ankle pants, topped off with a Mediterranean blue silk tunic sweater, and a pair of Manolo thongs in orange crush. Satisfied with her rush job, she headed up to the lido deck to meet her southern gentleman.

She had to remind herself this trip was work, not pleasure. And while she did have to play the part of tourist, she also had to keep her eye on the Imperial brass ring.

Nathan. Just a pleasant distraction, nothing more. By the end of the cruise, she'd no doubt tire of him. At no time in her life had a man, not even Daddy Dearest, interfered with her goals, and a man wasn't about to start now. Even one whose kisses knocked her Louboutins off, made her spine turn to jelly when he said her name with that 'Cat on a Hot Tin Roof Southern accent,' and, as of last night, starred in her X-rated dreams.

She'd set her sights on him, and just like everything else she set her sights on and accomplished, she'd be kissing her dry spell goodbye. Then by the end of the cruise, she'd send him on his way, never to see him again.

She stepped off the elevator and rounded the corner.

Nathan stood at the rail looking out over the commercial port to the city of Marseille beyond, the wind ruffling his hair. The only two times they'd met, he'd been wearing a suit. Although last night after a few rounds on the dance floor, he'd stripped off his jacket and tie, and rolled up his shirt sleeves, revealing a tan throat and muscular forearms.

Today, he wore dark-wash jeans, a white button-down, un-tucked, and driving mocs, no doubt Italian. She tilted her head for a better view of his ass. And what a fine ass it was. *Le sigh.*

Damn, but the man knew how to wear a pair of jeans. Aviators covered his eyes, and a day's growth of stubble covered his jaw. Just your typical casual guy-wear, but he gave it an added dash of sex appeal.

No. He wasn't her typical 'prey,' as Josh so crudely liked to put it. But maybe she'd been in a rut, and it was time for a change.

Slipping on her sunglasses, she stepped up to the rail beside him. "Ah, Marseille, Gateway to Provence, one of my favorite regions of France." The salty air cleared the sleep-deprivation cobwebs from her head and energized her.

He turned, took a step back, and gave her an appreciative once-over that she felt down to her toes. Without her four-inch heels, she felt small in comparison to his height.

He raised a brow over his sunglasses. "No stilettos?"

"No. I can be practical when it's called for. And walking miles on paved streets calls for practicality."

"You've been to Marseille?"

"I came with my parents when I was a little girl—too young to enjoy it, really—and then again when I was a sullen teenager, angry that I couldn't go to camp with my best friend instead." Laura laughed and shook her head. "I was such a little bitch."

Nathan chuckled.

"But after college I took another trip over, and discovered what I'd missed the first two times. Wine. And while most people head for the countryside, I prefer the grit of the city."

"Wine, huh? I like wine," he said.

"Well, you're in for a treat. Although known for their rosé, I prefer the spicy, full-flavored reds. And of course no visit to Marseille would be complete without dining on bouillabaisse."

"Sounds like I've hooked my wagon to the right train. You can be tour guide for the day."

"All right. We can take the Petit Train de la Bonne Mère—"

"You say that like you mean it." He looked impressed.

Laura made a face. "I speak fluent French, Spanish, and Italian. My mother insisted. I also speak fluent sarcasm, when the occasion warrants. Which my mother had nothing to do with." *Unless you count her very existence.*

"I see. But do you speak Southern?" His lips curved into a sexy smile.

"No. But I'm a fast learner." Her gaze flicked to his mouth.

"I'm sorry, I interrupted your review of the itinerary."

She blinked, distracted. His lips were so close to hers. "Yes. Anyway. We can take the Little Train," she said with a smirk, "up to the hilltop basilica Notre Dame de la Garde and its breathtaking view of the city, then back to the Vieux Port, or we can take the path less traveled, the Corniche Président JFK, along the rocky Mediterranean coastline. If I recall, even the sullen teenager in me appreciated the views."

"Why do we have to choose?"

Smiling, she said, "Good question. I like the way you think."

———

The panorama from the Notre Dame de la Garde was breathtaking with all of Marseille spread out before them, and the sparkling Bay of Marseille beyond. Some five hundred feet below, the city's white stone buildings with their terracotta-tiled roofs fell in a jumble at their feet, like a child's discarded building blocks. Above, a sky so clear and blue, it almost hurt to look at it.

The splendor of the scene outside competed with the magnificence of the basilica's interior. Nathan had never seen anything like it. The church's mosaics had fascinated him with their brilliant palette of colors and depth of detail. He wasn't a religious man, but that didn't mean he couldn't appreciate the architecture and artistry of the Neo-Byzantine structure.

"I'm not often rendered speechless, but this does it," Laura said as she gazed out over the vista.

"Ditto."

The salt tang drifted in on the breeze, and Nathan filled his lungs with it. As work assignments went, this one was off the hook.

He and Laura stood in companionable silence, too awestruck to do anything else. She removed her sunglasses, lifting her face to the sun, eyes closed, a slight smile on her face. The breeze teased a few strands from her braid and fanned him with the scent of her perfume. He could see the pulse in her neck, enticing him to press his lips to her sun-warmed skin.

"You should know I'm not opposed to a shipboard fling."

He glanced up and into her open eyes. *Yeah.* The chemistry couldn't be denied. He'd felt it the instant he'd wrapped his hand around the ankle of her imprisoned foot. Should he forego the opportunity fate presented to him on a silver platter? He'd regretted not asking for her phone number that day and now here she stood offering him what any man would be crazy to refuse.

She turned to face him. "I'm a big girl, Nathan. I'm not dreaming of white dresses and china patterns. I'm receptive to a purely physical relationship with no strings. Clearly there's attraction here."

Sweet Jesus.

She stepped closer, but didn't touch him. Didn't matter. His body responded as if she had. Yep, crazy. So let the romancing begin. Snaking an arm around her waist, he drew her in for a kiss sure to be as soul-searing as their first.

He touched his lips to her sun-drenched mouth, tasting the heat and desire there. Clutching her hips, he felt her sway toward him, her hands pressed to his chest. Vaguely aware of the crowd, he sought to deepen the kiss without making a public spectacle. His tongue tangled briefly with hers, before he withdrew, taking a tender nip of her lower lip as he retreated. He gazed down into eyes so blue and unwavering they gave the sky a run for its money.

She flicked her tongue over her lips before sucking her lower lip into her mouth.

He groaned, closing his eyes. "God, woman, you're killing me."

She smiled, slow and seductive. "Wait 'til I get you to bed. Hope your insurance is paid up." She lifted a shoulder. "Just saying."

His knees threatened to buckle. But wait he would, and so would she. The patience he'd learned as a boy on the streets of inner-city Atlanta, then later in the hills of rural North Georgia, had taught him as a young man that the anticipation of obtaining the object desired only heightened the experience once it was obtained. And he had hours left in the day, and the evening, to romance her. And romance her he would.

———

Nathan shook his head as he studied the view.

"What?" Laura asked, confused.

"I feel as if I'm on the set of a movie or something. It just can't be real."

Their table at Chez FonFon in the picturesque Vallon des Auffes, a small fishing port off the Corniche, overlooked the little harbor where colorful wooden fishing boats bobbed at their moorings.

Earlier they'd walked along the Corniche JFK, tracing the rocky coastline of the Mediterranean, stopping to appreciate the beauty of the villas and gardens that dotted the route.

Then they'd ordered what was touted to be the best bouillabaisse in Marseille, and at Laura's recommendation, to accompany it, a fine red from the Bandol region of France.

"Mmm." Nathan swallowed the wine he'd just sipped. "Great recommendation." He swirled the wine in his glass. Watched as the dark legs ran down the side.

"I'm glad you like it." She gazed out at the view. "There's so much of the world to see and experience. And so many fabulous foods and wines to be tasted."

"Here's to fabulous food and wine."

Laura lifted her glass and tapped it to his. Taking a sip, she closed her eyes, and held the wine on her tongue, before swallowing. "Black fruit, vanilla, cinnamon, and leather. Full-bodied and rich."

"You're quite the connoisseur."

Laura lifted a shoulder. "I appreciate the craftsmanship that goes into nice things, be they stilettos or fine wine."

"I've come to appreciate stilettos myself." A slow grin spread over his features. "Especially when they grace a pair of legs like yours."

"Are you flirting with me?"

"No. Definitely not. I don't flirt. I woo." He winked.

"Woo. Now there's a word I haven't heard in, well, ever. Unless you count the occasional steamy historical romance novel."

The waiter brought the first stage of the traditional bouillabaisse, the saffron-rich broth topped with croutons, accompanied by a fragrant roasted garlic clove and *rouille* for spreading on the croutons.

Nathan lifted a dubious eyebrow.

"The fish is served separately," Laura supplied.

"I knew that," he said with a sheepish grin. He lifted his spoon, sipped the broth, and nodded. "Delicious."

"I'm hurt. You doubted me. Do I look like someone who would steer you wrong in anything to do with the finer things in life?" She waggled her spoon at him.

"No, ma'am."

———

Why did that Southern courtesy send a little tingle through her? she wondered. "Speaking of sex and that shipboard fling." *Wow.* She just gave *herself* mental whiplash.

He choked on his bouillabaisse, and placing his spoon in the bowl, wiped his mouth with his napkin. "Give a guy a little warning."

"I have a few rules, so there are no misunderstandings." She set her spoon carefully in her bowl.

"Rules are good. Let's hear 'em."

"Rule Number One: I won't be the other woman." She let that sink in. "I don't have flings with married, or otherwise attached, men."

"As we've already established, I'm not married or otherwise attached."

"Good. Rule Number Two: Just because we're having sex doesn't mean you get to monopolize my time. Sex is sex, and the rest of our time is our own, unless we mutually agree otherwise."

"Understood."

"Rule Number Three: This is just a fling. It ends with the cruise, so don't expect anything once we're back in the States."

"Agreed."

"Rule Number Four—and this one's important: No personal questions. I'm not going to share my deepest, darkest secrets and I won't expect you to share yours. No stories about our dysfunctional families, our formative years, or our teenage traumas."

"Fair enough. Anything else?"

She thought about it a moment. "Rule Number Five: I pay my way."

"No. That's a deal-breaker."

"I won't have you paying for my meals, or anything else for that matter. I didn't come on the cruise expecting to find a Sugar Daddy, even if he is Southern. You pay your way, and I pay mine. Then no one is beholden to the other."

When he didn't respond, she ran her foot up his leg almost to his crotch. He jumped at the intimate contact then closed his eyes and groaned.

"If you want some of this"—she swept her hand up her body—"those are my conditions."

"Damn, sugar, you drive a hard bargain."

She laughed. "I'm worth it. I promise."

He groaned again. "Fine. I'm afraid to ask if there's anything else?"

"That about covers it. What about you? Any rules?"

"Just one. I don't do sleepover."

"Fine. Rule Number Six: No sleepovers." She could accept that, even though she had no issues with waking up to a warm naked man with a morning hard-on.

She raised her glass of wine. "To a no strings, Ship of Dreams fling."

He smiled at her across the table and lifted his glass to hers. "I can get onboard with that."

CHAPTER SEVEN

"How's the cruise?" Darcy asked.

"Fine." Laura shifted the phone so she could open an email on her laptop. She'd barely glanced at her smartphone all day. Unusual for her, but she'd been preoccupied with Nathan. Having fun and all that. Thinking about dinner with him tonight. Followed by her version of dessert.

She'd called Darcy while she was still in port and had a signal, but she also needed to reply to emails. Good thing multi-tasking came naturally.

"Have you hooked up with an Italian? I don't think you've ever, er, dated an Italian."

"There was that guy from Sicily, oh, what was his name? You know, the Formula 1 racecar driver."

"If you can't keep all your conquests straight, how do you expect me to? Maybe you should keep a spreadsheet. And you didn't answer my question. Any accented hotties on the ship?"

Laura bit her lip. For some reason, she didn't feel like discussing Nathan. "It's like an AARP convention.

Everyone here is old enough to be my father. And a few, my grandfather."

"Oh, that sucks. What a drag for you."

"Well, it isn't a vacation after all."

"I know, but all work and no play makes Laura a very bitchy girl."

"Ha, ha. So, what's new with you and Josh? You settling in to connubial bliss?"

"Happy as clams."

"Really? And just what makes clams happy?"

"We're redecorating some of the rooms on the upper floors, and I'm secretly working on an office for Josh. You know, the junk room on the third floor? I've been stripping wall paper and painting while Josh is at work."

"Sounds dreadful." Laura couldn't imagine performing backbreaking labor for herself, much less someone else. "Why don't you just hire someone?"

"Then it wouldn't be as special. Doing it with my own two little hands makes it mean more. It'll be great when it's finished."

"Shouldn't you be working on your next book instead?" Laura frowned over an email from Celeste, the head of the creative team, regarding the drink company's campaign.

"Oh, I am. And it's going like gangbusters. Who knew how productive wedded bliss would make me. It's like a six-pack of Red Bull for my creativity."

"You leave next week for California, right?"

"Yes, and as much as I hate leaving Josh, I'm so excited about the trip. Did I tell you how awesome you two are?"

"Well, I am anyway."

"Oh, Fudgesicle, there's the bell. I've got the upholsterer coming over with some fabric swatches."

Laura laughed at Darcy's go-to F-bomb substitute.

"Okay. Go look at your swatches. Tell the ambulance-chaser hello."

"Laura."

"Yeah?"

"Don't work too hard. Enjoy yourself a little."

She thought again about the afternoon she'd just spent with Nathan, and the evening to come. "I'll try."

Hitting 'end,' she checked her watch. She still had time to jot down some of her thoughts on her Imperial experience so far. Then she'd take extra care with her appearance, because unless her signals had gotten crossed, her drought would meet its end tonight.

———

Scrolling through emails, Nathan caught up on those that couldn't wait. A question about the creative brief for the new tech company campaign. An issue with the media buying for a local Mercedes dealership. Just the typical day-to-day fires that had to be put out. Thankfully all were little hot spots, and not conflagrations.

A text from Amanda asked how his first day in France was. After giving it some thought, he replied, "Well, it didn't suck."

Disasters averted and business handled, he stepped out onto his balcony to breathe in the fresh scent of the water and enjoy the remaining rays of the sun before it set.

The ship had left port over an hour ago and was headed for St. Tropez, followed by Monte Carlo a day later. Nathan tried to envision spending an evening in the Casino de Monte Carlo, home of many a James Bond film. Shaking his head at how far he'd come, he grabbed a chair from the bistro table and propped his feet on the ship's railing.

From the mean streets of inner-city Atlanta to the mountains of rural North Georgia. From the Southern hospitality of Atlanta to the hustle and bustle of New York City. And now, the glamour and beauty of the Mediterranean. What would his grandmother think of him now?

And then there was the gorgeous, intelligent, and worldly Laura Danforth. He'd dated some beautiful women. Smart, capable women. But Laura shined like the Hope Diamond among a display of third-rate fakes. Their afternoon together had been entertaining for many reasons, chief among them, the chemistry between them.

He'd been pretty good at chemistry in school, and not just the sexual kind. Tonight, he'd mix the perfect blend to produce a chemical reaction, preferably a highly combustible one. One part atmosphere, one part romance, and one part heat. The result should be a chemical reaction of epic proportions.

For the atmosphere, he'd reserved a table at the intimate onboard restaurant, La Presse du Vin, which featured wine flights from around the region. For the romance, he'd give her roses, and for the heat, well, from what he'd gleaned so far, a touch was enough to ignite the heat. Mother Nature could take it from there.

———

The waiter placed the white linen napkin on Laura's lap. She gazed across the candlelit table at Nathan, his white dress shirt open at the neck revealing a tanned throat. A single red rose lay on the table at her elbow.

He'd arrived at her door promptly at seven-fifteen bearing an armload of red long-stemmed roses, and wearing a charming grin. She'd rarely received roses, or flowers of any kind for that matter, from a man. Romance had nothing to do with what she wanted from men. She'd been shocked by her reaction to his thoughtfulness. A flutter in her chest, and a pleasant warmth in her belly.

The restaurant's understated décor provided a welcome respite from the high glamour of the rest of the ship. Vintage winepresses stood around the room beneath down-lighting like works of art. Wine corks in a herringbone pattern covered an accent wall, while the other walls were a rich Merlot color. A large glassed-in wine room with rotating racks provided ample storage for the diverse collection of wines available. Small pub tables topped with old wine cask lids stood near a mahogany bar accented with wrought iron.

An eight-glass wine flight waited at their table when they'd arrived. She'd glanced over at Nathan, confused, thinking that the *maître d* had escorted them to the wrong table.

"I thought you'd like to sample some of the region's other wines. Some rosés as well as the reds you love."

Another thoughtful gesture that left her off balance. "Ah. I thought you just wanted to get me drunk."

"A gentleman never gets a lady drunk." He indicated the glasses. "But it is all part of the seduction."

"Seduction?" She drew back in surprise, then leaned forward and said in a conspiratorial whisper, "Let me make it easy for you. I don't need seducing. I'm a sure thing."

"Maybe I'm not."

"Well, then. Maybe I should be seducing you instead."

"That sounds intriguing. We'll try that tomorrow."

"It's just meaningless sex." *Dammit!* Did she just say that out loud? It was meant to be a reminder to herself.

He frowned, his brows drawing together, as he gave a

shake of his head. "Nothing you do in life should be without meaning, least of all sex. Otherwise, what's the point?"

"All right. It's just sex then."

This time his eyebrows shot up. "Just sex? Again, what's the point if the act is, well, pointless. Sugar, for someone who says she appreciates the finer things in life, your view of sex is rather . . . jaded. Sex should be savored, just like a fine wine"—he selected a rosé—"or a rich bouillabaisse."

She lifted a brow in response.

"Fair warning," he continued. "Sex with me will be neither meaningless nor pointless."

Laura's breath caught as he pinned her with his gaze. Her breath shallowed as she watched those full lips caress the rim of the wineglass. Biting her lip, she pressed a hand to her bouncing knee. Men, even those with whom she expected to have sex, did *not* make her nervous.

He took a sip of the wine. "Mmm. Try this." He handed the glass to her.

Their fingers touched as he passed the wine to her and she felt it like a bolt of lightning. All this talk of sex, meaningless or otherwise, had simply heightened her reaction. At least that was what she told herself.

Suppressing a shiver, she took a mouthful of the wine, let the flavors explode on her tongue before swallowing. "Crisp. Refreshing." She tilted her head. "What did you taste?"

He looked thoughtful a moment, and a little self-conscious. "Let's see. Citrus, red berries, and . . . peach."

"You have a connoisseur's discerning taste buds."

He shrugged. "I just know what I like." He reached across the table and took her free hand, rubbing the back with his thumb.

Goose pimples crept up her arm, as her lips parted.

"And I like how your lips taste." His eyes drifted to her lips. "I can't wait to taste the rest of you."

Holy Rhett Butler!

———

They sampled several more glasses of wine before ordering. But rather than savoring her meal, Nathan could tell Laura was chomping at the bit to get the dinner over with. He enjoyed watching her squirm in her seat and smiled over the jittery leg bounce beneath the table. "Do you always do that when you're nervous?"

"Do what?"

"Bounce your leg." Not getting an answer, he chuckled. "Good things come to those who wait."

"What?"

"You know . . . patience is a virtue."

Laura snorted. "In case you haven't noticed, I'm not exactly virtuous."

She sure as hell didn't look virtuous in a sleeveless dress with a neckline that dipped south of her sternum, baring lots of luscious skin, including the curve of her breasts, her hair pulled back in her customary tail.

First on tonight's agenda, sliding the tie from her hair and running his fingers through it. Next, tasting all that skin. Heat flared in his abdomen, and he admonished himself about the aforementioned patience.

"What do you think of the ship's décor?" he asked, redirecting his thoughts. Might as well pick her brain.

"I appreciate Art Deco as much as the next person, but like Christmas decorations, a little goes a long way."

He nodded in agreement.

"I'd prefer something in relaxing neutrals, something

contemporary but warm." She waved her hand at their surroundings. "Something like this."

He made a mental note. Laura's sophisticated taste level couldn't be ignored, and he'd been thinking the same thing himself. The new ship needed a more relaxed feel. "I can't help but think I've stepped into a Fred Astaire movie." He chuckled over a fond memory of his grandmother watching the old black and white movies after a long day on the farm. She'd always been a very practical woman, but her face turned dreamy when she watched Fred and Ginger glide across the screen.

"Or Jean Harlow," Laura offered.

"You a classic movie buff?"

"No, her image is in the ad for Indulgence, one of my favorite perfumes."

"Oh, right. Great ad. Saw it in *GQ*, I think." He tilted his head. "So, what should we order for dessert?"

"Dessert?"

"Of course. We can't pass up the decadent desserts offered." He almost chuckled at the petulant expression on her face. "How about we split the melting chocolate cake? You like chocolate, right?"

"I'm female."

"That you most definitely are." He signaled the waiter and placed their order for dessert and coffee. As their plates were cleared, he asked, "Do you live in Manhattan?"

"Yes." She picked up her wine glass. "And you?"

"Yes."

"Are you from New York?"

"Born and raised." She squirmed a little more in her seat.

"Do you have any brothers or sisters?"

"That's Rule Number Four. No personal questions."

"Right. Sorry. Just making conversation."

She set her glass down. "Look, Nathan. I appreciate all the effort to make this a romantic evening, but I'm not interested in baring my soul to you or anyone else. I'm interested in . . ."

She hesitated, and he knew she'd been about to say 'meaningless sex' but thought better of it. "A fling. Nothing more."

Nathan nodded. He didn't know what made him ask those questions. Even if they were superficial, he didn't usually go there. And he appreciated it when no one tried to take him there. "You're right."

She flashed what appeared to be a smile of relief. "Now, about that fling." The smile transformed to seductive, as her eyes glittered with desire.

Nathan jumped when her bare foot snaked its way up his leg, getting closer to his crotch by the second. He latched onto her ankle before she reached her goal.

"We'll pass on dessert," he ground out as the waiter approached with their coffee.

———

Nathan towed Laura along the empty corridor to the elevator and impatiently pressed the up button. He pulled her in for a kiss that quickly turned sultry. So much for patience.

"Your place or mine?" Nathan asked between kisses.

"Mine," Laura breathed as she nipped his lower lip.

"Mine's closer." Nathan changed the angle of the kiss.

"I have the penthouse." Laura groped his ass.

He pulled back. "Really?"

She nodded.

"Yours. Definitely yours." He'd just pressed his lips to hers again when the elevator *dinged*.

The door opened on a blissfully empty elevator. Reaching out, Laura grabbed Nathan's jacket lapels, hauling him into the corner as the doors slid shut. She wrapped her leg around his, pressing her hips against his, feeling his impressive erection. She groaned as she pressed hot kisses along his jaw.

Nathan slipped his hand inside her dress, baring a breast, and eliciting a gasp from her. "What happened to patience?"

The elevator came to a gentle stop and Nathan pushed away from her, then, reaching out again, covered the delicious breast he'd just bared. Both were panting like they'd just run a marathon, and Laura's hair was mussed where he'd had his fingers in it.

An older couple stepped on, gave them a knowing glance. The woman leaned over to her husband and said in a stage whisper, "Remember the first time we had elevator sex? Of course the elevators moved much slower in those days."

Laura's hand flew to her mouth to cover an unladylike snort as she shot Nathan a look.

He ran his fingers through his rumpled hair and stifled his laugh with a cough.

The elevator stopped on the next deck and the couple stepped off. The man gave Nathan a thumbs-up as the elevator doors closed.

"Wasn't that the man in the fitness center this morning?"

Nathan nodded. "Mr. Cybex."

———

Nathan grappled with the key card, cursing when he missed the slot. Finally the green light came on and he threw the door open.

Laura stepped into the room, softly lit with lamplight, the blackness of the Mediterranean Sea beyond the picture windows. Before he could say a word, she'd slipped her dress from her shoulders, where it glided to the floor, leaving her standing in nothing but a pair of strappy silver stiletto sandals.

"Have mercy!" He nearly choked. "You—you've been naked except for that dress all evening?"

She simply lifted a hand. "As you see." The corner of her mouth lifted, bringing out the dimple he'd wanted to kiss since the day he met her.

His body told him to dive in. His brain told him to savor everything about her. All that silky skin, beautiful breasts, firm tummy, and those legs. Yards of lean sexy legs. His gaze traveled over her as she stood brazen and unrepentant. His eyes met her deep blue ones, hooded now with desire. *Breathtaking!*

"Take your hair down."

She complied, lifting her arms, she freed her hair , spreading it around her shoulders, covering her breasts. A modern-day Lady Godiva. As his breath came out in shallow huffs, he had to remind himself again to take it slow. She licked her lips, and he stifled a groan.

He approached her, taking her hips in his hands. She reached out for his belt buckle. "Uh-huh." He cuffed her wrists and held them behind her back, making her breasts thrust forward. "We're on Nathan-Time now. Slow and easy like a southern summer."

"But—"

"No 'buts.'" He spun her around and steered her toward the bedroom and got an eyeful of a glorious tight ass for his trouble, lifted even higher by those killer shoes.

The bed had been turned down and the lights were low. Laura tried to spin around, but he held her. "No." He snaked an arm around her waist and drew her against him, pressing her delicious derriere into his erection. He skimmed his other hand up her breasts, sweeping aside her hair, before cupping the column of her throat, and gently held her there while he rained kisses down her neck to her shoulders. She tasted better than any fine wine. Like hot, juicy summer peaches.

He inhaled her scent, the same expensive perfume she'd worn when they'd had a chance encounter on a busy Manhattan street. But this time he could smell the woman underneath. Heady and erotic.

Her hands reached behind her back for him. He grasped her wrists again and dragged them back in front of her. "Am I going to have to tie you up?"

"Been there, done that." Her breath came out in ragged gasps.

His stomach knotted with desire at the image of Laura laid out on a bed, hands tied. Almost on the verge of sensory overload, he turned her in his arms and gazed into a face so sensual, lips still swollen from his kisses in the elevator, eyes blurred and drowsy. He cupped her jaw. "Laura, look at me."

She raised her eyes to his.

"It may take all night, but I'm going to kiss every inch of you. You think you can handle that?"

She nodded.

"Good. I think I'll start here and work my way down." He pressed his lips to the dimple at the corner of her mouth.

CHAPTER EIGHT

Laura groaned. Her standard romps were a frenzy of heated kisses, discarded clothes, and lecherous gropes. Your basic wham-bam-thank-you-ma'am encounters. Couplings so physical and unemotional they might have been between two wild animals.

But this. This was delicious torture. Like slowly roasting alive, while enjoying every minute of it. Nathan knelt in front of her, his mouth and tongue leaving hot trails across her bare stomach, while his hands performed wicked delights in their wake. Grasping her hips, he pressed his face to her core. Her legs buckled and she collapsed onto the bed.

How had Nathan taken control? How had she *let* him take control? Control was her middle name, and the bedroom was no exception. But as she lay back on the bed, she realized she liked it. Giving over to someone else was just as heady as taking control. She indulged in a languorous stretch while she watched as Nathan removed his jacket and shoes, unbuttoned his shirt. His eyes never left her. She could feel them caressing her like a lover's hand.

Peeling off his shirt, he tossed it on a chair atop his jacket, revealing a muscular chest and a tight belly. A light-brown patch of hair trailed down his abdomen and disappeared into his waistband. She licked her lips when his hands dropped to his belt buckle, the evidence of his desire for her straining against his zipper.

He stepped out of his trousers and boxers and stood in all his long, lean, naked glory.

As he approached the bed, she reached for him.

"Oh no. I'm not finished," he said, his voice raspy with desire.

She groaned both in exasperation and anticipation.

He grasped her ankles and began kissing his way up her legs, stopping at her Achilles, then her calves, finding a sensitive spot behind her knees she never knew she had, where he licked and nipped until she thought she might spontaneously combust. When he reached her thighs, she could no longer lie still. "Please, Nathan," she panted.

Nathan slid his body up hers, abrading her heated skin, eliciting shivers of pleasure. He took her mouth in a scorching kiss as she opened her legs to him.

He filled her in one smooth thrust, inhaling her gasp of pleasure as his tongue tangled with hers. "God," he groaned against her mouth. "You feel so good."

She wrapped her legs around his waist, clutching his hips, urging him to move. But he didn't. He reveled in the feel of her, focused on her breathy sighs, the sensual feel of her bare breasts against his chest.

"Nathan. You're killing me. What are you doing?" She bucked her hips against his. "Why aren't you moving?"

"Shh. All in good time." He leaned down, took her mouth with his, once, twice, three times. Soft gentle kisses. Then he dove in, and as his hips began to move, his tongue mimicked his movements. Laura released a throaty groan, her tongue caressing his, her fingers grasped his ass and squeezed.

Breathy moans and sighs, whispered naughty endearments, and groans of pleasure filled the room. She raked her fingers up his back, panting with each thrust of his hips, tangling those same fingers in his hair. "Nathan. Nathan."

His name on her lips was almost his undoing. The heat built into a conflagration as they soared ever higher, his blood a molten river. He grasped her face with his hand. "Laura. Look at me. I want to see you."

She opened her eyes, dark with desire, and gazed into his, as they reached the pinnacle, a rapture beyond anything, before falling into the abyss.

———

Laura's pants subsided, as her heartbeat returned to normal. Nathan rolled off of her, but drew her with him, settling her head on his shoulder. His hands skimming along her arm to her shoulder and back down again. Drowsiness set in, her body a boneless heap. Safe to say, that was the best sex she'd ever had. Something to be said for Nathan-Time. Slow and sensual. Delicious.

"You alive?" Nathan asked.

Her only response, a nod. Words seemed beyond her at the moment.

He chuckled, a rumble deep in his chest. Then he

kissed the top of her head. The tenderness of the gesture wasn't lost on her.

Pull yourself together, Laura. She raised up on her elbow and gazed down at his handsome face, looking as relaxed as she felt. Skimming a hand across his chest, she smiled. "Well, Nathan. Seduction complete. What do you have to say for yourself?"

His lips lifted in a cocky grin. "I think my actions spoke louder than words. Much louder. In fact, I think they heard you on the captain's bridge."

She tweaked his nipple.

"Ow."

"Don't get cocky. Or I might have to show you a thing or two."

He lifted a brow, intrigued. "Woman, give me a moment to recover, and you can show me anything you want."

"Careful there, hotshot. Playing with fire will get you burned."

He tilted her chin up and covered her mouth with his. His other hand glided up her rib cage, across her breast as she nipped at his tongue.

"Are you recovered yet?" She trailed her hand down his abdomen, enjoying the quiver of muscle beneath.

"Yes."

Her mouth followed the path of her hand. "Don't say I didn't warn you."

"Burn, baby, burn," he murmured, as she headed south.

———

The ship had docked in St. Tropez, on the French Riviera, sometime between Nathan creeping out of her room around two a.m.—but not before another couple of rounds of slow, sizzling sex—and sunrise. Her dry spell had come to an end. And in a glorious, bone-melting way.

They'd begun their day in St. Tropez with a particularly lame guided tour of the city—something she intended to point out in her report—later ditching it to spend the morning strolling the Quartier de la Ponche, with its maze of streets and its buildings in soft terra-cottas, warm peaches, sun-drenched pinks, accented with the occasional sky-blue, all beneath an endless azure dome.

They'd dined on Provençal beef stew at Le Café, on a terrace overlooking the Place de Lices, and sipped on cold French *pastis,* an anise-flavored liqueur. Well, she had at least.

After a sun-drenched day, she and Nathan had parted ways to go to their respective staterooms to dress for dinner.

As she checked her emails, she laughed at the memory of Nathan's face when he first tasted the licorice-tasting drink. The way he'd squeezed his eyes shut before swallowing like he'd taken foul-tasting medicine. And then grabbed the jug of spring water meant for diluting the *pastis,* and pouring it into an empty glass, before gulping it down. Licorice, as he'd explained once he'd washed the taste from his mouth, wasn't high on his list of flavors.

They'd tried their hand at *pétanque,* a game similar to bocce, playing against one another, with sexual favors on the line for the winner. Her skin warmed at the thought of paying up tonight. The acts she'd anted up were no hardship to perform on a man that looked, . . . and tasted, smelled, and felt like Nathan did.

Laura didn't know what to make of Nathan's affectionate gestures. He'd reached out for her hand on more than one occasion, clasping her fingers with his and gently swinging their arms between them. She liked the sweetness of it, but it also made her uncomfortable. To her mind, they were more the actions of a boyfriend, than a fling.

Stepping into her luxurious shower, she turned on the body jets and let them pound away at her while she lathered her hair and tried to put the more troubling aspects of their fling out of her head. She had more . . . charming aspects to focus on. Like Nathan's mouth. And his hands. And other tantalizing regions below the equator.

After last night, Nathan Maxwell filled her thoughts. She'd managed to tamp down her lust while they lunched, when she'd let her feet do the talking beneath the table. But she had plans for the evening, which didn't include dining in any of the ship's fine establishments.

———

Nathan whistled a cheerful little tune as he ambled down the corridor, anticipating another evening in the presence of one Laura Danforth. He couldn't remember when he'd enjoyed someone's company so much. And he didn't really know anything about her given Rule Number Four. All he knew was she was a trust-fund baby, by her own admission, she lived in Manhattan, she liked to run her foot up his legs, and she had a sweet spot behind her knee that he wanted to taste more of. Oh, and she served on some sort of fundraising committee.

The only reason he knew that last bit was because while they were enjoying the sites in St. Tropez, she'd received an urgent email from a committee member, she'd said, about a big gala in September. She stepped away for a minute to make a call and returned, stating simply, "Emergency resolved."

She'd nearly done him in that afternoon, especially at

lunch when she'd grazed her foot up his leg, heading north in one of her favorite moves. He'd jumped like a man on a live wire before cuffing a hand around that trim little ankle and halting her erotic ascent.

Still whistling, Nathan knocked on the door to Laura's stateroom. The whistle died on his lips when she opened the door wearing nothing but a little black silk robe and those hot-pink satin stilettos of hers. Her long, silky hair flowed around her shoulders almost to her waist. "Sugar, you're, uh, not dressed."

"Observant, aren't you?" She propped her hand high on the door, raising the hem of her skimpy robe to just below her pearly gates. He checked the corridor for any unwelcome observers, as he struggled to form something other than a Neanderthal grunt. "Er, are we, uh, going to dinner?"

"I thought you might like a piece of this instead." She peeled aside her robe to reveal a black and hot pink lace corset and matching panties that left little to the imagination. Her robe whispered down her body to pool at her feet, and all the blood in his body went with it.

As soon as he could get his tongue off the floor, he stepped into the room, closing the door behind him. "I'd like more than a piece of that." His eyes roamed over her from her beautiful head to her satin-encased toe. "I'm a glutton. I want it all." His arm snaked out, hauling her firmly against him, as he claimed her mouth with his.

Breaking the kiss, she said, "I thought you might like an evening in with just me and La Perla."

"As much as I admire, uh, La Perla, I'm afraid three's a crowd."

"That's a crying shame, but if you insist." She unfastened the hooks at the front of the corset and dropped it to the floor. Her breasts spilled out, making his mouth water.

"Sweet Jesus," he muttered. He filled his hands with her. She groaned, throwing back her head allowing him easy access to the tender spot below her ear. He took advantage, pressing his lips to the erratic pulse in her neck. He knotted his hands in that long luxurious hair. Breathed it in. She smelled of jasmine and sex. And heaven. Pure heaven.

"It's my turn to seduce you," she murmured.

"Sugar, you're doing a mighty fine job." He bent, took a taut nipple into his mouth, lathing it with his tongue.

Fisting her hands in his hair, she held him to her.

He released her breast to blaze a trail up her neck to her full lips, where his tongue explored the hot recesses of her mouth.

Yanking his jacket off, she tossed it on the floor, then ripped his tie open and began unbuttoning his shirt, planting hot kisses down his chest to his abdomen.

"Woman, unless you want this to end before we even get started, I'd advise against going where you're headed."

She smiled against him, and instead went to work on his belt buckle, making short work of it before unbuttoning his fly and plunging her hands down the front of his pants. His knees buckled.

"I've been wanting to touch you like this all day," she panted.

"Good Lord. You're trying to kill me."

She laughed, deep and throaty, sending a shot of heat to his already overheated groin. "I warned you about your insurance."

He boosted her up, his hands planted on the bare ass revealed by her thong. Wrapping her legs around him, he carried her to the bedroom, his mouth firmly on hers.

She proceeded to undress him, her touch excruciating in its sensuality. Shoving him onto the bed, she crawled atop him, straddling him. She was something to behold. Bare breasted, hair tumbling around her, eyes hooded with desire. And her lips parted, swollen and moist.

"Seduction complete." He grasped her hips and rolled her beneath him. "Now, I'll take it from here."

———

After dining on room service—lobster, followed by plump chocolate-covered strawberries, and champagne—Laura sat back in her chair, her black silk robe around her. Replete. The first word that came to mind. Suggesting to Nathan that they have a fling was the best idea she'd had in a long time.

He'd displayed an aptitude in that department. More than a few times. She sucked chocolate off her thumb as she eyed his bare chest across the table from her.

Rising from the table, she swiped her finger in the bowl of chocolate sauce, and straddling him, smeared it across his lips. Diving in, she proceeded to lick and nip the chocolate off.

His hands splayed across her back as he allowed her entrance to his mouth. His fingers laced in her hair. Breaking the kiss, he reached for his glass of champagne, and with a wicked grin tipped it, spilling it across her chest. "Whoops."

Squealing as the cold bubbly spread, running down her belly and into her belly button, she yanked the wet robe away from her skin. "What the hell?" She stood, stripped off the robe.

"Mission accomplished," he said.

"If you'd wanted me naked, all you had to do was ask."

Reaching out, he snagged her around the waist. "What

would be the fun in that?" He drew a champagne-soaked nipple into his mouth and suckled it. "Excellent vintage." Drifting lower, he slurped the pool of champagne out of her belly button, making her giggle.

Lifting her up, he placed her across his lap, legs straddling him, and slipped inside her. She threw her head back in ecstasy.

He always managed to turn the tables on her. Just when she thought she was in control, he flipped the switch. As he drove into her in smooth, solid thrusts, she gladly gave way to him, knowing she would be far from disappointed.

———

Nathan rested his chin on Laura's shoulder as they floated back down to earth, covered in sticky champagne, her hot body pressed to his. What more could a man ask for?

Bedding Laura was the highlight of the trip. No priceless antiquities, no spectacular hilltop views could compare with the feel of her wrapped around him.

He didn't want the evening to end. He, who never stayed with a woman for the night, preferring to avoid the whole awkward morning-after thing. "How about a bath?"

She lifted her head, her brow furrowed. "What?"

"A bath. You know, bubbles, candlelight. I thought you women craved baths."

"Not me. I'm a shower kind of gal. Faster."

"Not tonight." He lifted her off him, and rose from the chair, heading toward the stateroom's luxurious bathroom, complete with picture window overlooking the dark Mediterranean. "Shame to waste this pool-sized bathtub. Just wait there, I'll call you when it's ready."

Turning on the tap, he rummaged around and found the complimentary Bulgari bath products. Pouring some beneath the stream of hot water, he tested the temperature. Perfect.

Whistling the same tune he'd started off the evening with, he laid out fresh towels. Catching his reflection in the mirror, he considered the man looking back at him. Bare-chested, hair mussed, lips swollen. Yep. That was the face of a sexually-satisfied man. His mouth spread into a wide grin.

He walked back out to the living room to find Laura standing in all her naked glory, pulling her hair up in that messy twist only women knew how to do.

"Bath's ready."

"I don't know why we don't just take a sh—"

He planted a kiss on her and, scooping her up, carried her into the bathroom. Stepping into the steamy water, he lowered them into the cloud of bubbles. After situating her in front of him, he pulled her back against his chest and began soaping up her breasts, his hands slipping and sliding along her slick skin, over every delicious curve.

Sighing, she relaxed against him, gave herself over to his ministrations. "Okay. I'm beginning to see the merits of a hot bath."

"I thought you might." Her rinsed her off, kissing her neck, caressing her breasts, as they gazed out into the night. The light of a moon almost full, kissed the black waters of the Mediterranean.

"Beautiful," she breathed.

"Yes. But not as beautiful as you." His hand slipped between her legs.

"You know, I've never had sex in a bathtub."

"Then, sugar, we'd better rectify that travesty right quick."

CHAPTER NINE

The next morning, Nathan followed Laura into the ship's casual dining room for breakfast before disembarkation into Monte Carlo for the day. He'd quickly broken his one and only rule about sleeping over.

He woke that morning, Laura in his arms, legs intertwined, butt nestled against his morning hard-on. He'd put that to use before she could even open her eyes. Yessiree, what a way to start the morning.

When they were seated at a table for two, Laura leaned over and whispered to Nathan, "Is it me, or is everyone looking at us?"

Nathan glanced around. "No. I think you're right. Everyone is looking at us."

Laura glanced down at her chest.

"What are you doing?"

"Just checking to make sure the girls hadn't popped out to say hello."

Nathan chuckled. "Sugar, if your, er, girls had popped out to say hello, rest assured I'd be the first to greet them."

"Such a gentleman."

"You know it."

———

After placing their order, Nathan handed his menu to the waiter. "While you were drying your hair, I had the concierge make reservations at Le Louis XV for dinner tonight. Thought a double-oh-seven evening of martinis and gambling suited Monte Carlo."

"Look at you, going all cruise director on me."

"What"—he pulled back—"that doesn't sound fun to you?"

"It does. It sounds intriguing." The thought of seeing Nathan in a tux made her toes curl. He did more for a man's suit than Armani. Nathan in a tux—well, it was beyond words.

"Did you bring an evening gown?"

"Please." She waved her hand as if he'd asked if she'd brought her toothbrush. "Of course I brought an evening gown."

The waiter delivered their breakfast, and Nathan dug into his eggs benedict. "What would you like to do today?"

"What? No itinerary? You're falling down on the job."

He lifted a brow. "My time was otherwise occupied, if you'll remember."

"That's no excuse." But Laura remembered quite well how he'd occupied his time. In the shower. Lathering her all over. Before pinning her against the shower wall, and—

"Well, I understand there are some beautiful museums in Monte Carlo, if you're so inclined." The knowing look in his eyes as he gazed into hers told her, her trip down memory lane was written all over her face.

"Sure. I could use a day of culture."

———

Museumed-out, she and Nathan boarded the ship to change for dinner.

"I don't know about you, but if I have to look at another piece of Grace Kelly memorabilia, I'm going to poke my eyes out."

Nathan's rich laugh sent quivers of delight up her spine, and she couldn't resist the urge to tug him beneath the ship's exterior stairs for a quick grope session.

She tangled her fingers in his hair and drew his lips down to hers.

His hands glided up her butt to the small of her back, where they slipped beneath her blouse.

Leaning into him, she pressed her breasts against his chest, as her hands slid down his back to his fine ass. "Um, your butt's buzzing."

"Hmm?"

"Your butt. It's buzzing."

"Ignore it. I intend to." He changed the angle of the kiss, and before long Nathan's butt wasn't the only thing buzzing. Now she had a delicious little foreplay buzz going.

"I'll come by your room at six-thirty."

"Or we could go back to my room now," she purred, running her fingers up his chest.

"You said you had some emails to handle for the gala."

"Party-pooper. We'll pick up where we left off."

"Looking forward to it."

Before tackling those aforementioned emails, some about the gala, some about work, she laid out the evening dress she'd packed for just such an occasion—dinner and gambling at the Monte Carlo casino. The halter style dress in classic black made her appear even taller than her five-foot eight inches, and emphasized her curves. The pair of strappy silver Manolo's and a Judith Leiber handbag in the shape of a Fabergé egg finished off the ensemble. Other than a pair of diamond stud earrings, she'd go *sans* jewelry tonight.

Her phone buzzed. Seeing a text from Katie, she frowned.

CAREFUL. THERE'S A SPY ONBOARD.

WHAT THE HELL ARE YOU TALKING ABOUT? Laura texted back.

SOMEONE FROM HAWK MEDIA IS ONBOARD.

Damn. She paced into the living area, scanning through the passengers she'd encountered so far, and discarding them without a second thought. Most were well-past retirement age—too old to be with Hawk Media. And any person with Hawk Media wouldn't be traveling first class. Another reason she'd booked the penthouse.

Closing her eyes and tapping her temples to focus her thoughts, she skidded to a halt. "No!" Nathan. He was the right age. She didn't know what his accommodations were, but he traveled alone, like herself.

Could she be sleeping with the enemy? *Damn.* That would really suck if she couldn't hook up with him again. Then again, what was that saying, *Keep your friends close, and your enemies closer?* Couldn't get much closer than having wild . . . scorching sex . . . all night long.

No. That's a win-at-all-costs tactic her father would use. And she wasn't her father. If Nathan proved to be the enemy, no more sex. Which would be a damned shame, since it was the best sex she'd ever had. And considering how much sex she'd had, that was saying something.

Focus, Laura. Returning to her dissection of Nathan as the potential enemy, she recalled his Cartier watch. The cut of his suits. The Italian leather shoes. Hermès ties. His ad exec salary might cover such expenses, but his rent in New York would eat up a chunk of it. He didn't strike her as careless with his money. Plus, she hadn't heard anything about Hawk Media hiring someone new.

Still. He stayed on her list of potential candidates until another more suitable candidate won out.

Pacing again, she continued her passenger inventory. "Wait a minute." The middle-aged guy with glasses. He'd chatted her up a few times. "What was his name?" George? Gary? Something with a 'G.' Greg? Greg. That's it.

He'd asked her several probing questions about her experience on the trip so far. How she liked her stateroom. What she thought of the food. Whether the service met her expectations. She'd also seen him carrying an electronic tablet around with him. Not very subtle. But then again, maybe he hadn't expected to encounter his competition on the ship.

She recalled his wedding ring. That tipped the scales in his favor. A married man on a cruise alone meant a) He was on the prowl, in which case, he'd remove his wedding ring, or b) He was traveling for work. "Ding, ding, ding, ding. We have a winner."

She texted Katie back. THANKS FOR THE HEADS UP. I THINK I'VE FIGURED OUT WHO.

Momentarily her phone buzzed again. DAMN YOU'RE QUICK.

DAMN RIGHT, she texted back. Too much was riding on this account not to be all-in. She'd just keep an eye on Greg.

———

The Casino de Monte Carlo teemed with tourists and jetsetters alike, of all nationalities. The palatial landmark, with all the opulence and grandeur of the *Belle Époque,* took Nathan by surprise. The movies he'd seen didn't come close to capturing the sumptuous decor, gilded details, and crystal chandeliers. Outside, they'd passed cars that cost more than his annual salary with pedigrees like Mercedes, Bentley, Rolls, Maserati, and Ferrari.

He paused to take it all in, trying not to act the starstruck yokel that he was.

"Oh, look. There's Roger Moore," Laura said, as if she rubbed elbows with famous actors who were Knights of the British realm all the time.

"Double-oh-seven himself," Nathan murmured. "Is that —" He pointed to a leggy blonde to their right.

"Yes. That's her," Laura said, talking about the *Sports Illustrated* swimsuit-model-turned-actress.

"Well, I'll be."

"She's beautiful if you like that sort of . . . perfection."

"Did I say she was beautiful? She pales in comparison to you." He pulled her close, and nuzzled her neck, savoring her shiver and sharp intake of breath. She smelled warm, feminine, and sophisticated. Erotic.

"Good answer," she murmured.

When he'd picked her up from her suite, her beauty had overwhelmed him. She'd skipped her favored sleek ponytail for loose flowing waves that spilled over her shoulders and down her back. He'd wanted to fist his hands in that sexy bedroom hair, bury his face in it, let it fall like a curtain around them as she rode him into oblivion.

Later, he'd told himself. Something to look forward to. Her dress fit her like a glove, the slit up the side revealing a leg he couldn't wait to feel wrapped around him again as he buried himself deep inside her.

Groaning, he retreated to whisper in her ear, "Sugar, I'm of a mind to take you to the nearest dark corner and show you just how gorgeous I think you are."

"You keep calling me sugar, and I'll lead the way."

Chuckling, he took her hand and guided her toward the Le Bar Américain for a drink before checking out the casinos.

They'd dined at Le Louis XV in the Hôtel de Paris on a meal so sublime Nathan doubted he would ever experience its like again. Pulling out all the stops, they'd ordered caviar and Mediterranean sea bass, indulged in poached pear, with lavender honey *crémeux* and emulsion for dessert, and gone through two bottles of wine.

He'd winced when he received the bill, and felt a stab of guilt at the money he was spending. If Hawk didn't fire him when he received the credit card bill, it would be a miracle. Good thing Laura had Rule Number Five about paying her way. The gentleman in him didn't like it, but with the mortgages on the farm, he'd cut back on his spending, no new suits or shoes, no new Hermès ties, and her dinner was one expense he could do without.

Enough of that. According to his grandmother, life's too short for regrets. Tonight was a once-in-a-lifetime adventure. *Enjoy it.*

———

Le Bar Américain boasted an elegant ambiance with soft lighting, leather-upholstered armchairs, rich wood, and live piano music.

Laura approached the bartender and ordered a Cosmo.

"Sir, what can I get you?" the bartender asked Nathan.

"A martini—shaken, not stirred."

Laura groaned, and the bartender rolled his eyes.

"I've always wanted to say that." A roguish grin spread across Nathan's face.

"Like he hasn't heard *that* before."

"I wish I had a euro for every time I've heard it," the bartender returned in a heavy French accent. "I'd be living on the French Riviera by now."

Laura stepped back and gave Nathan a once-over. Damn, if he didn't look scrumptious in a tux. She patted his rock hard chest, "You could give James Bond a run for his money." She tilted her head. "Maybe instead of the traditional British spy, they should consider a southern James Bond. Shake things up a bit."

"And instead of a martini, he could drink a mint julep," Nathan replied with a grin.

"Yeah, something like that." She shook her head.

"What should we try our luck at tonight? Roulette? Black Jack? Craps?"

"Hmm." She sipped from her Cosmo. "Why do we have to choose?"

"Good point."

A short time later, they stepped into the noise and buzz of the casino. Laura's gaze drifted over some of the world's most glamorous people. Movie stars rubbed elbows with royalty. Rock stars partied with business moguls. The tourists were easy to spot. Mouths agape, eyes wide, pointing out this notable personage or that diamond-studded neck.

She cut a glance at her escort, as he placed a hand at the small of her back, directing her to a just-vacated Black Jack table. Nathan Maxwell held his own. He possessed a quiet confidence. Nothing flashy, but nothing to be ignored either. Polite. Polished. Debonair.

She couldn't help notice the way women looked at him when he entered a room. And the man knew his way around a woman's body, too. She could attest to that. Yessiree, her dry spell was over and in a big way.

———

Nathan stood at the craps table in the Salle des Amériques, an ever-growing stack of *cheques* in front of him. "Give me a kiss for luck." She'd kissed him before every roll of the dice, and it seemed to by paying off. Why stop now? "Come on, baby needs a new pair of shoes." Or in his case, sister needs two mortgages paid off.

"Seven!" the stickman called.

The crowd that had formed around the table cheered, and he cupped Laura's neck, hauling her in for another deep steamy kiss.

They'd played Black Jack first, and Laura had won a few hundred dollars, while Nathan had lost nearly the same amount, then they'd moved on to roulette, where she'd promptly lost her winnings. Lady Luck finally smiled on Nathan at the craps table.

Eyeing the stack of *cheques* on the table, he'd decided not to push Lady Luck's generosity, and called in his winnings, to the disappointment of the crowd. He figured he'd won close to ten thousand euros. While it wouldn't pay off the mortgages, it might keep the wolves at bay for a time. He'd wire the money to his sister at his earliest convenience.

Tipping the boxman, he and Laura gathered his *cheques* to cash them. Folding the check the casino paid him with and slipping it into his jacket pocket, he guided Laura out of the casino, into the cool night air.

"What a way to end the evening," Laura said, laughing, her eyes bright.

"Sugar, this evening isn't even close to over. I've got a few more things in mind."

"Like what?"

He leaned in and whispered something naughty in her ear.

Her eyes widened. "That's a new one," she replied.

———

The ship's horn blasted as they ran for the port and up the gangplank. Breathless, Laura grabbed Nathan's hand and dragged him toward the elevator, eager to fulfill his wicked fantasy.

"Whoa, Nellie! We have to wait until we're out to sea," Nathan said with a laugh.

"But nothing's stopping us from a little foreplay." She reached up and tugged on his bow tie, untying it, giggling as a passing couple cast a reproachful eye.

Giggling! Where had that come from? Laura Armstrong didn't cry, and she certainly didn't giggle. The giddiness she experienced now was far better than any alcohol buzz, and the thought of getting Nathan in her room and out of his tux left her lightheaded.

When they finally made it inside her stateroom, she pressed him against the door and ran her hands up his chest, to his hair, tangling her fingers in the silky brown tresses. "I want you, Nathan Maxwell." She molded her lips to his, her tongue grazing his lips.

The ship's engines started.

Moaning, he pulled her hips against his, then reaching around, squeezed her ass. "Dear God, woman. Your fore-play will be the death of me."

Taking each end of his bow tie, she led him into the bedroom. "Why don't I give you a little striptease? That should pass the time until we're out of port."

He closed his eyes as if in pain. "Sugar, if you're wearing what I think you're wearing underneath that dress, your striptease won't last until the anchor's weighed."

She laughed, deep and sexy. "Maybe you're right. So I'll sit here"—she dropped into a chair, and crossed her legs, the slit revealing every inch of her bare leg—"while you do a striptease for me."

He choked out a laugh. "Oh no. I don't think so."

"Oh sure. You were all onboard when it was me doing the stripping. Now I'm asking you to strip, and you go all shy on me."

"Not shy, just self-aware." He chuckled, looking a little self-conscious.

"Come on, Nathan. Let me see you strip. Nice and slow, then before you know it, we'll be out at sea. I'll make it worth your while, I promise."

She untied the halter straps at her neck, dropped first one, then the other.

"You're a brazen hussy, you know that?"

"And you love it." She flashed him her most seductive smile.

He groaned, but began to slowly remove his tie. Then moved to his cuff links before removing his jacket.

"Turn around."

"What?"

She twirled her finger in the air. "Turn around."

He complied.

"Now remove your shirt." In control again. It felt good. "That's it."

He slipped the shirt off his shoulders, glanced over his shoulder, and flashed her a grin.

"You may have missed your calling. Nathan Maxwell, Male Stripper."

He chuckled, the sound scraping deliciously over her aroused nerves.

"Shoes and socks next."

"Are you going to tell me how to undress?"

"Yes."

He sat on the bed, toed off his shoes, slid off his socks.

"Now the pants."

He obliged her, slowly unzipping his fly, the sound rasping in the quiet stateroom. She bit her lip in antic-ipation.

Stepping out of his pants, he tossed them on the floor.

She lifted a brow. "Apparently stripping for me was a turn-on for you." Her gaze slipped below his waist to his erection.

"You sitting there bare-breasted was a turn-on for me."

"Now it's your turn."

She stood and shimmied out of the dress, and stood in nothing but her birthday suit and silver stilettos.

"Good God," he breathed. Tugging the blanket off the bed and taking Laura's hand, he led her out onto the balcony for a little love beneath the stars.

CHAPTER TEN

"I don't know about you, but I'm starved," Nathan said.

They'd opted to spend their day in the port of Portofino in the small old resort town of Santa Margherita Ligure, with its candy-colored buildings and *trompe-l'oeil* frescoes, embraced by the sea on one side and the mountains on the other.

"I could eat. If you can hold out a bit, there's a hilltop restaurant overlooking the town," Laura offered.

Nathan shrugged and grinned. "I'm game."

His phone vibrated in his pocket. Taking it out, he glanced at the screen and frowned. "I need to take this, do you mind?"

"No, of course not."

"Hey, Amanda," his voice going all sweet. "Thanks for calling me back. I forget about the time difference." Nathan stepped into a tiny square where a fountain bubbled cheerfully.

Amanda? Hmm. Who was Amanda? Laura wondered. Did she need to remind Nathan that she didn't play 'the other woman?'

He turned his back to her. She didn't like eavesdropping, and while she wasn't close to him, she could still hear his end of the conversation. Laura strolled over to the fountain, away from Nathan, and perched on its low wall.

"Listen, I had a big win last night at the craps tables in Monte Carlo—what? No, I haven't started gambling. It was just for fun. Amanda—chill. I'm not going to have to join Gamblers Anonymous when I return."

Nathan paced over to the fountain, as if he were oblivious she was there. So much for offering him privacy. Oh well. If he didn't want it, she wasn't inclined to give it to him. Especially when the conversation was just getting juicy.

"I wired that money to the farm account this morning. Yes. I want you to use it to pay on the mortgages. I know it's not enough, but maybe it will hold the lenders at bay a little longer."

So *that's* why he'd wanted to find a bank. She thought he'd just wanted to deposit his winnings.

He paused, propping his leather-clad foot up on the wall next to her, listening to the other end of the conversation.

Laura dipped her hand in the cool water, trying to appear as if she wasn't clinging to his every word. He'd wired last night's winnings to a farm account and asked this *Amanda* to pay on the mortgages? Plural? Nathan didn't strike her as the farmer type. And what lenders did he need to hold at bay?

"Okay," Nathan continued. "I miss you, too."

Laura clamped down on her reaction. *Missed her? Who was this woman?* Wincing, she realized that sounded a lot like jealousy. And she wasn't the jealous type. Just selfish. She wanted to be the one and only, if only for a short time.

"I'm sorry to leave you with this mess, but it will pay off in the end. I promise. I'll call you in a day or two." He ended the call and slid the phone back into his pocket. He stared straight ahead for a moment, before searching for Laura as if he didn't know where she was. "Sorry about that. Family business."

Family business? Rising, she walked over to him. "Look, Nathan, we agreed, Rule Number Four: No personal questions, but we also agreed, Rule Number One: I'm not the other woman. So, I have to ask, who is Amanda?"

Nathan stepped into her, and cupping her face said, "Amanda is my baby sister. I promise there is no other woman." He lowered his mouth to hers, taking her lips in a warm kiss, before retreating. "Now, I thought you were starving."

Laura sighed. Nathan Maxwell sure knew how to kiss. "I am, but not for food anymore."

A slow smile spread across his face. "Sugar, don't tempt me."

———

Laura had spent a good bit of the afternoon thinking over Nathan's baffling phone conversation, trying to put the pieces together. She didn't know why it mattered so much to her. Was Nathan in financial trouble? If so, why was he on this expensive cruise? Did he have a gambling problem, despite what he'd told his sister? To her knowledge, he hadn't spent any time in the ship's casino, and he hadn't suggested they go there either.

And what was the deal with this farm? If he had a farm, what was he doing living in New York? Dressed like he belonged on the cover of *GQ*? She couldn't imagine the urbane Nathan Maxwell in coveralls and a flannel shirt.

Her curiosity was eating her up, but she reminded herself of her own rules.

Her thoughts circled back to The Spy and she questioned again whether it could be Nathan. But no. She'd seen Greg talking with other passengers, taking notes on his tablet. Nathan hadn't spent any time with other passengers—at least not that she knew—except in her presence.

"There's an app for that," Laura offered, responding to Nathan's comment about people who couldn't demonstrate even a modicum of courtesies.

She opened the door to her stateroom, Nathan's laughter following her into the room. Glancing down, she saw an envelope on the floor, as if someone had slipped it under her door. The recipient name on the envelope read: LAURA ARMSTRONG. Before Nathan could see it, she flipped the enveloped and slid it open.

"It's a telegram," she muttered, confused, answering a question Nathan hadn't asked. Skimming to the end, she saw her grandmother's name.

"I didn't know they still sent telegrams."

"Me neither." She wandered over to the picture window to read it.

"Not bad news, I hope?" Nathan asked, still standing near the door.

"Hmm? No," she replied, distracted. "No, it's not bad news, unless you consider being disinherited bad news." Now why had she blurted that out?

She released a mirthless laugh. So the old bitty had finally done it. Apparently, it was official.

Her grandmother had been so pissed that Laura had missed her eightieth birthday celebration that she'd met with her team of lawyers and revised her will. She sighed, and collapsed into a nearby chair. Clearly the flowers, the bottle of *Krug Clos du Mesnil* champagne—her grandmother's favorite—and the card did nothing to mitigate the woman's wrath.

"Laura? Are you okay?" Nathan knelt in front of her, taking both her wrists in his.

Still stunned, she gazed out the window. "Yes. I'm fine." Not really. Not yet. But she would be. She'd survived without her father's love and her mother's affection, she could survive without her grandmother's money.

"No, you're not." Nathan said, his voice soft and understanding. "I can't say I know what it feels like to be disinherited, but I imagine it doesn't feel good. Why would your grandmother do that?"

Laura could feel tears stinging her eyes. She. Would. Not. Cry. *Especially* in front of Nathan.

And dammit. It wasn't the money. She didn't need the money. She wasn't afraid of hard work, and her salary and the money from her grandfather would support her quite comfortably. But the inheritance was just one more connection with her family, tenuous as it was, that was now broken. As far as her father was concerned, she didn't exist. And now her grandmother felt the same way.

She swallowed the tears building in her throat, and gave Nathan a watery answer. "Because she can."

"Ah, sugar." He took the paper from her hand and laid it on the side table. "Come here." He pulled her up and took her place in the chair, and drawing her into his lap, nestled her head beneath his chin.

It felt so damn good to nestle into his lap. To be held with such tenderness. Such . . . caring. She couldn't resist burrowing in, pressing her face into the warmth of his neck.

Other than as a child, when Darcy's mother or father comforted her, she couldn't remember the last time someone had just held her. Certainly not the men she met. The men she had meaningless sex with. The only holding they wanted to do involved some form of sexual contact. Not this unbearable tenderness.

He stroked her hair, pressed a kiss to the top of her head. "Do you want to talk about it?" he asked.

"Not really. Rule Number Four."

He chuckled, the sound rumbling in his chest. "Okay. What would you like to do?"

She raised her head and gazed into his kind eyes. "I'd like you to make love to me, Nathan."

He held her gaze, then claimed her mouth with his. His fingers traced a lazy pattern across her back. Soothing and arousing all at once. He moved to cup her face in his hands, and she wrapped her hands around his wrists. His kisses were slow and thoughtful. Tender and sweet.

Sighing into his mouth, she relaxed into him. Let herself go. For once, just bared her soul and let herself be.

He unbuttoned her blouse, kissed her shoulder as he peeled back the silk. He popped open the front closure on her bra, baring her breasts to his touch, his mouth. Closing her eyes, she let him sweep her up and away. Lifting her off his lap, he stood her in front of him, removed her remaining clothes, before rising from the chair himself. "Sit."

He knelt at her feet, gazing up into her face, his eyes liquid gold, warm. Spreading her legs, he tasted her, taking her breath away. She gripped his hair, fingers tangling, grasping. The pleasure almost unbearable. The climax burst upon her, taking her by surprise, making her cry out with the sheer glory of it.

After shedding his clothes, he lifted her from the chair

carried her into the bedroom. Taking his mouth with hers, she tasted herself there. Gathering her close he slipped into her, a sigh on his lips. Lifting her hands above her head, his fingers intertwined with hers, he breathed her name.

"Look at me, sugar. My beautiful Laura."

She opened her eyes to find him gazing into hers. Her heartbeat against his, their bodies joined, her soul laid bare to him. And she flew above it all, forgetting the pain, reveling in the unbearable sweetness of him.

———

Nathan lay with his arm around Laura, her head on his chest, his hand drawing circles on her back, as their breathing returned to normal.

Something happened this time. Something more than physical. Something simultaneously wonderful and frightening.

Wonderful, because he'd never experienced that connection with another woman before. Frightening, because, well, he'd never experienced that connection with another woman before. He wondered if Laura had felt it too.

Seeing her so distraught over that telegram had affected him. More than he'd like to admit. Who disinherited their own grandchild? He'd wanted to pick up the phone and give this woman who would so coldly use money as a weapon against her own flesh and blood a piece of his mind.

He had no idea how much money was involved, whether Laura would be able to provide for herself without it. He only knew that she was, in her own words, a trust-fund baby. Was that the trust fund she'd been referring to?

Laura kissed his chest and hummed in appreciation.

He hugged her close. "What would you like to do for dinner tonight?"

"Could we just stay here, in the room?"

"Are you sure?"

He felt her nod of confirmation.

"All right. After sex like that I couldn't deny you anything. How about I go pick up some of that raw fish you're so fond of, and I'll pick up a juicy artery-clogging burger from the grill and bring it back to the room? Maybe a bottle of wine?"

Laura sat up, her hair mussed, sliding over her shoulder to cover those perfect breasts. "That sounds . . . wonderful."

"Your wish is my command." He rose to find his pants, Looking around in confusion, until Laura said, "Living room."

"Oh, right. Thanks."

He bent down to kiss her. "I'll be back shortly. Keep the bed warm for me."

She smiled, a sexy, drowsy smile, and smacked him on the ass as he turned to walk away.

———

After hearing the soft click of the stateroom door closing, Laura flopped onto her back and stared at the ceiling. Her grandmother had always been a bitch, ruling with an iron fist and using money as a stick rather than a carrot. No wonder her father was emotionally stunted. Even so, she never thought she'd actually follow through on her threats to disinherit her.

She rose from the bed, the post-sex buzz all but gone, and walked naked to the living room to retrieve the hateful telegram before Nathan could read it. Ripping it to shreds in her frustration, she then balled up the remnants and tossed them in the trash.

Angry at herself for telling Nathan, she went to the closet and yanked her robe off the hanger. As if telling him wasn't bad enough, she'd almost cried in front of him too. And did it end there? No. She'd gone and *needed* him. And *told* him she *needed* him.

She hated needy. Working herself into a good mad, she paced the room.

But, God, she sighed. The mad ebbed. He'd been so tender. So . . . supportive. So unlike any other man she had ever slept with.

They were breaking rules left and right. She'd broken Rule Number Four after reading the telegram. He'd long since broken Rule Number Six by spending the last four nights in her bed. He even paid for her lunch today when she went to the ladies' room, breaking Rule Number Five.

Little sneak.

And she'd been breaking Rule Number Two by spending every waking—and sleeping—moment with him.

She glanced over at the bed, the rumpled sheets, the comforter lying halfway on the floor. And what the hell happened there earlier? The sex hadn't felt like just sex anymore. It had felt like . . . more. Exactly what, she couldn't put her finger on. But something . . . deeper. More meaningful.

"Oh, hell no." She paced away from the bed. She was not breaking Rule Number Three. This was just a fling. Nothing more.

That settled it. Tonight, after dinner, she'd tell him she wanted to be alone. That he needed to go back to his room. Nathan had proved to be a bigger distraction than she'd planned and it was time to refocus her energies on the Imperial account.

Her grandmother thought she'd won, but all she'd succeeded in doing was reigniting the fire under Laura. She was more determined than ever to get the account, and with it the VP position.

———

On the train for the ninety-minute trip to Florence, Laura gazed out over the rolling hills of Tuscany.

She'd caved last night. Once Nathan got her back in bed her resolve crumbled. So much for tiring of him before the end of the cruise. How could she tire of a man with so many skills at his disposal?

Only three more days, she rationalized. Three more days of his clever mouth and his cleverer hands. Three more days of his laughter, his warmth, his sex appeal.

Enjoy it while it lasted, she told herself. Because there was no way in hell she was breaking Rule Number Three. Once she returned to New York, she had to get her head back in the game. She and her team would only have six weeks to finalize the pitch. There was just no room for Nathan in her life right now.

That she was even thinking about him in her life later, after the Imperial deal closed, was something she brushed aside. For now. She'd ponder on that later.

Satisfied with her decision, she resolved to enjoy the day in one of her favorite cities. People sang the praises of Paris, but she'd take Florence over Paris any day of the week. The art, the architecture, appealed to her appreciation for fine craftsmanship. All surrounded by the beautiful Tuscan landscape.

She quickly checked her phone for any fires that required dousing. An email from Katie with a few questions, but nothing that couldn't wait until later. She tapped out a quick reply to Havi on the technology team about an issue with the drink campaign, then as she was tucking away her phone, it buzzed. Darcy.

"Hey, girlfriend!" she answered.

"You don't call, you don't text. Was it something I said?" Darcy teased.

"Sorry, I've been a bit . . . busy," Laura replied.

"Translation, I met a guy. So, what accent does he have? French? Italian? Ooh, or maybe Eastern European?"

"Southern."

"Southern what? Italy? I didn't know their accent was different."

"No Southern U.S., as in *Gone with the Wind*, as in Rhett Butler."

"You're on a ship in the middle of the Mediterranean, and you met a man from Georgia?"

"You got it, sugar."

"Wait, you said all the men were old enough to be your grandfather."

"Okay, so I wasn't exactly truthful."

"He's a passenger on the ship?"

"Yes. But I actually met him in New York. Before I left."

"You invited a stranger on the cruise with you? Did I teach you nothing about stranger danger?"

"I didn't invite him. He just happened to be on the cruise."

"Do tell. What's he look like? Is he rich?"

"He's handsome, polished, gentlemanly—"

"Other than the handsome part, he doesn't sound like your type at all."

"Funny, I thought the same thing, but he grew on me."

"How did you meet him in New York? A bar?"

"A sidewalk."

"A what?"

Laura told Darcy the story of her rescue.

"Aww! How romantic," she sighed.

Laura could just see Darcy's face going all dreamy. Ever the romantic.

"He's your knight-in-shining-armor. Your Prince Charming with the glass slipper."

"Sugar, I don't do knights-in-shining-armor like you."

"Sugar? Is that what he calls you? How, well, sweet." Darcy giggled on the other end of the phone.

"What's new with you?" Nathan appeared with a cup of coffee in his hand, prompting Laura to change the subject.

"Oh! I almost forgot why I was calling, *Holly's Heroes* is an RT Book Reviewer's Choice Best Book!"

Laura remembered Darcy struggling with that particular book while she was on the hunt for Mr. Perfect. "Congratulations, Darcy! We'll have to celebrate when I get back." A Reviewer's Choice was like the ADDY of the romance writer's world. Other than a RITA, it didn't get much better than that.

Not wanting to share too much personal information in front of Nathan, Laura ended the call with a promise to call Darcy when she returned to New York. "Have fun in Wine Country!"

CHAPTER ELEVEN

Nathan handed Laura one of the cups of coffee in his hands. "Nectar of the gods, just the way you like it, hot and sweet."

"True that." She took a sip. Sighed. "Thanks."

"You didn't need to cut your call short. Sounded like your friend had some good news to share."

Laura gave him a curious look.

"You were offering congratulations when I sat down."

"Right. She's a romance writer and her book was nominated for a top award in the industry."

"Well, congratulations then."

"So, what's on tap for today, Mr. Cruise Director?"

Nathan settled his hand on her thigh, clearly at ease with the public display of affection. "I thought we'd go to the top of the Duomo, look out over the city. Then over to the Uffizi. And we can't miss the *David*, so we'll head over to the Galleria dell' Accademia after that."

"I need to get some shopping in. Souvenirs for the folks back home."

"Then let's set aside some time to visit the Ponte

Vecchio. Did you know that it's the only remaining medieval bridge in the world with shops built into it?"

"Will there be a quiz on this later? How do you know all this if you've never been to Florence?"

He shrugged. "I read the ship's bulletin."

"You do?"

"Sure. Why not? You mean you don't?"

"No. I guess I'm more of a digital gal. I'd rather have it in an email or something."

"Hmm. Not a bad idea, actually."

"Well, I have been known to have the occasional good idea. Take us for instance." She waggled her finger between the two of them. "We go to together like, well, coffee and cream." She took a sip of the aforementioned beverage.

"Like biscuits and gravy."

"Strawberries and chocolate."

"Buttermilk and cornbread."

"What?" She drew back. "Ew. No."

"Okay, fine. But I happen to like buttermilk and cornbread."

"I'll just overlook that little flaw. Anyway, admit it. This fling thing was a brilliant idea on my part."

"You may have been the one to toss out the idea, but I'd have worked my way around to it eventually."

She tilted her head. "Really?"

He leaned over, kissed the dimple at the corner of her mouth, tasted the coffee there. "I wanted to do that from the moment you turned around to thank me for prying your heel out of the sidewalk."

"Seriously?"

"Seriously. And when I saw you sitting at the bar that first night on the ship, I knew I had to find a way to make you mine"—he placed his finger over her mouth before she could remind him of Rule Number Three— "if only for a short time."

———

Laura had been to Florence a few times in the past, visited all the must-see sites, but seeing them through Nathan's eyes was a new experience, and one she wouldn't soon forget.

He drank it all in. Nothing jaded about his view of life. It was so refreshing.

She felt light. Giddy even. And she didn't do giddy.

They'd huffed up the four hundred sixty-three steps to the top of Duomo, took in the city's tiled roof buildings nestled against the Tuscan hills beyond. Strolled the exhibits of the Uffizi, and gazed upon the magnificent works of Titian, Caravaggio, and Michelangelo.

After lunch in a crowded noisy *trattoria* not far from the Uffizi, they'd backtracked to the Basilica di Santa Croce, where she'd purchased hand stitched crocodile and ostrich key chains from Scuoloa del Cuoio for her co-workers, and a burled calfskin business card case for the Shyster to put his business cards in. For Darcy's father, a calfskin eyeglass case. Unable to resist, she'd purchased a decadently luxurious butter yellow reversible suede and lambskin trench coat with a python belt for herself.

They'd stumbled upon a shop near the Piazza Santa Croce that carried rare books with a hand-tooled leather-bound volume of Dante's *Inferno*—in English, no less—on display in the window that had Millie-the-Braniac's name all over it. She'd read it no doubt, but this would serve as a collector piece.

That damage done, they turned their steps in the direction of the Ponte Vecchio, where Laura found a beautiful framed cameo pendant perfect for Darcy, and a lovely pair of cameo earrings for Darcy's mother.

"You're very generous with your friends."

Laura shrugged. "Goes back to my appreciation for fine craftsmanship."

"Uh-huh. Or your appreciation for those close to you."

Uncomfortable with this observation, she didn't respond.

"Nothing for your family?" he probed.

"Trust me, they don't want for anything." Except warmth. Love. Affection. "What about your sister?"

"Oh, I picked up a little something for her."

"When did you do that?"

"When you were buying the cameo."

"Oh." Laura almost asked to see what he'd purchased, but really, what was the point? She didn't know his sister, and likely never would. Nevertheless, she was curious what he'd picked out for her.

"What do you say we finish off the day with the *pièce de résistance* of Florence."

"That's French," Laura pointed out.

"Whatever," he said, with an eye roll. "You get the point."

Taking her hand, they crossed the Ponte Vecchio and headed in the direction of the Galleria dell' Accademia.

As they circled Michelangelo's seventeen-foot sculpture of *David*, mouths ajar in awe, their silence spoke volumes. It didn't matter how many times she beheld the colossal figure, it never ceased to amaze her.

"He's really something," Nathan observed.

He barked out a laugh when Laura leaned over and

whispered a size comparison between him and the naked statue. "I'll take that as a compliment.

———

Exhausted after a jam-packed day in Florence—not to mention the blazing sex he'd just experienced—Nathan rested his chin on Laura's head, his arms wrapped around her, and listened as her breathing became even with sleep.

He gazed down at her face, soft and relaxed. His hand drifted down her rib cage, splayed across, feeling the deep rise and fall with her breath. All her sharp edges blurred, softened. He enjoyed her like this. But he also enjoyed her sharp edges.

Three more days. That was all he had left with this amazing woman. When he'd boarded the ship, he'd had no expectations for the cruise beyond accomplishing some primary research, seeing some sights, and squeezing in a little rest and relaxation here and there. That he'd see the damsel-in-distress he'd rescued on a Manhattan sidewalk, not so much. That he'd spend seven days with said damsel, even less. But here she was, her leg wrapped around his, her breath soft on his chest.

She intrigued him. And though his relative ignorance of all but her most basic demographics could account for that, it wasn't the only reason. Fast, as his grandmother would have said, he thought with a satisfied smile, but also generous, kind . . . and vulnerable despite her money and obvious privileged upbringing.

She had some sass in her, but her manners were polished, her public conversations cultured, her knowledge of art and history were all, no doubt, the product of a very expensive private school education.

And yet for all that, he could see uncertainty beneath it all. That feeling of not being quite good enough. As one who experienced that same uncertainty, he could spot it easily in others.

He thought about the earrings he'd purchased for her today when he'd purchased the pair for his sister. Nothing flashy or expensive, just a little *memento* of him and this trip. Tucked safely away in his stateroom for now, he'd give them to her on their last night on the ship.

He could break Rule Number Three. What the hell? They'd already broken all the other rules. He could ask to see her again in New York, and maybe she'd say no. But, there was also a chance she'd say yes. And he'd never been one to pass up an opportunity.

———

Laura had suggested that they take another guided tour for the city of Pisa. For one thing, she'd never been, and for another, she needed to experience more guided tours to help with her research. They couldn't all be as lame as the one in St. Tropez, right?

Watching as the passengers ahead of her boarded the bus for the short trip into Pisa, Laura's business brain took over. What if you could do interactive guided tours specially designed for the demographic Imperial was targeting?

Her phone buzzed with an incoming text. She took it out, glanced at the screen. Katie. Tapping out a quick reply an idea struck. What if Imperial offered its passengers free apps for the different ports of call? The tours could be categorized by length, interests, and agility levels. Making a note to herself for later, she tucked her phone away. *Genius!* Biting her lip to hide her smile.

"Good news about the charity gala?" Nathan asked.

"No. Why?"

"You're smiling."

"Oh. No." Damn, he read her too easily. "Just a quick question, and a reminder to myself to handle something when we get back to the ship."

Taking her hand, he helped her onto the bus—always the gentleman.

They got off the bus at the first stop on the tour and the most famous site in Pisa, The Leaning Tower.

As they milled around waiting for everyone to climb off the bus, Nathan pulled Laura close and said, "Watch for pickpockets."

She snorted. "I'm from New York and Georgia Boy here is telling me to watch for pickpockets."

"Even so. See that young boy over there?" Nathan pointed across the Piazza dei Miracoli.

"The one entertaining that couple?" The little boy performed a little song and dance.

"Yes. He's the distraction."

"What do you mean?"

"It's called the Diversion Heist. The little boy distracts the mark while the adult accomplice swoops in and steals the wallets, jewelry, and any other valuables they can get their hands on."

"We should do something." She laid a hand on Nathan's arm.

"No need." He drew her attention back to the couple, where a roaming police officer shooed the kid away.

"How do you know so much about those schemes?"

"The same schemes are used on unwary people in the U.S."

"Again, how do you know?"

"I didn't grow up in the best environment."

The tour guide called for everyone's attention, effectively ending their conversation.

———

She and Nathan boarded the ship, planning to part ways until dinner. She had a few emails that needed her attention, but she told Nathan they involved the Silver Linings Gala. Not a total lie—one of them did. This was her second year serving as the chair of the marketing committee for the Silver Linings Gala, which raised money for the Women's Legal Fund of Harlem, and she loved the work. The fact that it was Josh's chosen charity had nothing to do with it.

"Let's do something casual tonight," Laura said as she took her stateroom key from her pocket.

"I could go for a juicy burger myself."

"Sounds per—"

Her words were cut off when one of the passengers, a man in his seventies, missed the bottom step and fell, his head narrowly missing the stairs.

"Oh!" she cried out.

Nathan bolted forward, knelt beside the man. "Sir, are you okay?"

"I'm fine." He struggled to sit up.

"Easy. Give yourself a minute."

Laura squatted next to Nathan. "Should I call for help?" She took the man's hand.

"No," the gentleman said. "I'll be fine. Damn Parkinson's," he muttered.

"Parkinson's?" Nathan asked.

"Makes me a little unsteady on my feet sometimes."

"Yes." Nathan helped the man sit up. "My grandmother had Parkinson's."

Something in his tone of voice drew her attention back to Nathan. He wore a look of sadness.

"I'm Nathan. And this is Laura."

"Laura, Nathan, I'm Henry, Henry Riggers."

"Are you sure you don't need medical attention? I could take you to the ship's infirmary."

"No, son. The only thing wounded is my pride." He gave a wan smile.

When the man started to rise, Nathan took his arm. "Here, let me help you back to your stateroom." He turned to Laura. "I'll meet you at seven?"

"Sure."

As she watched Nathan help Mr. Riggers to the elevator, her heart gave a little squeeze. His grandmother would have been proud.

Nathan's comment came back to her. *I didn't grow up in the best environment.* What had he meant by that? He behaved like a gentleman, but knew about pickpocket schemes. He talked about his grandmother with the utmost respect. He clearly cared for his sister and "the farm." And yet that comment called to mind a hoodlum or gang member. And just now, the kindness and respect he showed Mr. Riggers. She shook her head. There was that perplexing mix of disparate qualities again.

As much as she hated to admit it, she'd like to break Rule Number Three and get to the bottom of Nathan Maxwell.

———

The next day, wrapped in a luxurious terry cloth robe, Laura stretched out on a chaise lounge in the spa's relaxation room to wait for her pedicure. She'd just been massaged, scrubbed, and buffed into a boneless blob of bliss. The perfect way to spend the day at sea. She sighed in anticipation of Nathan's mouth and hands on her spa-fresh silky-smooth skin.

It wasn't entirely for her pleasure. Of course not. It was work, and hard work at that. After all, she had to know what the spa offered. See if it met the expectations of her demographic. And, she was pleased to report that it did. *Damn, her job was tough. She really should look for something less stressful.*

And—bonus—she'd spoken with Veronica the Vampire, and Natalia Brusca, who'd both been in the spa earlier, about their experience on the cruise.

Picking up an American tattle rag from the side table, Laura flipped through the pages of stories about not-so-secret affairs, star-studded weddings, and baby bumps. Keeping a finger on the pop culture pulse was as important to an ad agency executive as intelligence briefs were to a world leader. You never knew when a tidbit might come in handy in a pitch.

Laura glanced up as Mrs. Cybex entered the room, belting her robe around her considerable frame. Stopping by the refreshment station, she plucked a couple of biscotti out of the basket and settled back with a cup of tea.

She and her husband had introduced themselves earlier in the week as Robert and Lillian Shelton, but Nathan's nickname for him stuck. And had extended to his wife.

Glancing at the magazine cover, Mrs. Cybex said,

"What a shame about Gwyneth and Chris. They made such a nice couple. Speaking of nice couples, you and that handsome young man have another date tonight?"

Another? What? Was Mrs. Cybex keeping tabs on her?

"I couldn't help but notice the way you two interact. You make a very attractive couple you know. I'm not the only one who's noticed. The whole ship is talking about it. He only has eyes for you. And you, well, it's clear to anyone with eyes that you're into him. In fact, there's a pool over whether you'll leave the ship engaged."

Engaged! As if. Maybe Mrs. Cybex had been sniffing too much hair dye.

Without waiting for a response from Laura, she continued. "My husband told me when he saw you and the young man in the fitness center that first morning that the chemistry between you two was off the charts. And, honey, it was rolling off you in waves that night in the elevator. Let me tell you, I needed a cold shower after that encounter."

She chuckled at Laura's horrified expression. "What? You think I wasn't young once? I remember the feel of those hormones coursing through me. Remember what it was like to be in lust and in love."

Love? Yep. She'd definitely been sniffing the hair dye. Should she set the woman straight—not that it was any of her business. "It's just a fling." She waved her hand dismissing the notion of anything more.

"Honey, that's what I said about my husband—before he was my husband, of course." She dunked her biscotti in her tea before taking a bite. "Let me tell you," she continued around a mouthful of cookie, "we were smokin' hot in the sack."

Laura winced at that visual. *Can you say TMI?*

Mrs. Cybex's face had gone all dreamy. "We couldn't

get enough of one another. I thought it would just flame out, you know, like paper tossed into a furnace. But the next thing we knew, we'd fallen for each other. Hard." She shook her head. "That was over fifty years ago. And we're still going strong." She winked at Laura as she took a sip of tea.

Laura glanced over at the door. Never a good nail tech around when you needed her.

Mrs. Cybex reached over and patted Laura's knee. "Just roll with it, honey. Have fun. But don't be surprised if the connection you have in bed spills over to your heart."

"Ms. Danforth." The nail tech stood in the doorway.

Laura jumped up from the chaise as if it had bit her.

"See you two at dinner," Mrs. Cybex chimed.

CHAPTER TWELVE

With so much to do and see in Rome, and only one day to do and see it, Nathan and Laura got an early start, much to Laura's dismay. Clearly, *someone* was not a morning person, because when Nathan yanked the covers off of her gorgeous naked body at six-thirty a.m., Laura made several threats to his manhood, cursed his offspring, and otherwise set his ears ablaze with her potty mouth.

A peace offering of sweet, hot coffee had done the trick and put him back in her good graces.

Then, she'd pissed him off when she surprised him by hiring a private car and driver for the day. They'd agreed to pay their own way, but she refused to allow him to pay his half of this extravagance.

But one look at the traffic, and the drivers, in Rome changed his mind.

First stop, the Sistine Chapel, where he and Laura craned their necks to gaze upon Michelangelo's awe-inspiring ceiling, and equally impressive *Last Judgment* altar fresco.

"That someone who was such a brilliant sculptor," Nathan said, thinking of *David*, "could also paint such beautiful frescoes is extraordinary."

After a whirlwind tour of Vatican City, they'd headed for the Colosseum.

Standing on the viewing platform looking out at the ruins, Nathan said, "The world's first sports arena."

"Yeah," Laura snorted. "If you like watching battles to the death."

"What? You have something against two guys beating the living shit out of each other?"

"Yeah, I'm funny that way."

Nathan snorted, then without a segue said, "I'm starved. All this sightseeing makes a man hungry. Let's ask Franco what he recommends for lunch." Franco, their private driver, had turned out to be so much more than just a driver. He was a wealth of information, not only on the history and architecture of Rome, but also on the local culture.

Franco recommended a busy little wine bar in the shadow of Trajan's Column that served hot and cold dishes. And with strong *grappa* to wash it down, Nathan was feeling no pain after lunch.

Weaving a little as they walked over to where Franco sat with the car, he remembered one of his grandmother's favorite movies, *Roman Holiday*, he said, "Hey! Ever been to The Mouth of Truth?"

"You mean La Bocca della Verità?"

"Yes, Miss Smarty Pants."

"No."

"Then *andiamo*, Franco!"

Fifteen minutes later, they stood in front of the iconic carving. "According to the movie *Roman Holiday*, The

Mouth of Truth acts as a lie detector. Anyone given to lying who puts their hand in the mouth will have it bitten off."

Laura rolled her eyes. "Yes, yes. I know."

"So, go ahead."

"Go ahead, what?"

"Put your hand in the mouth."

"Why me?"

"Because I'm a gentleman, and ladies always go first."

"You and your chivalry." Laura hesitated.

"Scared?"

"Don't be ridiculous," she sniffed. "It's just a silly legend."

"Then you have nothing to worry about." He lifted an eyebrow in challenge.

———

Laura swallowed hard, then stepped closer to the mouth of the carving and raised her hand. She glanced up to see a grinning Nathan. With some trepidation, she slid her hand into the mouth, half-expecting to have it bitten off at any moment given all her recent lies.

Having met his challenge, she yanked her hand from the orifice and breathed a sigh of relief. "Your turn."

That wiped the grin from his face. "What?"

"Oh, no." She shoved him closer. "If I did it, you have to do it, too."

"Fine. Whatever."

Nathan lifted his left hand toward the mouth.

"Aren't you right-handed?" Laura asked.

"Yes."

"Afraid you'll have your hand bitten off, so you're willing to sacrifice your left?"

He snorted, "Yeah, something like that." He sighed. "Okay. Fine." Raising his right hand, he inserted it halfway into the mouth.

"No cheating. All the way in." Laura waved her hand at the carving.

Nathan shoved his hand in the mouth before jerking it out.

Laura's laughter rang out in the enclosed space. "Not easy, is it?"

"I don't know about you, but that sobered me right up."

"Where to next?" Laura asked.

"Do you want some gelato?"

"Is the Pope Catholic?"

Franco took them to San Crispino for arguably the best gelato in Rome.

Sitting on the wall of the Trevi Fountain made famous in movies like *Three Coins in a Fountain* and *La Dolce Vita*, Nathan and Laura gorged on the cold treat. Hazelnut for Nathan, *stracciatella* for Laura.

"Mmm. Taste this," Laura said, holding out her dish of gelato. "The bitter chocolate, the sweet cream. Delicious."

Rather than taking a spoonful of gelato, Nathan leaned in, kissing her mouth, then licking his own lips. "Mmm. It *is* delicious."

Laura laughed, pushing him away. "I think you're still drunk on *grappa*."

Nathan just grinned and polished off the rest of his gelato. Standing, he took a coin from his pocket and held it out to Laura.

She lifted a brow. "What? Is that my tip for last night?"

"Hardly. It's for you to throw into the fountain."

Laura stood and took the coin. Nathan grabbed her by her shoulders and turned her away from the fountain.

"You have to toss the coin in with your right hand over your left shoulder. The legend is that throwing a coin into the fountain will guarantee a return trip to Rome. So go ahead."

"Uh-huh. And just how do you know this?"

"My grandmother was a classic movie buff. I kept her company." Nathan gave a sheepish shrug.

Laura's heart squeezed thinking about Nathan as a teenager, keeping his grandmother company as she watched *Three Coins in a Fountain*. She didn't know why, but she felt a little self-conscious with him watching her. Taking a breath, she tossed the coin over her left shoulder.

Nathan held out a second coin for her. "If you throw a second coin into the fountain, you'll discover romance."

Okay, she just got an odd tingle down her spine. Laughing it off, she said, "You're crazy."

"Fine." Nathan took the coin from her hand.

She couldn't say why, but just before he could throw it, she stole it back and tossed it over her left shoulder.

He snagged her around the waist and pulled her in for a deep, terrifyingly intimate kiss. Easing back, he gazed into her eyes, almost as if he were searching for . . . something. Laura broke the hold.

The moment gone, he said, "How about we reprise the fountain scene from *La Dolce Vita?*"

Laura backed away. "How about we head over to the Pantheon instead?"

Nathan prowled Laura's living room, waiting for her to finish dressing. His fault she was running late. When he'd arrived at her door to take her to dinner, and found her in nothing but a flesh-colored lace bra and panties, he'd been too tempted to resist.

As he headed for the bedroom, to ask whether he should change the time for their dinner reservations, he heard the blow dryer. Since he'd learned her routine in the last week, he knew it wouldn't be long before she was ready. For a woman that always looked so put together, it didn't take her long to achieve that image.

Laura's phone buzzed from where it sat on the bedside table, indicating an incoming text message. Thinking it might be important regarding the charity gala she'd been working on, he picked up the phone. The words 'Hawk Media' caught his eye.

Imperial wants to schedule a pre-pitch meeting with us and Hawk Media as soon as you get back. Should I schedule it?

"What the—" He couldn't quite wrap his head around what the text meant. He stared at it another minute, then collapsed to the bed as the truth dawned on him. Laura Danforth worked for Giddings-Rose. And, more importantly, was going after the very same account he was after. She was his competition!

The realization that he'd been sleeping with, romancing, spending every waking hour with—and enjoying the hell out of every minute of it—the very woman who could stand in his way of the Imperial account, and the farm-saving bonus, hit him like a sucker punch. "Ho-ly hell," he muttered. Scrubbing his hands through his hair, he collapsed onto the bed.

He felt sick. Heart sick. She'd lied to him. Told him she was a trust-fund baby—her words—talked about a charity gala she was working on. And all along she'd been communicating with her agency, no doubt.

While he'd been busy romancing her, she'd been busy spying on him. A twenty-first century Mata Hari. Beautiful, sexy, capable of luring a man to her bed in the hopes of gaining his secrets.

He thought back over their conversations. Had he said anything to her to tip her off? Had he revealed any thoughts on his approach to the account? Had he left his phone out where she could see emails? Text messages? No on all accounts. And thanks to her rule prohibiting exchange of personal information, which now made perfect sense, he'd refrained from sharing too much with her. At least there was that.

Now what? Should he continue her ruse? Maybe even throw some false leads her way? No. She might not have a conscience, but he did. He couldn't pretend. And he sure as hell couldn't sleep with her again. Not knowing this.

Had sleeping with him been part of her plan? Get him to let his guard down? After all, she'd initiated the fling, and wasted no time in doing it. She'd thrown it out there, the second day on the cruise on the Notre Dame de la Garde in Marseille.

Well, she hadn't succeeded. At least not at getting information out of him. What she had succeeded in doing was getting under his skin.

———

"You've got a text message. Since it's about the Imperial account, I figured it must be important." Nathan stood in the doorway of the bathroom, his voice quiet, holding her smartphone out to her.

She looked down at the phone and then back up into his face and she knew. He was the spy, not Greg. The jig was up. And so was her ruse. Her heart picked up its pace, moving into a sprint.

When she didn't take the phone, he set it on the counter with all the care he would a ticking time bomb.

So many emotions to deal with, none of them good, and a few of them unfamiliar. Anger at herself that she'd been sleeping with the enemy the whole time. Anger at Nathan for his duplicity. Frustration that she'd let great sex blind her to reality. Possibly even talking herself out of seeing Nathan as the spy.

And then, something deeper, stronger. Something she couldn't put a finger on. Betrayal? Certainly. Disappointment? Possibly. Heartache? Before she could name it, he continued, his voice soft, but angry.

"So, the whole trust-fund story, the disinheritance—was that all a lie, too?"

"No. That was true."

"And the charity gala?"

"True."

His disappointment in her enveloped her like a wet wool blanket. The feeling so familiar.

Then she drew herself up, got her feet back under her. "*Et tu*, Nathan? Before you get all holier than thou on me, Mr. Maxwell, you didn't exactly tell me the truth either. So, pot meet kettle."

Ignoring her comment, he rounded on her. "Did you *plan* to spy on me from the beginning?" He threw up his arms, released a laugh devoid of humor. "Did you really get your heel stuck in the sidewalk? Did we really end up on this ship together as a coincidence? Or did you orchestrate it all to distract me? To get information out of me?"

Throwing off that wet, wool blanket, Laura jabbed a finger at his chest. "Me? What about you? Mr. Corporate

Relations. And what about Amanda? Is she really your sister, or his she your *wife*? The flowers, the romantic dinners, the gestures? And what about that Rhett Butler accent? Was that part of your act, too?"

"Sugar, nothing about me is an act. What you see is what you get. Trouble is, you don't *want* to see too much. Better to remain ignorant. Can't develop any attachments that way. Not that it matters now, but corporate relations is part of my job, as an ad executive you should know that, and Amanda is my sister. I never lied. Too bad I can't say the same about you."

He opened the stateroom door, and looked back at her. "Rest assured, I'm going to get the Imperial account, and I'm going to use every weapon in my arsenal to do it."

"You're going to need them . . . *Sugar*." She shot back as she followed him to the door.

Instead of slamming the door shut behind him, as she expected, he pulled it closed with a quiet *click*, leaving behind a deafening silence. Except for the thudding of her heart.

———

Pacing the confines of his room, Nathan growled in frustration. With her. With himself. How could he have let his guard down? Everything about her should have sent off warning bells. Not that he knew anyone from Giddings-Rose was on the ship, but dammit. First, he pries her heel out of a sidewalk seam in front of Imperial's offices.

Then, she's on the same ship where she initiates a fling —no doubt in the hopes he'll reveal something about Hawk Media's plans for the account. She has all her convenient rules about no personal questions, paying her own way, and no contact after they return to New York.

"Christ Almighty!" There'd be hell to pay when Hawk finds out.

Simmering down, he opened his balcony door and stepped out into the brisk wind coming off the water and sat staring out, seeing nothing.

Then disappointment set in. Laura had been the first woman he thought he could have a serious relationship with. The first woman who he thought he could care about.

"Ha!" How would he know if he could care about her? How could he tell the difference between the real Laura and the act that she'd put on? Then he thought about the vulnerability he'd seen in her eyes the day she'd received the telegram. That was difficult to fake. He ought to know.

"What the hell difference did it make, anyway?" It was over. He'd be better off focusing this anger and frustration on the Imperial account, because the competition just got a whole lot tougher.

———

Twisting her still-damp hair into a bun and knotting it, Laura padded barefoot into the living room, slid open her balcony door and inhaled the fresh salt air. She needed to clear her head, cool her temper, and regroup.

"Son-of-a-bitch!" she yelled into the blackness beyond. She was as angry at herself as she was at Nathan. She should have listened to her instincts. They'd always been dead-on. Instead, she'd let a man cloud her judgment. A really hot, charming— "Okay. Enough!"

She had an account to snare, and snare it she would. Picking up the phone she ordered dinner to her room, grabbed her laptop and opened the file she'd started on Imperial. Making notes on the interactive tour app, real-time Twitter updates, and digital bulletins, she put Nathan's treachery out of her thoughts. And tried like hell to ignore the emptiness of the stateroom without him. And if the stateroom felt empty without him, it was only because he'd made himself at home these past few days.

Nothing more.

The emptiness in her heart was another matter.

CHAPTER THIRTEEN

The next morning, Laura signed up for another guided tour. This one a tour of Naples and its surroundings.

The city itself seemed to tumble down the stone cliffs to the edge of the sea, as if stopping at the last moment. She'd originally planned to sit this port-of-call out, still so angry over Nathan's deception, but she'd be damned if she'd let him get in the way of the Imperial account any longer. She'd let him in, let him distract her from her goal. Well no more. This was war.

Her idea to create interactive tour apps had taken hold and she'd made voluminous notes the previous evening, throwing herself into her work, and telling herself she wasn't hiding from *him*. No siree. She just wanted to give the creative team details so they could develop visuals for the pitch.

Mr. and Mrs. Cybex walked past her down the aisle of the bus, smiling and nodding a greeting.

And right behind them, Nathan. *Damn.* She'd hoped he'd either chosen another tour, or decided to stay on the ship. Ignoring him as he made his way down the aisle, she rummaged in the messenger-style bag with her belongings, a notepad and pen, and her phone. No point in hiding who she was and what she did for a living. She'd found her spy. Right under her nose. Or should she say, right under *her*. *Over* her. *In* her.

Stop! Not a good line of thinking at the moment. She didn't want to remember how amazing he felt in any of those positions.

When they reached their first stop on the tour, Laura let everyone get off the bus first, so she could distance herself from Nathan. Naples was a big city. If he stayed away from her, she'd stay the hell away from him.

———

D*ammit.* She missed Nathan. Missed him on the island of Capri when she took the funicular to Capri Town, the hilltop village. Missed him on the ferry ride to the town of Sorrento where she had lunch. Alone. And she missed him now, as she sat sipping her *limoncello*, watching the chaos that was Pompeii.

She had wisecracks aplenty at the ready every time she saw a statue of an erect penis, which in Pompeii were as common as taxis in New York, and she had no one to share them with. At least no one who would appreciate them the way Nathan would.

Exhausted from a very long day, she polished off her drink, and stood to take some photos outside the archaeological ruins of Pompeii. Damn Nathan and his charming personality. She had work to do.

———

Standing a few feet away, her back to him, Laura made some notes in the small notebook she carried. Nathan couldn't help himself. He watched her, as he'd done all day. Keeping her in his sites.

She flipped that long silky ponytail over her shoulder, then sliding the notebook under her arm, raised her smartphone to take some pictures of the walls of Pompeii, the vendors' tables lining the entrance, doing a brisk business as the tourists crowded around looking for bargains.

Distracted, Laura didn't notice the man that had sidled up next to her, appearing to take photos himself.

Out of instinct, Nathan crept closer. The flash from a knife propelled Nathan forward, shoving people aside, but before he could reach her, Laura cried out, dropping her phone and her notebook.

The thief ran off with Laura's bag in his hands, the cut strap dangling down his thigh, dodging the crowd as he went. He couldn't have been twenty feet in front of him, so using his smartphone Nathan took aim at his head and hurled it. The phone struck its intended target, nailing the guy in the back of the head, before clattering to the ground. His pitching skill had come in handy.

The impact stunned the man, making him drop Laura's bag as he reached around to grab the back of his head. He never looked back, breaking free of the crowd, he just kept running like the hounds of hell were nipping at his heels.

Nathan scooped up the bag and phone and returned to find an ashen-faced Laura. "You okay?" He grasped her tense shoulders and ran his hands down her arms. His fingers snagged in a cut in her blouse. Tensing, he peered inside the tear and saw blood. The knife had grazed her rib cage. "Jesus!" he hissed. "You need medical attention."

"I'm . . . fine." Her voice shook as much as her body did.

"No, you're not. He cut you." The yearning to draw her into his arms and comfort her—comfort himself—was so strong it resembled a gravitational pull. She gazed into his eyes, clearly confused. Shock maybe?

"Nathan, I—"

People from their tour group began to gather round, and then the tour guide pushed through the crowd. "*Signorina*, you are injured?"

"She's been cut," Nathan said. "She needs medical attention."

"*Sì*. We will see to it, *pronto*. You are her husband?" the tour guide asked.

"No." Nathan turned and walked away. He didn't know what he was to her.

———

Someone handed her a clean handkerchief, which she used to staunch the bleeding while waiting for emergency medical personnel. Mrs. Cybex sat with her arm around her, comforting her while she gave a statement to the *Polizia Municipale*. Laura couldn't provide a description given she never saw the man except from behind as he ran away from her.

Through the crowd, she could see Nathan talking with the authorities, but he never looked her way. He scrubbed his hands through his hair, as she'd seen him do when he was frustrated. Probably just wanted to get back on the ship and forget it ever happened.

When medical personnel arrived, she refused to go to the hospital, only allowing the *soccorritore*, the Italian version of EMTs, to clean and bandage her wound. No stitches, but they recommended that she get antibiotics from the ship's infirmary if she didn't want to go to the hospital.

Once they released her, the tour guide called a taxi to take her back to the ship. When she stood, the shock of the purse snatching set in, and she began to shake. Mrs. Cybex joined her in the taxi, and gathered her close against her ample frame.

As the taxi sped away, Laura turned to search for Nathan, but he was gone. Her lover, her competition, and now her enemy, he'd come to her rescue, and her aid, then faded into the crowd.

And while he'd retrieved her bag, something was still missing. Him.

———

Nathan arrived back at the ship after dark. After returning from Pompeii, he'd walked the streets of Naples for hours, playing the incident over and over in his head, second-guessing what he'd done, and what he should have done. If he'd just gotten to her sooner, she wouldn't have been hurt.

If he'd tackled the guy, he wouldn't have gotten away. Asshole had cut her, stolen her bag, and gotten away. Nathan's only satisfaction, meager as it was, was that the jerk-off would have a good-sized lump on the back of his head, and she'd gotten her bag back.

Taking his smartphone out of his pocket, he frowned at the shattered screen. He'd replace it as soon as he returned to New York. For now, he'd have to communicate the old-fashioned way—landlines.

Opening the door to his stateroom, he noticed the

message light blinking on his phone. Punching the button, he listened to the message:

"Nathan, I . . . thank you." Laura's voice still trembled, making the dull ache in his chest flare. "I'll never be able to express how much your courage today meant to me. Even after . . . well, I can't thank you enough." The message ended with a soft *click*.

He'd done what anyone would have done in the same situation. Nothing more. He resisted the urge to call her. Check on her. He chose not to examine why.

Putting the incident aside, he began packing his things for the trip home. If he'd left anything in Laura's stateroom, he'd just have to live without it. Sliding open the top dresser drawer he pulled his shirts out and something fell on the floor. The box holding the earrings he'd bought for Laura.

Slumping to the bed, he pressed his hand to an empty spot in his chest, stared down at them. "Well, shit." Maybe he had left something in Laura's stateroom, after all. His heart.

CHAPTER FOURTEEN

Back in New York, Laura's feet beat against the pavement in time to Muse blasting through her earbuds. Her phone buzzed at her hip. "This is Laura," she huffed, breathless from her run.

"Laura! Hey, Jack Jeffries."

"Jack. Hi."

"Did I catch you at a bad time?"

"No, just out for a run in Central Park. What's up?"

"Now that you're back, I'd like to take you to dinner."

Laura stopped in front of the Met, stunned. She'd forgotten about his previous request to take her dinner. He hadn't wasted much time calling her after she returned to New York. Two days to be precise.

Perfect. Maybe she could finally get Nathan off the brain. Since Rome she'd spent far too many brain cells on memories of him, his Southern drawl, his sexy grin, and his kisses. Oh yeah, his kisses. "Sure. I'd love to."

"How's your schedule look for Saturday?"

"Like I'm having dinner with you." She couldn't hide the smile in her voice.

"Great! Text me your address, and I'll pick you up at seven."

"See you then." She hit 'end' and resumed her run. Dinner with Jack, some reminiscing about the good ol' days, followed by drinks at her place. And, if she played her cards right, a nice tumble in the sheets. Just what the doctor ordered to cure what ailed her: an acute case of Nathanitis.

———

Jack pulled Laura's chair out for her. Just that simple gesture reminded her of Nathan, her Southern Gentleman. Well, not *her* Southern Gentleman. Not anymore. Not ever, really.

Jack had picked her up in his new Maserati Ghibli and driven out of the city and into the village of Hastings on Hudson, to a favorite restaurant of his. The restaurant offered gorgeous unimpeded views of the Hudson River and the Palisades beyond.

"I'm glad we were finally able to have dinner," Jack said as he took his seat.

Laura leaned in, giving him her best flirtatious smile. The one she'd perfected since those days of the country club. "Me, too."

The waiter came over to take their drink orders. Jack selected a crisp Napa Chardonnay.

"Tell me everything that's happened to you since we last saw each other . . ." He appeared to be running a calculation in his head. ". . . thirteen years ago."

From their table on the patio, they dined on locally-grown produce, some from the restaurant's own garden, sipped on excellent wine, watched the sun set over the Palisades, and caught up on each other's lives. If Jack didn't say much about his divorce, Laura assumed it was still a touchy subject for him, and she respected that.

He hadn't made any overt gestures, and any time he'd touched her, it had been with the utmost courtesy. A hand on the small of her back, taking her hand to assist her out of his car.

By the time he opened the passenger door for her for the return trip to Manhattan, she felt they'd established a connection, and while it lacked the spark she and Nathan had shared, it had the depth of history behind it. "I had a very nice time tonight, Jack." Laura reached out and placed her hand on Jack's thigh. He flinched.

She assumed it was a shudder of desire, but when he glanced at her with a wary frown, she removed her hand. Maybe he liked to take things a little slower. Patience was not her strong suit, as Nathan often reminded her.

Now why had she thought of Nathan when she had a handsome guy next to her?

"I understand you were on the *Nave dei Sogni*. How'd you like her?"

"She's quite a ship, but I'll save my thoughts for Giddings-Rose's pitch."

He laughed at that. "Fair enough. But you can tell me about your land-based experiences."

They spent the remainder of the trip back to Manhattan discussing France and Italy and travel abroad in general. The earlier tension dissipated.

When he pulled up in front of her building, the doorman came out to assist, but Jack waved him off. "Thank you for having dinner with me. I can't remember when I enjoyed an evening out with a woman as much as this one."

She waited for him to make his move—to kiss her, invite himself up to her apartment. But he didn't. Not one to sit idly by and wait, she slid over in her seat and leaning across the console pressed her lips to his. This time the flinch was clearly that. A flinch.

She recoiled, hurt, and not a little shocked. She'd rarely been rejected by a man, her father excepted, especially with such . . . obvious disgust. After all, he'd asked her out, hadn't he? Did she need a breath mint? Maybe it was the onions in the salmon ceviche.

"Well. Thanks for dinner."

Jack grabbed her wrist when she turned to open her door. "God, Laura. I'm sorry. I don't know why, but I thought you knew."

"Knew what?"

"You're right." He sighed. "We haven't seen each other in over a decade, and I expect you to know I'm gay."

Oh, snap! "Gay? You?" How'd she miss that?

"Yes," he said, his voice barely audible even in the quiet confines of the car's dimly lit interior.

She couldn't deny his confession came as a shock. She knew plenty of people who were gay. But this was Jack, the high school quarterback that had taken them all the way to state finals. The guy who was the subject of every teenage girl's wet dream. The guy who married Miss New York, for Christ's sake!

"But—how long have you known?"

"It's hard to put a specific age on it, but probably since I was about fifteen. All the guys were talking about boobs and asses, and . . . well, you know"—he waved his hand in the general direction of her crotch—"and I just . . . had no inter-est. At first I thought it was because I was focused on sports. But when a guy's body held more interest for me than a girl's, I kind of knew."

"Oh, Jack." Laura reached across and placed her hand

over his and gave it a squeeze. At least he'd never had to face the ridicule of his teenage classmates.

"But what about Stephanie and your marriage?" And the subsequent divorce? *Light bulb moment.* Well that explained it.

He shrugged with an air of regret. "I really tried at first. I thought I could make it work. I thought maybe it was just a phase." He laughed and shook his head. "But I was miserable, and I made her miserable right along with me."

"And your parents?"

"They took it far better than I thought. Better than I could have hoped, really. Funny thing is, so far I haven't met anyone I thought I could have a relationship with. So here I am, gay, out—sort of—and no one to love."

She sat back and looked Jack over. She'd really had no clue. Not that she expected to see it tattooed across his forehead, but seriously, a hint might have been nice. Save her the humiliation. *Okay, enough about me.* "Did you ever think that maybe your, um, non-gayness was the problem?"

"No. We know. Trust me."

"Okay. Then it'll happen, Jack. A guy would be crazy not to snap you up."

"Thanks, Laura." He gazed down at her hand on his. "I hope we can be friends." He turned his palm up so they held hands.

"Give me the Imperial account and I'll be whatever you want."

"How about I give you a *fair shot* at the Imperial account?" he responded with a grin.

She released a dramatic sigh. "If that's the best you can do, I guess I'll take it."

"One more thing. While I'm not trying to hide my sexual orientation, I don't exactly advertise it."

"No kidding."

"So, I'd appreciate it if you didn't, you know, spread it around." He fiddled with the cocktail ring on her left middle finger.

She raised her right hand and crossed her finger over her heart. "Advertising executive/client-to-be privilege."

"So, how was it? Tell me all about it. How's Rhett Butler?" Darcy started in as soon as Laura sat down at the little sidewalk café in the Theatre District.

"Oh, you mean The Liar?" Laura placed the napkin across her lap and picked up the menu.

"What?" Darcy narrowed her eyes. "He isn't married, is he?"

"No. Worse."

"What could be worse?"

"He's the competition."

"The competi—" Darcy gasped. "He works for—" She waved her hand, unable to come up with the ad agency.

"Hawk Media. Yes. He's the VP of Business Development, and he's heading up the pitch for Imperial's account."

Darcy sat back in her seat, mouth agape. "When did you find out?"

"Rome."

She sat forward again. "Wait a minute. What did you tell him about yourself?"

Laura fiddled with her flatware and tried to still her bouncing leg. "Not much. You know my rules."

Darcy rolled her eyes. "You had crazy monkey sex with a guy, for what? Ten days?"

"Nine, but who's counting?"

"Apparently you are."

Laura rolled her eyes. "And what exactly is monkey sex, anyway?" She lifted the glass of ice water to her mouth.

"And didn't tell him what you did for a living?" Darcy continued, ignoring Laura's rhetorical question.

Laura shrugged. "It didn't come up."

Darcy snorted.

"We were busy having sex." Laura smirked.

The waiter chose that moment to walk up to the table. "Ahem, should I come back?"

"No," Laura said.

"Yes," Darcy interrupted.

He raised a brow, before beating a hasty retreat.

"So it was a lie by omission," Darcy pointed out after the waiter left. "And clearly he omitted what he did for a living, or he wouldn't have taken you by surprise."

"No. He *lied* about what he did."

"What did he say?"

"He said he was in corporate relations."

"So, Ms. Armstrong"—Darcy folded her arms on the table—"as an ad agency executive, is corporate relations not part of your job?"

"You've been spending too much time with the Shyster."

"Just answer the question."

"Yes," Laura muttered.

"Then he didn't exactly lie."

"Fine. I hate when you turn all lawyer-like on me."

"Did I tell you my new hero is a litigator? Josh has been instructing me on the fine art of cross-examination. Comes in handy."

"Perfect. Can we just order, and forget about The Spy?"

"The Spy?" Darcy set her menu down again. "You think he intentionally spied on you?"

"What else could explain the chance encounter in front of Imperial's offices, and then his appearance on the ship?" Laura had been giving this some thought. Nathan thought *she* was spying on *him*, but she thought he said that just to throw her off.

"I thought you got your heel stuck in a sidewalk seam. Are you saying he orchestrated that?"

"No. It just worked to his advantage, that's all. I was a sitting duck."

"And how would he know which ship and which itinerary you'd chosen?"

Damn, she hated it when Darcy got all logical. She counted on her more ditzy side in conversations like this.

"I don't know. How does any spy find out . . . things? Anyway, let's talk about something else. I had dinner with Jack Jeffries last night."

"Imperial's Crown Prince? Isn't that some sort of conflict of interest for him . . . or you?"

"Pfft. We're not lawyers. Besides, we've known each other since we were kids."

"And as I recall, you had a crush on him in tenth grade."

"I did not. Besides, he only had eyes for Miss New York."

The waiter returned to take their order.

After he walked away, Darcy said, "So how was it? Your date with Jack?"

Laura hesitated. She couldn't share Jack's secret, even with Darcy.

"You didn't sleep with him, did you?" Darcy whispered across the table.

"No." Though not for lack of trying.

"Well, that's good. All you need is for the competition to think you slept your way to the account."

"No chance of that. There's just no spark there." *And, oh yeah, he's gay. More's the pity.*

Laura was convinced that if she slept with someone else, she'd forget Nathan Maxwell. Trouble was, other than Jack, no one floated her boat, and he'd barely floated her boat above the minimum draft.

"Moving on. How was your trip to California Wine Country?"

———

B right and early the following Friday morning, Laura smoothed her hands over her skirt as she walked down Imperial's carpeted hall. She'd gone with a classic white silk blouse, black pencil skirt, black patent Louboutin platform pumps, and simple silver jewelry. Professional and poised, with a hint of sexy. *Eat your heart out, Nathan Maxwell.*

Taking a deep breath, she entered Imperial's boardroom for the pre-pitch meeting. It wasn't the meeting that had her nerves on edge. It was seeing Nathan for the first time since Naples.

Ridiculous. He was just a man.

But what a man. Nathan already sat at the table with a couple of other members of the Hawk Media team, including Hawk himself. Nathan chuckled at something the woman said. His eyes crinkled at the corners and Laura's stomach did a back dive off the Empire State Building.

Light-gray suit, white shirt, navy tie. She remembered with startling clarity what the superb cut of that Italian suit covered.

Ever polite, he nodded a curt greeting to her.

She studiously ignored him, turning to Celeste, the head of the creative team who'd be working on the pitch. "Laugh."

"What?" Celeste looked up in confusion.

"Laugh. I want the Hawk Media team to think we're just as relaxed as they are."

"But—"

"Just laugh," Laura ground out.

"All right. Sheesh." Celeste obliged with a cackle.

Great. She'd forgotten Celeste's laugh sounded like the Wicked Witch of the West. Taking a seat opposite Hawk, she opened her iPad case, and tried to quell her bouncing leg.

Jackson Jeffries entered the room, followed by Jack. After the men circled the room, shaking hands with everyone, they took seats, Jack at the head of the table.

"I'd like to thank everyone for coming." Jack began, nodding to everyone in the room. "Why don't we get started?"

Nathan tried to keep his head in the game, but he found himself all too aware of Laura's presence. Hair in her usual ponytail, conservative blouse, black skirt. But those oh, so sexy legs and those skyscraper pumps blew that prim image right out of the water. She rocked the sexy secretary look, and then some.

She took notes on her iPad, glancing up at Jack with interest. Jack glanced her way and smiled as he explained what the cruise line was seeking in its agency and in its campaign.

The purpose of the pre-pitch meeting was to help focus the pitch and campaign planning.

"I don't have to tell you, we don't hire an idea, we hire an agency," Jack continued.

The meeting took about an hour, and after an opportunity to ask questions, everyone packed up their belongings. Nathan noticed that Laura hung back.

He reluctantly followed Hawk and Julia, the head of the creative team, out into Imperial's Lobby.

"Julia, do you mind if I have a word with Nathan alone?" It was phrased as a question, but was more of a command.

Julia frowned a moment. "No. I'll just catch a cab and meet you back at the office."

"Thank you." Hawk waited until Julia stepped into the elevator, before pressing the button for another one. Once on the elevator alone, Hawk turned to Nathan. "You and Laura know one another?"

Nathan hesitated a moment wondering how Hawk knew.

"You couldn't keep your eyes off one another," Hawk supplied.

Well damn. Time to face the music. "You could say that." In the biblical sense. "We were on the cruise together."

"You're dating a woman heading up our competition and took her on the cruise with you?"

"No. Of course not. She happened to be on the same cruise as me—a reconnaissance mission like mine—only I didn't know that until Rome."

"And Rome was at the *end* of the cruise?"

"Yes."

"And just how did you find out?"

"I, uh, saw a text on her phone."

"How would you have seen a text on her phone?"

"It was on the table . . . by her bed." Best to come clean before it leaked out.

Hawk stumbled back. "Ho-ly hell! You slept with our competition?"

"No. I mean yes. I mean I slept with her but I didn't know she was the competition at the time. As soon as I found out, I ended the affair."

"I should hope so. Exactly how long did this affair last?"

"Nine days."

"Nine! Jesus, Nathan. You didn't share any state secrets with her?"

"Of course not." Nathan tugged at the collar of his dress shirt.

"You do know who she is, right?"

Nathan didn't have a good feeling about where this conversation was headed. "She's Laura Danforth, obviously the account executive handling the pitch for Giddings-Rose."

Hawk gave him a strange look. "She's Laura Danforth *Armstrong.*

"What?" Nathan's question came out as a strained whisper.

"She's Milton Armstrong's daughter."

Nathan took the sucker punch straight to the gut. When he regained his breath, he scrubbed his hand through his hair. "Armstrong. As in Milton Armstrong? As in Great Lakes Shipyard Armstrong? One of the world's richest men? Builder of the very ship we were on, not to mention all the other ships in the Imperial line?"

He paced away in the tight space of the elevator. "Priceless. Absolutely priceless." Paced back. She'd conveniently left out that little tidbit. But then again, she'd left out a lot.

Thunderclouds built in Hawk's usually placid eyes. "And her father is Jackson Jeffries' good friend."

"Son-of-a-bitch!" Nathan ground out. He felt as if his pants were down around his ankles.

"Add to that, she's one of the top account executives in New York. She's played an instrumental role in landing some of the agency's biggest accounts."

Nathan scrubbed a hand through his hair again. "Christ, Hawk. I didn't know."

"I should take you off the account."

Hawk's statement hit him like another punch to the gut. "No, you shouldn't." Not that he blamed Hawk. He'd do the same thing if he were in Hawk's shoes. But he couldn't lose the bonus. He couldn't stand by as his sister was turned out of her home.

"Give me one good reason why I shouldn't"

"Because I'm the best man for the job. You thought so, too, or you wouldn't have hired me. Wouldn't have given the account to me."

"You're right. But no one is indispensable."

Nathan looked Hawk in the eye. "I'll get the job done."

"Then, for God's sake, keep it in your pants."

CHAPTER FIFTEEN

A fter a day from hell, Nathan stripped off his sweat-soaked T-shirt and climbed into the shower. Even the balls-to-the-wall workout he'd just put himself through didn't ease the tension.

He pressed his hands against the shower wall and let the spray pound his head.

With everything he'd been up against growing up, he'd never believed his efforts were futile. But this time, the odds were not in his favor. In fact, the outcome was almost a forgone conclusion.

How could he compete when Laura *Armstrong* had an 'in' to the whole business? He ticked off the list of things weighing heavily in her favor.

The daughter of the shipbuilding magnate who built, and continued to build, Imperial's ships, headed up the pitch team.

Her father, that same shipbuilding magnate, also happened to be Imperial's CEO's best friend.

Check. And check.

What more leverage did she need?

The following Monday, ten sets of eyes stared at Nathan waiting for his report and his directions for the various teams working on the pitch. One pair of eyes in particular unnerved him a little: Hawk's.

He'd spent the entire weekend working on the presentation, developing the angle, distilling his thoughts into manageable sound bites, something his teams could take back to their desks and work with.

"After hearing what Imperial wants in a campaign and an agency, and after my experience aboard the *Nave dei Sogni*, I'm proposing an overhaul of Imperial's public image, starting with their latest ship. A new line, a new name, one that appeals to their target demographic. I'll entertain ideas from anyone who has one—this isn't just the creative team's domain. So, start thinking about that."

Nathan clicked his laptop and a photo of a bright green Braniff Airways plane displayed on the screen behind him. "The Braniff 'End of the Plain Plane' campaign was revolutionary in its scope and in its results. For those of you fuzzy on this particular feat of advertising creativity, Jack Tinker and Partners, through their account leader, Mary Wells, hired an architect, a fashion designer, and a shoe designer to overhaul Braniff's tired image. The result—a revolutionary turnaround for a failing airline.

"I contacted Great Lakes Shipbuilding. Since the building is still in the early-stages, we can look at revising the deck plans, and nothing has been done with interior design at this point, so it's a blank slate."

Nathan continued, "I'm recommending we hire a top interior designer and space consultant. Like their other ships, this should be an all-suite ship. No cramped cabins." He let that sink in a moment.

"We're targeting those with deep pockets, but not deep enough to afford their own private yachts. The point is to make the demographic feel as if they were on their own yacht. Spacious accommodations, the highest space per passenger ratio available." The nodding heads around the table offered encouragement.

"A completely non-structured cruise, optional private land-based tours. And for dining, special requests are welcome. We cater to the vegan, the dairy-free, the gluten-free, and everything in-between. Want something specific for your scheduled cruise? Prefer Evian bottled water? Add it to your profile and Imperial will get it for you."

He glanced at Hawk to gauge his reaction so far. He was furiously taking notes. His *boss* was taking notes! Either he loved it, or he was listing the reasons to fire him.

"Speaking of profiles. Guests complete an online profile with all their preferences. Everything from food and beverages to music and bath products."

"And because the size of the ship is much smaller than the rest of the fleet, Imperial will be able to offer interesting ports-of-call. Ports off the beaten path that much larger ships can't access."

"The campaign will flow from the ship's design, the offerings, the *feel* of the cruise experience that Imperial will offer its guests."

"Now, with only four weeks to the pitch, we're up against the wall for a campaign of this magnitude, so time is of the essence. I'd like to hear some ideas by end-of-day tomorrow. If you have any issues or questions, my door is always open." Nathan stood, signaling the end of the meeting. As he gathered his notes, Hawk came up to him. He slapped a hand on Nathan's back. "That's an ambitious campaign."

"Imperial's got ambitious goals," Nathan returned.

"And I think you'll exceed their goals with this campaign." Hawk strode out the door.

Nathan released the breath he hadn't realized he'd been holding.

———

Having worked on her presentation until the wee hours of the morning, Laura was confident in her proposal to the group. Incorporating the goals and objectives of Imperial based on the pre-pitch meeting, along with the ideas she'd noted on her trip, Laura sat down with her teams, and laid out her proposal.

"Let's begin with my vacation slide show." Laura clicked the button on her laptop and the selfie of her on her balcony flashed on the projector screen, followed by a few chuckles.

"But seriously, while the décor of the *Nave dei Sogni* was gorgeous, it was a bit over the top." Laura clicked to the next slide with photos of the ship's dining room, lounge, and other public areas. There were lots of *wow's* and *oh my's*, along with some confused looks.

"Where's Fred and Ginger?" Claudia asked.

She clicked to a collage of photos from her stateroom.

"Holy shit!" Havi said.

"Exactly. This is more like it." The photos showed her penthouse stateroom from various angles. "Elegant. Comfortable. Welcoming." She clicked again, showing a photo of La Presse du Vin. "Quiet, warm, relaxing. A place of respite, with all the creature comforts."

"You heard the CEO. The new ship will be designed to feel like your own private yacht. This is what the demographic wants. Unobtrusive pampering. Champagne upon boarding. Their luggage picked up at their home and delivered right to their stateroom. No schlepping luggage to the airport, no hassles with customs. The line will offer no fuss travel."

She continued, "But even with that warm, welcoming atmosphere, our target doesn't want to completely disconnect, right? We still want our Twitter, Facebook, and Instagram. We want up-to-the-minute updates. Information at our fingertips. So, the experience will appeal to the digital demographic, a demographic who doesn't want to unplug from social media on vacation, but prefers to share their experiences in real-time via social media."

"As we know, Imperial's social media is currently dying on the vine. I propose we revive it. Big time. With real-time Twitter updates. Docking in Portofino today? We've got you covered with the weather report, recommended restaurants, not-to-be-missed sites, and sites that may be closed for repairs. Shopping on the Ponte Vecchio and don't know where to grab lunch? Send a tweet with a specific hashtag. The social media experts will send links and directions to the recommended restaurants in your area. Instead of the environmentally unfriendly daily paper ship's bulletins, which usually hit the trashcan shortly after delivery, you can sign up to receive them via email.

"And speaking of digital media, I went on some pretty boring city tours. Stuck one out, bagged another one." She didn't want to think about what happened on the one in Naples. "The problem with organized tours is we all take things in at our own pace. Some of us like to read every placard in the museum. Stand in front of *David* until the docent's escort us out. Others of us prefer to get the high-lights and move on. It's difficult to please both types of tourists.

"That's where the Concierge Tours App comes in. Created exclusively for Imperial, the app will be an interactive tour guide for ports-of-call and their surrounding areas, complete with subway maps. You select the sites you want to visit. You decide how much information you want at those sites. Then you move on.

"Those are my initial thoughts. I'm open to any suggestions, comments, or questions. Oh, one more thing. The ship has yet to be named. That's where we come in. The name should symbolize what it has to offer."

Celeste slapped her hands on the table and said, "Let's do this."

———

The following Monday, Laura's phone rang and reaching for it she saw Jack's name on the screen.

"Hi, Jack."

"Wednesday. You. Me. A benefit."

"Ooh, you really know how to show a girl a good time."

"Come on, it's for The Skills Project, and you'll know just about everyone there. Plus, I could really use your help fending off the cougars."

Laura laughed. Jack's Ralph-Lauren-model-looks, warm engaging smile, and rumored net worth made him a favorite among the unattached 'mature women' crowd. Laura wasn't the only one that hadn't had a clue about Jack's sexual orientation. "Keep up your sweet-talk and you'll have me eating out of your hands."

"Great. I'll make sure to wash my hands before I pick you up at seven."

Hitting 'end,' Laura opened her calendar app and entered the event.

Even with all the hours she was putting in at the office, Nathan still managed to creep into her thoughts on a regular basis. She found herself wondering what he was doing. And even more pathetic, wondering if she ever crossed his mind. She relived her cruise with every meeting on the pitch and every task in support of that pitch.

Maybe a night out would take her mind off the frustratingly charming and great-in-bed Nathan. Even if her escort was gay.

———

Late Wednesday afternoon, Nathan made some notes as he conversed with the owner of a local bookstore who'd scored a book signing with a hot new best-selling author. They needed a quick and dirty campaign to advertise the event. He was just finishing up the call when Hawk stuck his head in the door. Nathan gave him the 'hold-on' sign, then said his goodbyes to the woman and hung up.

"What's up?" he asked as Hawk sauntered in and lowered his six-foot four-inch frame into a chair across from Nathan's desk, legs splayed out.

They were back on solid ground after his confession.

"Was that Mia on the phone?"

"Yes. She's desperate for our help."

"She's a good friend, so let's make it happen. She really pulled off a coup getting Sam Workman for a book signing. People are saying he's the next Stephen King."

"If the other teams are too busy, I'll take care of it

myself," Nathan assured his boss. "I still remember a few things from my days working in the trenches."

"I know it's short notice, but do you have plans tonight?"

"You mean other than your friend's ad campaign? No, why?"

"I've got a ticket to The Skills Project benefit, but Michael is sick, so I need to go home and relieve Melissa." Nathan must have made a face because Hawk continued, "It's Jack Jeffries' pet project. It'll give you an opportunity to schmooze him."

"Sure. Where and what time?"

Hawk handed him the ticket. "It's all on there." Hawk rose and headed for the door before turning back. "Thanks, Nathan. I appreciate it. And you'll meet some interesting people."

———

Laura stepped off the elevator to see Jack waiting in the lobby of her high-rise. He looked very *GQ* in a black suit, black dress shirt, and hot-pink tie—Hermès no doubt.

"Damn, woman. You look good enough to eat." He took her hands and gave her the once over. "You might have me swinging in the other direction." That infectious grin had melted many a girl's heart.

"You look pretty edible yourself."

He took her elbow and guided her to the glass doors at the front of the lobby.

"You're making my job tonight very difficult." At his confused expression, she continued, "You know—fending off the cougars."

"The way you look tonight, I think I'll be the one who's busy. I'll be beating the men off you with a stick."

"And who asked you to?"

He laughed. "Right."

———

The warehouse-sized loft in a trendy section of SoHo buzzed with the kind of conversation only heard at events attended by the top one percent. Nathan had no point of reference for the topics under discussion, everything from tedious renovations on an Aspen vacation home, to adding on to a five-car garage to house the latest purchase of an Aston Martin special edition Vanquish, to the latest dining sensation, edible air, whatever the hell that was.

With no sign of Jack Jeffries, Nathan sipped his scotch and tried to appear interested in one of the sculptures up for auction that evening—a concoction of rusted and twisted metal that resembled the mangled wreckage from a multi-car pile-up rather than a six-figure-priced work of art. Whoever buys that has more money than sense, he thought, good cause or not. Just make a donation and leave the pile of metal for the scrap heap.

Circling back to the room at large, his step faltered when he spotted Laura standing in the entrance. She looked stunning, especially in a Jezebel-red dress that hugged every curve, and those damned erotic stilettos—some kind of snake this time.

But then again when didn't she look stunning? Even at first morning light, eyes blurred with sleep, hair mussed, a feline smile of satisfaction on her lips, she dazzled. Before the pre-coffee grumpiness set in, that is.

She turned to speak to someone behind her, then Jack Jeffries moved to her side.

Nathan's jaw clenched. Right. Talk about throwing a bucket of ice water over his head.

Taking his arm, Laura let him escort her into the crowd, where she appeared perfectly at home playing kiss-kiss with the *hoi polloi*. The daughter of one of the world's wealthiest families would no doubt attend such functions on a regular basis. She probably cut her teeth on the backbiting that goes on when those at the top of the wealth food chain gathered.

But what rankled even more was the lengths she would go to, to get the Imperial Cruise account, including sleeping with the founder and CEO's son and the company's Vice President of Customer Relations. It wasn't enough that her father and Jackson were best friends.

He heard the hammer hit the last nail in the coffin.

Jack and Laura made the rounds before heading over to the bar for a drink. Well, he'd promised Hawk he'd schmooze with Jack and schmooze he would. And as for Laura, the gloves were off.

———

Laura ordered a martini and drummed her fingers on the bar. She dreaded these events like a shopaholic dreaded the words, 'Your credit card has been declined.' Not that the event wasn't for a good cause, but all the glad-handing and ass-kissing that went on made her long for a shower. She glanced around the room. Jack was right. She knew most of the people there, and couldn't count a genuine one among them. She felt a hand on the small of her back. Jack was the exception. Like his father, money hadn't tainted him.

She winced at her hypocritical thoughts. What was that saying, *People in glass houses shouldn't throw stones?*

"Jack."

Her hand froze in the process of reaching for her drink. She knew that voice all too well. The voice that had whispered delicious naughty phrases in her ear on so many occasions she'd lost count. *What the hell was Nathan doing here?*

"Nathan." Jack reached out his hand to give Nathan's a shake. "How are you?"

"I'm good. Quite the event you have here," he said, indicating the throng. He'd yet to look Laura's way.

"Thanks. It's our fifth year, and we're set to break another fundraising record. Nathan Maxwell, you remember Laura Armstrong. Laura, Nathan Maxwell." He gestured between them.

"I remember." Nathan's eyes glittered like two hard stones, so different from the warmth she'd grown used to seeing there. "But when we met, you had a different last name."

She winced, and slid Jack a glance. "Yes." She played down the nerves, played up cool, taking a sip from her drink, even though she burned inside.

He looked as urbane as usual in his well-tailored black suit, white shirt, and royal-blue tie. Where Jack appeared every inch the metrosexual, Nathan appeared every inch the testosterone-loaded male. Why she ever thought Nathan wasn't her type, she'd never know.

Jack laughed. "Well, this must be awkward."

"Not really," Laura said. "What's a little competition between friends?" She lifted an insolent shoulder.

"Especially when that friend will stop at nothing to win."

"Every weapon in the arsenal, right, Nathan?" She

lifted her glass, as if in a toast. She relished a challenge. Like facing a well-skilled opponent in a chess match, it only made the victory that much sweeter.

Jack slipped his arm around Laura's waist. Nathan's eyes cut to Jack's arm and then narrowed. *Proprietary much? So Nathan was a little territorial, was he?* She didn't know how she felt about that.

Part of her wanted to express her outrage at being considered an object to be possessed. Another part of her wanted to make him jealous. And yet another part of her . . . *liked* it.

"And maybe some that aren't." Nathan turned his attention to Jack. "Hawk sends his regards. He had a conflict and couldn't make it tonight."

"I'm sorry to hear that, but glad you could make it instead. Come, let me introduce you around." With his possessive hand still at her waist, Jack guided Laura along while he shepherded Nathan through the gauntlet of New York's doyen and doyenne.

She had to admit Nathan's Southern charm disarmed even the most hardened hedgefunders and corporate raiders. It had worked on her, hadn't it? And as charming as he was out of bed, he raised it to the tenth power in bed.

She recalled one moment in particular, hands cuffed in his above her head, his body joined with hers. She felt an irresistible urge to fan herself. *Was the air-conditioning on the fritz?*

"Laura? How about you?" Jack interrupted her torrid little walk down memory lane.

"Hmm?"

Jack chuckled. "Where were you?"

"Oh. I'm sorry. What did I miss?"

Nathan's gaze said he knew exactly where she'd gone.

Jack shook his head at the other men in the circle, as if to say, *women*. "We were talking about a game of golf this Saturday at Manhattan Woods. Nathan here hasn't played since he left Atlanta. What do you say? Want to join?"

Her first inclination was to decline, but then on second thought, did she really want Nathan and Jack palling around without her? "Sure. What time?"

"I'll see about a nine a.m. tee time. Anyone else care to join? Fill out the foursome?" Jack asked the others in the group, including a state senator who'd just recently been accused of sexting his children's nanny. *Ick.*

A chorus of disappointed *no's* followed.

"Well. Looks like a threesome, then," Jack said with a smile.

"Super," came Nathan's lackluster reply.

Laura grinned. *Check.*

CHAPTER SIXTEEN

S tepping out onto the Manhattan Woods Clubhouse terrace, Laura took in the view of the New York City skyline. Laura's parents had been members of the private club since it opened in 1998. In fact, it had been the scene of Laura's futile flirtations with Jack. It had also been the scene of the golf lessons she and Darcy took. That is before Darcy got bored and ditched her for riding lessons.

Her mother had rarely played golf, if at all, preferring to sit on the terrace and gossip with the other country club wives. But she remembered her father bringing current and potential customers to the club to both impress and intimidate.

She hadn't been at the club in ages, choosing to avoid her parents and their haunts if at all possible. Besides, other than golf, the country club environment held little appeal for her.

She heard the sound of footsteps and the unmistakable click of golf cleats. Turning, she let out a reluctant sigh. Nathan stood wearing a green golf shirt and navy slacks, a cap pulled down low over his face, looking like he could conquer anything the golf course threw at him.

"Jack's on his way. He ran into someone in the locker room," Nathan said through tight lips.

Laura could see the muscles working in his jaw. Well, even though she'd agreed to participate in this little outing, it wasn't high on her list of where she'd rather be today either. She'd come out of self-preservation and a need to protect her territory. Nodding, she turned back to the view.

She felt more than heard his presence close behind her. He leaned in, and she smelled his cologne. Flashes of naked bodies, hot kisses, and even hotter sex darted through her brain. Why did the sense of smell have to trigger such strong memories? Her stomach clenched and she closed her eyes.

"You think you'll win the Imperial account by playing the sex card?" he said *sotto voce*.

She stiffened. That was rich. So he thought she was sleeping with Jack? And to get the Imperial account, no less. As if she'd need to sleep with him to get the business. If she weren't so insulted she'd laugh at the absurdity.

She could tell him he was wrong, but he wouldn't believe it. She could tell him about Jack, but he probably wouldn't believe that either. Who would, really? Even so, it wasn't her place to open that closet door.

She was grateful now that Jack had stopped her that night, *er*, well, that him being gay stopped her, because now that'd she'd seen Nathan again, she realized she probably couldn't have done the deed with Jack even if he wasn't gay. Nathan had apparently spoiled her for all other men.

Dammit.

Well, let him *think* she and Jack were doing the deed. What did she care?

Except that she did.

A little.

Okay, a lot. She cared a lot. And way more than she should.

"Yes." She faced him, pasting a brilliant smile on her lips. "I've been told that once men have sex with me they can't deny me anything," throwing what he'd once said to her back in his face. "Even multi-million dollar advertising accounts."

Before he could respond, Jack joined them on the terrace. "Good morning, Laura." He leaned in to kiss her cheek and she glared directly into Nathan's judging eyes.

"Good morning, Jack."

"Let's hit the driving range. I could use a warm up."

———

Nathan seethed as he followed Jack and Laura out to the driving range. He couldn't help asking himself whether he resented her sly machinations to win the account or if he was just jealous.

There was no denying his blood boiled to think of the two of them in bed. Of Jack's hands on her. His mouth.

Jealousy. Plain and simple.

Then he thought about the bonus drifting out of reach, and with it, the loss of his grandmother's farm. And the only stable home his sister had ever known. No. Definitely resentment.

Okay. Both.

If she'd had a penis, he wouldn't even be having this internal monologue. Of course, if she'd had a penis he wouldn't have experienced some of the best sex he'd ever had.

In his life.

Ever.

His hands fisted at his side. He liked Jack. Looked forward to working with him if—when—Hawk got the account—and he didn't want any tension between them.

Laura stepped up to the practice tee and addressed the ball, her long legs and taut ass displayed to perfection in the white shorts she wore. The sound of her club hitting the ball made a satisfying *whisk*. She had a beautiful swing, he had to give her that. And not too shabby on the distance, either.

Her hair, pulled back in her standard tail, draped across one shoulder. He remembered the silky feel of that hair, loose and tousled, as it draped across his face, his chest . . . and regions further south. He held back a groan.

"Nathan?" Jack interrupted his thoughts. "You going to hit some balls?"

"Yeah." Nathan shifted uncomfortably before dropping a few balls at his feet. He felt stiff, not having played in several months. Relaxing his shoulders, he assumed his stance, and tried to put Laura and her little games—and her hair—out of his head.

Like riding a bicycle, he thought as he found his swing. He watched as the ball flew past the three hundred yard marker.

Jack emitted a sharp whistle. "Damn, Nathan. I thought you said you hadn't played in a while. Even Tiger would envy that drive."

Jack stepped up to the tee and took a swing. The ball flew straight and true, landing just short of the three hundred yard marker.

The three hit a few more balls, switching from woods to irons. Nathan kept his head down. Focusing on nothing but his swing. And sometimes Laura's ass when she bent over to retrieve another ball. He was a man, after all.

"It's about tee time," Jack said as he dropped his eight iron back in his bag.

"I hear you're looking for a fourth."

Nathan heard Laura gasp and he glanced up into her ashen face.

"Father! What are you doing here?"

Ah, the venerable Milton Armstrong.

"I believe I'm a member of this club. I could ask the same of you." He leveled her with a glare as if she'd been caught red-handed stealing from the cookie jar. "Your grandmother sends her regards, by the way."

"Yes. I received her . . . regards on the ship."

Milt pointed at her. "That mouth is why she disinherited you."

"No. She disinherited me because she couldn't control me."

Jack stepped up and held out his hand to the tall, heavyset man with graying hair and a slight paunch. Good to see you, Milt." The two men shook hands. "I invited Laura to play."

"I'd like to introduce you to Nathan Maxwell," Jack continued. "Nathan recently moved to New York from Atlanta to join Hawk Media." Jack turned to Nathan.

Nathan shook Milton's hand. "Pleasure to meet you, sir." He shot a glance at Laura. At least she had some color in her face now. And that color was beet red. If looks could kill, her father would be six feet under about now.

Milton clapped Nathan on the shoulder as if they were old friends. "McCutcheon's told me about you. So you're the man who'll be handling the Imperial account."

Nathan pasted a smile on his face, uncomfortable with

Milton's presumptuousness. "Well, first I have to convince both the Jeffries and Imperial's board that Hawk Media is the agency for them."

Milton led Nathan away. "Oh, you'll win the account. You can take that to the bank." Nathan slid another glance at Laura. Her lips were pressed into a straight line, and her jaw looked like it would shatter if she clenched it any harder.

What the hell was going on here?

———

L aura stood frozen to the spot. She'd seen her father do some pretty underhanded things, but this topped them all.

"Laura, I'm really sorry." Jack stepped close, keeping his voice down. "I mentioned something to my father about our tee time and he must have told Milt. I had no idea he was going to be here."

"It's fine. It's not your fault." It was so like her father to insert himself into the group. He had no shame. At least *she'd* been invited.

"I could tell him you have a headache."

"No. Absolutely not." She'd been shocked at first, but pissed and then some had taken its place. She'd be damned if she'd let him have his way and run her off.

"All right, then." He slung his arm over her shoulder. "Let's go kick some golf course ass."

Nathan and her father were already at the first tee, and from her perspective looked to be yukking it up like two long-lost friends.

"How about we make this interesting?" her father said

as she and Jack approached. "Four person best ball, Nathan and me against you two. Losers buy lunch."

Laura rolled her eyes. *Gee. Competitive much? Who could I possibly have gotten that from?*

"Unless you're afraid of losing." Her father directed this at her.

She shrugged. "I've always been the better golfer."

Her father turned to Nathan, a smug smile on his lips. "Who wouldn't be better if they hit the ball from the girlie tees?" He followed up with a chuckle.

"All right, fine. I'll hit from the big-boy tees."

"And no handicap," her father added. "If you can't run with the big dogs, you'd better stay on the porch. Right, Nathan?"

———

Nathan didn't know what the deal was between father and daughter, but he didn't like Milton's treatment of Laura, regardless of what she'd done. As far as he could tell, Milton was shaping up to be a first-class asshole.

"Ladies first," Nathan said with as warm a smile as he could muster.

Laura grabbed a ball, a tee, and her driver out of her bag for the four hundred and twenty-six yard par four. After taking a couple of practice swings, she stepped up to the ball. She swung and drove the ball down the middle of the fairway about a hundred ninety yards from the tee.

"Looking a little rusty, there," Milt said as he took his position in the tee box without waiting for an invitation.

Jack walked over and squeezed her arm. "Good job."

Milt's tee shot sliced and landed just off the right fairway two hundred thirty yards out.

"Now who's looking a little rusty," Laura said with a smirk, drawing a glower from Milton. "He always had a problem with his slice."

Jack took his place and drove the ball down the middle several yards past Laura's.

Nathan slapped Jack on the shoulder. "Nice," he said then stepped into the tee box. He out-drove them all with a clean shot two hundred eighty-five yards down the fairway.

"Ha, ha. I knew I'd picked you for a reason," Milton said as he climbed into his golf cart, inviting Nathan to join him.

Laura breezed past and climbed into the cart with Jack, her nose in the air.

———

At the eleventh hole, Jack two-putted, giving Laura the hole, and putting them up by one over Nathan and Milton. She and Jack gave each other high fives, and she had to bite her tongue to keep from sticking it out at her father like an insolent twelve-year old.

Jack stepped up behind her and whispered in her ear, "Way to go, Laura, 'Jack Nicholas' Armstrong."

She laughed and smacked him on the arm. Thank God for Jack's soothing influence. Of course he was the one who'd gotten her into this golf game from hell in the first place. When this was over, there was a martini, or three, with her name all over it, or them.

Nathan had been quiet the last few holes, only interacting when directly engaged. Probably wishing he'd stayed home and avoided the whole dysfunctional Armstrong father-daughter experience.

The twelfth hole was a relatively short, straight-forward par three, except for the moat-like sand traps that surrounded the green. Selecting her four wood, she placed her tee and ball, took some practice swings, and drawing the club back, swung smooth and even, making contact with the ball. All eyes watched as the ball arced, hit the flagstick, and . . . landed in the cup.

"Holy shit!" Jack yelled. "Did you see that?" He whooped. "You just made a hole-in-one!"

Laura jumped into his arms and wrapped her legs around his waist as he swung her around. "Oh my God! I've never made a hole-in-one!" Her laughter rang out.

"I've never *witnessed* a hole-in-one!" Jack flashed an irresistible broad grin.

Laura grabbed the sides of his head and hauled him in for a kiss right on the mouth.

"Damned pure luck, nothing more," Milt grumbled. "Don't let it go to your head."

———

Nathan couldn't hold back his smile, even while watching Laura kiss the man who could be a key decision-maker about his future. And his sister's. But dammit. He couldn't help it. It wasn't often that you witnessed a hole-in-one. In fact, he'd never seen an ace first-hand, and it was damned impressive. No matter who made it.

He'd also never seen the reserved Laura so exuberant. Well, other than in bed, pressed up against the shower wall, oh, and in the bathtub. That Jack was the recipient of all that exuberance rankled a bit, but there was no denying her joy was infectious. And that she'd done it in front of her asshole father only added to the sweetness for her, he was sure.

Nathan's gaze slid to Milt, who sat in the golf cart going over his scorecard and pouting.

Jack set her on her feet, but Nathan doubted her feet actually touched the ground. He walked over and awkwardly patted her on the back. "Congratulations, Laura. I guess that means drinks are on you."

She released a throaty laugh that socked him in his gut. God how he missed that.

"I'll buy all the rounds you like."

Her eyes sparkled, her cheeks flushed with excitement. She looked beautiful. And he'd give just about anything to kiss that mouth and the tantalizing dimple that formed there.

He settled for teeing off instead.

Milt's cockiness ebbed following Laura's ace, and even though the game ended with him and Nathan the victors by two, he didn't stick around for lunch. Or celebratory drinks. Guess he didn't want to celebrate his daughter's ace. He'd simply shaken Nathan's and Jack's hands and left, without a word to Laura.

So much for sportsmanship. Or fatherly affection.

———

Laura recorded her ace with the pro shop for all posterity and she, Jack, and Nathan headed for the restaurant and seats on the terrace. The day had grown warm, the sun bright in a perfect, cloudless sky. She removed her light cardigan, enjoying the feel of the sun on her bare arms.

After buying the obligatory round of drinks—hers the martini she'd longed for out on the course—Nathan's and

Jack's a beer, she closed her eyes and savored the first sip, before looking over the menu.

Nathan sat directly across the table from her, and she could feel his eyes on her. Eyes that had once darkened with desire and longing as she caressed his skin with her hands and mouth.

She gave a mental snort. Nathan thought she and Jack were sleeping together. If only she *could* sleep with someone else, maybe she'd forget Nathan and his spell-binding sex.

He took a pull from his beer and settled back in his chair. "So, how long have you two been, um, dating?"

She slid her gaze to Jack just as he shot her a look. He must have read something in her face because he answered Nathan's question. "Oh, it's hard to remember. Right?" He glanced her way again. "We've known each other since we were teenagers. Our families go way back."

"How nice." Nathan picked up the menu, his expression closed.

But she could just imagine the thoughts running through his brain. Had she and Jack been dating when she'd been on the cruise? Or had she started dating Jack as soon as she returned to sew up her shot at the account?

"But don't think our relationship"—Jack gestured between the two of them with his beer bottle—"will have any influence on Imperial's decision on ad agencies. After all, the board members have a vote."

"I trust your unbiased judgment, Jack," Nathan said, gazing out at the golf course below. "But you have to admit, it looks bad. If Giddings-Rose gets the account, everyone will say it was a forgone conclusion."

"Perhaps. But you and I will know it wasn't." Jack's friendly demeanor took a decidedly chilly turn. "I won't end, or even postpone my relationship with Laura, so this discussion is moot."

"You do realize I'm sitting here, right?" While Laura appreciated Jack's defense of her and their . . . relationship, she didn't like being discussed as if she had no stake in the conversation.

"Of course. Just clearing the air," Jack said, his friendly tone restored.

———

They placed their orders with the waiter, and the conversation turned to a recap of the day's events, with a focus on Laura's ace.

"My dad is going to get such a kick out of your hole-in-one." Jack shook his head. "As much golf as dad plays, he's never made one. He'll be jealous for sure."

Nathan listened to the conversation with half an ear, more concerned with how to turn the tide in his favor.

He wondered how much influence Milton had over Jackson. To hear him tell it, Jackson relied heavily on him. He also wondered why that was. The reason from Milton's perspective was clear. He had something to gain. As long as his friend's business remained successful, he could count on building his ships.

But what did Jackson have to gain? From his meetings with Jackson, he'd found him to be as affable as his son, but with a layer of shrewd businessman underneath all that warmth. Why did he rely on Milton's advice, and what business acumen could Milton offer that Jackson didn't already have?

Their food arrived, and as he dug into his BLT, he continued his analysis of the situation.

Jack had said Imperial's board would vote on the agency, but Nathan wondered how many board members ran in Laura's social circle. How many were members of this country club, and others that Laura had access to? Then there was her father. Talk about "Old Boys Network."

Before meeting her father today, he figured Laura was a shoe-in for the account. He builds ships, his best friend buys those ships for his cruise line, and his daughter markets that same cruise line. Seemed a natural progression.

But clearly, there was no love lost between father and daughter. He scrubbed his chin. Took a swallow of his beer. An interesting dynamic, that.

His gaze drifted across the table to Laura, looking cool and reserved in her dark designer sunglasses and hot pink sleeveless polo. She'd had a momentary lapse in that composure when she'd seen her father standing there.

However brief, her body language had said intimidated. An emotion he'd not witnessed in the short time he'd known her. Vulnerability, yes, but intimidation, no. She'd just as quickly regained her equanimity, pulling the bravado mantle tight around her once more. Jack, on the other hand, had shown no intimidation in the face of her father's rude dismissal of her. In fact, he'd politely come to her rescue.

Jack snagged the pickle from Laura's plate before winking at her.

And the final nail in his coffin, she was sleeping with Jack.

That they had a history was clear in their mutual comfort level. The questions were what was that history, what was their current relationship, and how would that affect his chances of landing the Imperial account?

CHAPTER SEVENTEEN

The large glass-enclosed room looked out over the massive indoor dry dock of Great Lakes Shipbuilding where the next member of the Imperial fleet would be constructed. Senior officers of the vast Armstrong empire roamed the room, drinking scotch or champagne, schmoozing the senior officers of Imperial Cruise Lines, including Jackson and Jack Jeffries. Uniformed waitstaff carried trays of canapés and duck-filled turnovers, offering them to guests.

The venerable Milton Armstrong presided over it all like a grand potentate.

He and Hawk were deep in conversation, standing next to the computer graphic of the ship's exterior.

The train ride from New York's Penn Station to Philadelphia's Thirtieth Street Station took a little over an hour, and the whole trip Nathan was trying to figure out why he'd received an invitation to a reception meant to entertain Imperial's movers and shakers.

But more importantly, he wondered if Laura would be there. Either in her capacity as lead on the account pitch, or as daughter of Milton Armstrong. But he rather doubted she would be there as Milton's daughter, given their clearly strained relationship.

Even so, if Hawk Media were invited, Giddings-Rose should be invited, too. With no sign of Laura, or anyone from Giddings-Rose, for that matter, his confusion grew. He spotted the ship's architect that Hawk Media had been consulting with for the pitch.

He'd brought another idea for the campaign to Hawk last week—a video of the shipbuilding process—something to place on the cruise line's to-be-redesigned website to get the marketing ball rolling. Give potential guests a sneak peek at the latest, greatest ship from the ground, or dry dock, up. Whet the appetite for that exclusive maiden voyage. Hawk liked the idea, and would take it to Milton and Jackson for their approval.

Maybe that was what this was all about.

A stout man with salt-and-pepper hair entered the room, looking as if he'd just come from a back-room deal. He strode over to where Hawk and Milton stood, embracing Hawk with a masculine slap on the back, before shaking Milton's hand. Hawk waved Nathan over.

"Nathan, I'd like you to meet my father, Senator Mitchell McCutcheon."

"Senator." Nathan shook his hand. "Pleasure to meet you, sir."

"Nathan here will be running the ad campaign for your son," Milton interjected.

"Well, sir, first we have to land the account." Nathan laughed, again uncomfortable with Milton's presumption. "I'm facing off against Mr. Armstrong's daughter, and I understand I have a worthy opponent."

Milton muttered a curse. "My daughter," he scoffed. "Not much competition there, if you ask me."

"All due respect, sir, your daughter has earned the admiration of every ad agency in the state, and many around the country, and is fast on her way to becoming the youngest person—not just woman—in the history of Giddings-Rose to be named an officer of the agency. I, for one, am not going to discount her abilities." Nathan didn't know where that had come from, but he couldn't stand there and let Milton disparage his daughter. Even if she was a pain in his ass.

When time had permitted, he'd researched some of her work. He needed to know what he was up against, which is what he told himself. But the more he saw of her work, the more impressed he became. And the more his pride in her grew. *Dammit.*

In his research, he'd learned the very campaign they discussed their first night at dinner—the perfume campaign featuring Jean Harlow, and the brilliant placement of that ad in *QG*—had been hers. Along with the edgy Fiat advertising campaign that recently shook up the import market. No wonder she had a reputation for smart, innovative marketing strategies.

Oh, yes. She was a worthy opponent.

Hawk and his father moved off to join Jackson and Jack at the artist's rendering of the ship. Leaning over, Milton placed his hand on Nathan's shoulder. "This account is yours for the taking. Don't let my upstart daughter get in your way."

Milton left him pondering that cryptic remark.

———

"So what's this news that's so big it couldn't wait? Another bestseller? Another award? What?" Laura asked as soon as she and Darcy were seated at a table in a SoHo restaurant. "Should we order champagne to celebrate?"

Darcy shook her head, mute, but beaming, her smile so wide Laura thought her face might crack.

"What?"

"I'm pregnant."

Stunned, Laura took a moment to answer. "Pregnant! Wow, you two sure work fast. You've only been married a couple of months." How could she feel both elated for her friend, and sick to her stomach at the same time?

Darcy shrugged. "We didn't want to wait."

"I'll say. I bet your parents are fit-to-be-tied."

"And so is Josh's mom. She's thinking of moving here just so she can be close to her grandchild. Josh and I have been checking out real estate in Brooklyn. I have to admit it would be nice having a built in babysitter close by."

Recovering her composure, Laura said, "I expect to be named godmother."

"Goes without saying."

"When will we welcome the little shyster into the world?"

Darcy snorted. "He or she might not be a shyster, er, lawyer. He or she might be a writer like me. Either way, I'll love the little peanut." She rubbed her hand over her nonexistent belly. "I'm due in April, right around Josh's birthday."

Feeling guilty over her initial selfish reaction, Laura reached across the table, took Darcy's hand. "I'm happy for you, you know that, right?"

Darcy's eyes filled. "Yeah." She squeezed Laura's hand,

swiped at a tear with the other. "Hormones." She shrugged. "I'm starved." Picking up the menu, she perused it. "Another byproduct."

After ordering, Darcy dug into the complimentary hummus and breadsticks. "So, enough about me. What's new with you? How's work on the cruise account going?"

"Fine."

"That didn't sound convincing. What's up?"

"Nathan and I had a little run-in last week."

"A run-in? Do tell."

"Well, he came to Jack's fundraising event and things got a little testy."

"Did you exchange words, what?" Darcy asked, her eyes wide.

Laura told Darcy about the benefit, the golf game, her father. And Jack.

"So Nathan thinks you're sleeping with Jack." Darcy sat back, pointed a breadstick at Laura. "Can't say I didn't warn you."

"Yeah, yeah."

"But you told him you weren't so problem solved."

Laura hesitated, and Darcy looked up from swirling her breadstick in the hummus. "You told him, right?"

"No."

"Why not? Why would you want Nathan to think you'd gotten the account by being a slut?"

"First, that's not what's going to land me the account," Laura huffed.

"But that's what he's going to think." She pointed her hummus-covered breadstick at Laura for emphasis. "And who wants that? No one, that's who."

"Second, what do I care what he thinks?" Except she did. But she had a feeling that even if she'd said she wasn't sleeping with Jack, Nathan wouldn't believe her. He'd made up his mind about what kind of person she was the night he'd read that text message.

Darcy narrowed her eyes. "Are you trying to make him jealous?"

"No. Of course not." She wasn't *trying*, but if he *was* jealous, so be it.

Digging into her plate of pasta as soon as the waiter set it in front of her, Darcy shoveled a forkful in her mouth.

After swallowing her pesto-covered penne, Darcy continued, "So what do you plan to do about Nathan and Jack?"

"What do you mean? Nothing." She poked at her salad.

Darcy set her fork down. "You're still into him, aren't you?"

"Who? Jack?"

"No, and you know that's not who I mean."

"Pfft. Don't be silly. I think those pregnancy hormones have gone to your brain."

Darcy eyed her, making her uncomfortable. "Maybe those pregnancy hormones are giving me super powers instead."

"Something like that."

"Even if it's not super powers, I *am* a romance writer you know. I create the moment when the heroine knows she's in love."

"Love! Now I know you've lost it."

"Or at the very least, strong like. And that moment is written all over your face."

Laura carefully molded her features into a mask of stoicism. "What you see is a woman working her ass off †o get the Imperial account and achieve the next step in her Life Plan."

And then what? a voice asked.

Then she'd be happy, she answered.

Darcy pinned her with a stare. "Remember Samantha in *Her Hearts Desire*?" At Laura's clearly blank stare, Darcy continued. "She always talked about her sexcapades with her best friend. Until Flynn, you know, the hero." Darcy waited a beat, her head tilted, reading her like a short story. "You haven't talked once about your, er, exploits with Nathan. Why is that, do you think?"

"Um, because it's over?" Laura snarked.

"Whatever." Darcy rolled her eyes as she resumed eating.

———

Instead of going back to her apartment, or even into the office as she should, Laura got out of the taxi at Central Park, and craving peace, headed in the direction of The Mall with its tranquil tree-lined path.

The shade of the elms along the path offered a respite from the summer heat, and provided a slight buffer to the noise of the city beyond.

Watching Darcy today at lunch, seeing her happy glow, Laura felt a strange new emotion. Envy.

Darcy's pregnancy meant in nine months she'd be a mom. A wife, a mother, with little to no time for her. Darcy had moved on with her life. She had everything she'd always wished for, and Laura couldn't be happier for her.

But.

Laura sighed. She had few people in her life with whom she'd forged a deep, long-lasting relationship, and her relationship with Darcy was the deepest.

What would happen to their friendship once her

godchild was born? The impromptu lunches, the spa days, the booty bar classes, and the drinks after work, would all fall by the wayside. She'd already taken a backseat to Josh. Now she'd be in the trunk. She winced at the selfishness of her thinking.

Giving herself a mental snap-out-of-it slap, she changed direction, walking out of the park and up Fifth Avenue toward her office.

Suck it up. She'd be fine. She didn't need anyone, anyway. She had her work and her Life Plan.

———

The following Saturday evening, Laura put the finishing touches on her appearance, then inspected her reflection in the full-length bathroom mirror. From her hair, which hung in a long sleek curtain down her back, to her ruby-red Carolina Herrera evening gown with the plunging neckline skimming over her subtle curves, she approved.

It was high time for a night out. She'd been working too hard. Even the peace and solitude she'd always looked forward to coming home to now felt more like a prison.

Scooping up her beaded evening bag, she headed for the door just as her intercom buzzed.

She hit the button. "Yes?"

"Ms. Armstrong, your car is here."

Hitting the button again, she said, "Thank you, Marcus."

Unaccustomed to the nervous jitters in her stomach, she took the elevator down to the lobby of her building. It was an important night in the advertising business. Advertising's top agencies would be at the Sylbie Awards tonight, and she was up for her first award thanks to the success of Giddings-Rose's Fiat campaign.

The nervous jitters had nothing to do with seeing Nathan again for the first time since the golf match from hell. Nothing at all. Nor with the fact that her campaign was up against a Hawk Media campaign in the same category: multimedia advertising. Nope. Not at all.

When she climbed into the limo, she could see her crew had already begun the celebration.

Katie held a glass of champagne to her lips, Havi stuffed a mouthful of caviar into his mouth, while Celeste threw back a shot of something.

"That should calm the nerves a little," Celeste said as soon as she'd recovered her breath. "My first award nomination," she explained.

"Me, too," Laura said as she settled back against the plush leather seats.

"Then here." Celeste poured another shot. "It'll help."

"Thanks." Laura peered at the glass. "What is it?"

"Whiskey, I think."

Laura tossed back the contents, the warmth spreading down her throat to her stomach. Inhaling sharply, Laura set the shot glass aside. "Okay, then."

The Grand Ballroom at the Plaza Hotel served as the venue for this year's Sylbie Awards, the opulent room's mirrors reflecting the glitter and sheen of its occupants. Entering the room, Nathan set off in search of Hawk Media's table. Finding it, he barely recognized his team, decked out in their finery.

Hawk walked up with his beautiful wife, Melissa, a

former Buffalo Bills cheerleader. After the greetings were dispensed with, Nathan went in search of a drink. Well, that and a reconnaissance mission for one Laura Armstrong. He passed one of the Giddings-Rose tables, and wondered which one she would sit at. He also wondered if Jack would be with her.

Ordering a scotch, neat, he turned back to the entrance. And there she stood. Dressed to kill in a revealing red gown.

And she appeared to be alone.

His nemesis. His obsession.

That's what she'd become. His research into her advertising portfolio had turned into research into her life. He'd learned things on Google she'd never shared with him during their short fling on the ship. Nathan snorted. Which was next to nothing. Where she went to college, her family. Plenty of information out there given her name and connections.

She hadn't been lying about the gala, after all. He'd found photos of her standing next to the mayor at last year's gala wearing a silver gown and looking like a Greek goddess. Perused the event's website, no doubt created under her skillful eye, listing her as PR Committee Chair. The date and location for this year's gala.

He'd read news stories about her family. The death of her paternal grandfather. The promotion of her father to CEO of the company not long after. The stories of her badboy brother's escapades with starlets, high-paid escorts, and the occasional married woman.

Now she stood in the doorway, poised, confident, appearing to all the world as if she'd never wanted for anything in her life. Never been unsure where she comes from or where she's going. But he knew better.

She turned to say something to the woman behind her

and entered the room with all the grace her private school education afforded her. Cool. Self-assured. Beautiful.

As she headed in his direction, he debated whether to take his drink and retreat to his table or stand his ground. Choosing to stand his ground, he enjoyed her slight hesitation when she saw him. Regrouping, she continued toward the bar.

"Grey Goose Cosmo," Nathan said to the bartender, "for the lady."

"That was presumptuous," she replied with a sniff.

"How do you know it's for you?" he asked, his brow lifted in challenge.

She leveled him with an eat-shit look, and he chuckled, enjoying himself.

He took his drink from the bartender. "We meet again, in yet another challenge. I understand your Fiat campaign is up against Hawk's Patrón campaign."

"Maybe this time next year, we'll be back for the award-winning Imperial campaign," she returned with a smirk.

Wanting to wipe that smirk off her face, he leaned over, whispering in her ear, "With Hawk Media as the recipient, sugar," relishing the shiver his breath on her neck elicited.

He spun and walked away without a backward glance.

———

"Damn him," Laura muttered under her breath. Stubbornly, she left the Cosmo behind, refusing to accept a drink from him. How did he manage to make her toes curl by just whispering in her ear? And damn him and his 'Nathan-time' sex.

Scanning the room for her table she couldn't help but

notice how good he looked in that tux. She'd wanted to peel off his clothes and lick him from head to toe.

Taking a seat next to Katie just as the emcee took the podium, she turned up her nose and focused on the ceremonies. By damn, she was going to enjoy her first award nomination if it killed her. But first she had to make it through dinner and dessert before the agonizing anticipation would be over.

"Who *was* that gorgeous guy you were chatting up at the bar?" Katie asked. "He looks familiar."

"That would be Nathan Maxwell, VP of Business Development at Hawk Media, and our competition for the Imperial account."

"Da-yum! That's too bad. You two would be great together."

Laura pulled back as if Katie had slapped her. "Bite your tongue."

As the emcee droned on with the introductions, Katie narrowed her eyes. "He was the spy, wasn't he? The one on the ship."

"Pfft. No." Laura waved her hand, dismissing her comment.

Katie continued to stare, making Laura feel like a pinned butterfly.

"Okay. Fine. It was him."

"Well, don't look now, but he's sitting two tables to the right, and he hasn't taken his eyes off you."

"Really? I mean, don't stare," Laura hissed, picking up her water glass, and throwing a casual glance over her right shoulder.

"You two seemed pretty cozy up there." Katie took a roll from the breadbasket, broke it in half, and began to butter it. "Did you sleep with him on the cruise?"

Laura choked on her water. Snatching up her napkin, she covered her cough. Eyes watering, she glared at Katie, who wore a smug grin.

"I'll take that as a yes."

Laura grabbed her arm and tugged her close. "Don't you dare say anything. I know where you live."

"Yeah, yeah. Don't get your La Perla in a knot. I'm not going to say anything . . . if you answer one question."

Laura released her and sat back. "What question?"

"How was he?" Katie asked, eagerness written all over her face.

———

Hawk pushed his dessert plate aside and propped his elbows on the table. "You might want to pay attention to the program instead of staring a hole in Ms. Armstrong's back," Hawk whispered.

Well, shit. So much for subtle.

Hawk chuckled at his expression and slid closer to his wife, putting his arm around her.

Nathan picked up the program. Only two more awards until the Hart Multimedia Advertising Award. Then he could gracefully bow out. Provided Hawk didn't win, otherwise he'd have to stay for the post-ceremony celebration.

He had to get away from Laura. Just being in the same room with her brought back so many memories. Steamy memories, as well as tender ones. If he stayed, he'd wind up asking her for drinks, and drinks could lead to not keeping it in his pants per Hawk's orders. Assuming she'd agree to meet him. Which was a pretty bold assumption.

The emcee interrupted his thoughts. "Next up, the Hart Multimedia Advertising Award. This award is given for the previous year's best multimedia advertising campaign, utilizing all forms of media including TV, radio, digital and print content, as well as social media. This year's list of nominees encompasses some of advertising's most stellar agencies." With each agency and campaign named, the corresponding tables erupted into applause.

"And this year's Hart Award goes to—" Drawing out the anticipation, the emcee fumbled with the envelope. Nathan glanced around the table at all the hardworking members of his team who created the campaign pre-Nathan. Hawk clasped his wife's hand, the only sign of his emotions.

"Cooper Media Group for their 'Way to Go' campaign, Platinum Airlines."

Melissa leaned over, patted Hawk's cheek in consolation, and kissed him.

Disappointment settled over the table, even as they clapped for the winners who were making their way to the stage.

Nathan looked over at Laura's table. Okay. At Laura. Though she joined in the applause, her shoulders slumped a little, as if she could no longer handle the fatigue. Colleagues were patting her on the back, offering words of encouragement.

Dammit. Why did he feel like she'd been cheated? The Fiat campaign had smoked Platinum's hands down. Hell, the Fiat campaign had smoked Hawk's Patrón campaign.

After the acceptance speeches were made, and the emcee moved on to the next category, Laura rose from the table and headed for the door. He'd blame it on sour grapes, but he wanted to leave too.

He waited a few more minutes then stood, saying his goodnights to Hawk, Melissa, and the rest of the gang. He didn't expect to see Laura. She'd probably caught a taxi home, but he headed into the bar, hopeful. And a glass of scotch sounded good about now, anyway.

She sat alone in the corner, her back to him, a highball glass in her hand.

Ordering his scotch, he took it from the bartender and walked over to her table. "Mind if I join you?"

CHAPTER EIGHTEEN

Laura lifted her eyes to his, surprised to see him standing at her table. "Come to gloat over my loss?"

"Why would I do that?" Nathan sat across from her, ignoring the fact that she'd never responded to his question. "We didn't win either," he pointed out. "Maybe I've come to drown my sorrows, too."

She snorted.

"For what it's worth, your campaign blew everybody else's out of the water, including Hawk's."

Laura narrowed her eyes, wondering why he was being nice to her.

He continued, "It's true. The 'Find a Fiat' contest? Pure brilliance. And the social media blitz, inspired."

Still confused by his compliments, she did the thing she did best, sassed. "Damn right." She hoisted her drink, said, "But, to the winner go the spoils," then took a gulp and felt the heat.

"Where's Jack?"

Turning the glass in her hands as if the ice cubes fascinated her, she hedged before answering. "We're just friends."

"I see. Keeping him in your back pocket then?"

"Jack doesn't fit in anyone's back pocket. And what you're implying is insulting. To both Jack and myself."

Nathan sighed. "You're right." He took another sip of his drink. "You look beautiful tonight."

She lifted her own glass to her lips, gazing at Nathan over the rim. His eyes matched the whiskey in her glass, warm, golden . . . inviting. Heat settled in her belly, and it wasn't from the alcohol. Memories of being naked against that hard, sexy body flooded her brain. She'd rather drown her sorrows in him. Or rather with him *in* her.

What the hell. Sex with him might not cure what ailed her, but it would go a long way to making her feel better. Tossing back the whiskey, she held her breath until the burn passed. "Come on." She stood, holding her bag in one hand, taking his hand in the other.

"Where are we going?"

"You're going to be a gentleman and see me home."

As soon as she'd climbed in the cab and given the driver her address, she pounced, grabbing the back of his neck and hauling his mouth to hers. Stunned at first, he hesitated, then sank into the kiss, his tongue wrestling with hers. *Oh yes!* This is exactly what she needed after a big letdown.

Sliding her hands inside his jacket, she pressed them against that lean, hard chest, splayed them across his ribs, down his belly, taking pleasure in the muscles quivering beneath her touch.

Cupping her face, he withdrew, his eyes searching hers. She didn't need a soul-reader, she needed a very hot and bothered Nathan. Maybe this would help.

"I'm wearing my La Perla. You remember, the red satin."

He closed his eyes. "Sweet Jesus. The thong that barely covers your—"

"The very one," she whispered huskily.

"Driver, could you step on it?"

———

Nathan didn't even get a glance at the apartment before Laura shoved him against the front door and began removing his bow tie. What the hell, he thought. He wasn't in the mood for slow and easy, anyway. But he wasn't in the mood to let her take the lead either.

Hands around her ribs he quickly shifted so that her back pressed against the door instead. Her blue eyes simmered with frustration at the sudden power shift. He wrapped his hands in that long lustrous mane of hers, tilting her head back, giving him easy access to her throat, where he nipped and licked his way to her tender earlobe. Her breathy moans and pants filled the dark apartment, the only light coming from the city skyline outside her windows.

He spun her around again, so she faced the door, and unzipped her dress in one fluid movement. Peeling back the Jezebel-red fabric, he pressed open-mouthed kisses down her spine, reveling in the silky feel of her skin beneath his tongue, the exotic fragrance she wore filling his senses.

God how he'd missed this. All the anger, frustration, and jealousy over her relationship with Jack dissipated.

Reaching around, he cupped her full breasts, their weight delicious as they filled his hands. She moaned his name, setting him ablaze, the conflagration coursing through his veins like a molten river.

He slipped the dress from her shoulders, let it fall to the floor, and released a deep, throaty groan at the sight before him. Laura, naked except for a red satin thong and those sex-me-up stilettos she had a penchant for. *Thank you, Jesus.*

"Sugar, you look good enough to eat."

———

"**T**hen what's stopping you?"

Laura had waited long enough. She wanted Nathan and she wanted him now. She turned to face him and heard his sharp intake of breath, as his eyes roamed her body with the intensity of a laser, sending sparks shooting up her spine. Reaching out, she took hold of his waistband and tugged him toward her. Yanking his shirt out of his pants, she shoved her hands up it to his pecs, where she began a slow descent, scraping her nails across his skin. He hissed out a breath.

When she met resistance at his waistband, she made quick work of his fly and found the thing her body craved more than air at the moment. He was hard for her. So hard. As she cupped him, he released a low, throaty groan and grasped the back of her neck to pull her lips up to his and tangle his tongue with hers.

She walked him backward to the sofa, where she pushed him down. He landed with a soft *oomph*. Not bothering with the rest of his clothes, she straddled him, settling his erection between her legs and lowered herself over him.

"Look at me, Laura," he ground out. "Look at me."

She complied as she rode him, slowly at first, only picking up the pace when he gripped her hips and took control. She watched as his eyes glazed over, his expression intense, sensual, enthralled. Powerful in the knowledge that she did that to him, she rode him over the edge, shattering into a million pieces, as her name exploded from his lips.

———

What she'd intended to be a purely physical joining, a momentary distraction, had turned out to be so much more. And it scared the hell out of her. *Dammit.*

Her heart beat a staccato against his. His panting breath warm against her neck where he nuzzled her, pressing kisses against her skin. She shivered at the intimacy of the contact.

"God! I've missed that," Nathan muttered against her neck.

"You have?" Laura drew back in surprise. She wasn't the only one, then.

"Don't tell me you haven't." He scooped her hair away from her face.

She snorted, then buried her face in his neck, nuzzling him. Hiding, really, so he couldn't see what must be tattooed across her face: *I missed you.* "Since I all but attacked you, what do you think?"

He ran his hand down her hair, the gesture sweet and soothing. "Clearly this isn't over between us."

"What do you mean?"

He shifted so she lay next to him on the couch, spooning against him. He continued to stroke her hair, "I mean we aren't done with each other yet," he whispered in her ear.

"The night's still young."

"You know that's not what I mean."

Something fluttered in her chest. Heartburn, maybe?

"Are you saying you want us to see one another? After what happened on the ship?"

He drew in a breath. "Yes, that's exactly what I'm saying."

"But we're in a head-to-head battle for the same account. You called me a liar, you accused me of orchestrating the entire thing."

He placed his hand over her mouth, cutting her off. "I know. I was angry. Once I had a clear head I knew how ridiculous the whole thing was." He moved his hand from her mouth. "Having said that, don't think I plan to back off my pursuit of Imperial."

"I wouldn't expect you to, and I would hope you wouldn't expect me to either."

He sighed. "No. I wouldn't expect that."

Silence filled the room.

"I didn't know who you were," Laura said into the darkness. "I thought Greg was from Hawk Media."

It was his turn to draw back in surprise. "Greg, the travel critic?"

"Is that what he was?"

Nathan laughed. "Yes, he writes for *The New York Times*. He cornered me one afternoon, I think you were in the spa, and asked me about my experience on the ship. Nice guy. Tough critic."

"If you were so angry with me, why did you take out the purse snatcher?"

He squeezed her. "That took a year off my life. When I saw the guy with a knife, I tried to get to you, but I wasn't fast enough."

She shuddered against him.

He grazed his fingers along her ribs to the slightly raised

scar. "And when I realized he'd cut you, well, I wanted to hunt him down and pound his face into mincemeat."

"But you hated me."

"No. I didn't hate you. I was angry at you, but the fact is I would have done that for anyone."

"Oh." Laura was hard-pressed to explain the disappointment that settled in her chest at his response.

"Let alone you . . . someone I cared about."

———

L aura twisted to face him. "You cared about me?"

He nodded. "Still do, obviously."

She was silent for a few beats as she gazed into his eyes. "So what do we do now?"

"That all depends."

"On what?"

"On whether you want to see me again."

"Yes. I do. But we have to set new rules."

He huffed out a laugh. "I think it was the old rules that got us into trouble in the first place. If we'd shared more about our personal lives, we'd have found out sooner and in a more honest straightforward way that we were both going after the Imperial account. And maybe handled it as adults instead of like two kids fighting over the same toy."

"Maybe. But Nathan, we're working for competing agencies, we're sleeping together, we have to be careful."

"Okay. What are the rules?"

"Rule Number One: No discussing Imperial."

"Goes without saying. Next."

"Rule Number Two: We have to keep this"—she pointed between them—"our secret."

He thought about the promise he'd made to Hawk.

Guilt settled in his chest. "Agree. Rule Number Three: No Jack."

"But, we're just friends."

"No Jack," he repeated.

"Fine. Rule Number Four: When the pitch is over and the winning agency is announced, no hard feelings, and we'll reassess our, um, relationship then."

"And may the best man—"

"Or woman," Laura interjected.

"Or woman, win."

"Deal." Laura stuck out her hand.

Nathan took her hand in his. "Deal."

"That was frighteningly easy," Laura pointed out.

"Yeah. Now we can have more make-up sex."

———

They'd managed to make it to her bedroom for the next round, and she'd managed to get him out of his clothes. As she lay against him, her legs entangled with his, his even breathing signaling sleep, she wondered at her desire to not only reignite their fling, but to have a fling with a man who would be competing against her for an account that could lead to the next step in her Life Plan.

Then she thought about how good it felt to curl up beside him, feel his warmth, touch his skin, smell his spicy, masculine scent. She sighed in contentment.

Contentment. A new word for her. A feeling so alien to her that she almost didn't recognize it. But now that she had it, she could understand its appeal.

She'd always been striving for the next thing, always moving forward. Never really taking the time to enjoy the present, what she'd achieved thus far. Once she'd accomplished a goal, she looked ahead to the next one. And the one after that. Restless. Yeah, that was a familiar word.

Maybe it was time to savor the moment.

Nathan shifted, wrapping an arm around her in his sleep. Her limbs heavy, languorous, she drifted off to sleep.

———

The next morning, Nathan walked around the apartment, thinking how it suited Laura. Elegant, understated, and most of all, expensive. That pretty much summed it up. And the view! Spectacular!

But he was more interested in the personal side of Laura Armstrong. Wandering over to an ebony bookcase along the back wall of the living room, he picked up a photo of Laura with two other women. One with long golden brown hair smiling into the camera, a glass of champagne lifted as if in a toast, the other, a brunette, he thought. It was difficult to tell with her hair pulled back from her face. Brown glasses, which matched the rest of her brown wardrobe, framed intelligent eyes that stared into the camera with a look of disdain.

He moved down the bookcase to another photo of Laura with the same two women. At least he thought it was the same two. The brunette in this photo was attractive, not quite beautiful, but with an interesting face and sparkling brown eyes. Her lips turned up softly at the corners. If it was the same woman, it was quite a transformation. Amazing what a smile, however slight, could do. The one with the golden brown hair wore a wedding gown and a dreamy expression.

Returning the photo to the shelf, he picked up another one with Laura dressed in the Red-Carpet-worthy silver evening gown he'd come across on his Google search, a nice-looking guy standing next to her, his arm around her waist. Nathan felt an irrational stab of jealousy. A previous lover?

Next to that he saw the same guy wearing a morning coat pressing a kiss to the bride's cheek. Ah, so he must be the lucky groom. Relieved, the sting of jealousy fled.

Noticeably absent from the photos scattered around the living room were her family. He knew what her father looked like, and her younger brother, and that her mother was still living and married to her father, but none of the photos resembled these people.

Remembering her grandmother's actions, his heart ached for her.

He may not have had the best family. An anonymous father. An absentee mother. But he had photos of her, along with photos of his sister and his grandmother. They may have been a nontraditional family, but they'd been tight-knit just the same.

How could her family not see what an amazing woman she was? Cherish that? Encourage that? He shook his head at their perplexing behavior.

Laura found him standing in front of her dining room window gazing out at Central Park below. She could just eat him up. His hair rumpled, his tux shirt wrinkled where she'd shoved it up to get her hands on his torso. When he turned to her, the day's growth of beard made her want to take his face in her hands and rub her cheek against it.

"Morning," he said in a lazy drawl, as a slow grin spread across his face.

"Morning." For some reason she felt awkward, like this was her first sleepover. She wrapped her skimpy robe around her. "I have coffee, but I'm not sure what I can offer you for breakfast."

His lips lifted into a smile. "It's okay. I've got to get going anyway. I didn't want to leave without saying goodbye."

Yeah. With only two weeks until the pitch, she had work to do, too.

He approached her and placed his hands on her shoulders. "I know the next two weeks will be busy for both of us, so no pressure. Just let me know when you want to get together again."

She nodded. "Sorry about the walk of shame," she said with a smile.

"No shame in it for me. I spent the night with a beautiful, sexy woman. Where's the shame in that?" Stepping into her, he pressed his lips to hers.

She leaned against him, her fingers curled in his already-wrinkled tux shirt. When he retreated, she followed him, wanting more.

Chuckling, he pressed another kiss to her mouth.

"I'll see you later, sugar."

Picking his jacket up from the sofa, he draped it over his arm, flashed her another grin, and left.

CHAPTER NINETEEN

The next week and a half passed in a blur of long days and steamy nights. When she and Nathan weren't together, they were sexting one another or carrying on naughty phone conversations. The clandestine nature of their relationship raised the stakes and the excitement.

They avoided work-related conversations, but it became increasingly difficult for her. Something that surprised her. But if there was anyone who could understand her crazy, stressful, fun world, it was Nathan, and she longed to share the stories with him.

Instead, they'd begun to share a little about each other. One night, Nathan brought up her contentious relationship with her father. A topic she preferred not to discuss.

"Come on, sugar, help me understand what I saw on the golf course that day. You know what they say, getting it off your chest will make you feel better."

They'd just finished a late dinner she'd had delivered from one of her favorite restaurants and were sitting back enjoying their wine. Throwing back a mouthful of wine, she took a deep breath.

"Fine. My father and I have never had what people would call a loving relationship. I think my lack of a penis disappointed him."

Nathan snorted. "Well, I, for one, am *not* disappointed by that missing organ."

She couldn't suppress the laugh. His humor had already taken the edge off the conversation.

"When I was twelve years old, I tried out for and won a place on the school debate team. Up until that time, my father had shown me nothing more than indifference. He never came to any of my events, whether they were sporting events or not. I was captain of the volleyball and basketball teams—"

"I could see that."

"Academic events like spelling bees, or even parent-teacher conferences. He was always too busy, or more likely just couldn't be bothered. Anyway, he finally came to my first debate. God only knows why."

She took another sip of wine, followed by another calming breath, the moment so fresh and vivid in her mind, it was as if she were reliving it. "I stood at the podium to debate the pros of banning smoking in public places. My nerves jangled, but the butterflies only added to the excitement. I felt confident in my research and in my arguments in support of the ban, and my coach told me I had a voice made for public speaking.

"Then I saw my father walking down the aisle to take a seat next to my mother near the front. I didn't expect to see him, and now that he was there, those butterflies turned into an angry hive of killer bees.

"The moderator announced my name and told me I could begin. The notes in my hands blurred. I swallowed, trying to get a grip on my nerves. The audience grew restless, and the moderator said my name again. Taking a deep breath, I began with my opening comments, but the words were coming out all wrong. Jumbled. I took a moment to collect myself and started again.

"After a few more stumbles, I saw my father rise from his seat, glare in my direction, and stalk out of the school auditorium, leaving students and parents muttering in his wake."

———

She huffed out a laugh devoid of humor. "I finally recovered enough composure to complete my arguments, but not without feeling like a dismal failure.

"As if his public disgust weren't enough, later that evening, after the ever-painful family dinner, I overheard my father telling my mother, "'Well, Cherise,'" she mimicked her father's brash voice, "'that's quite a daughter you've given me. Can't even stand up and read from her own notes. And you wonder why I've never come to any of her activities. So I can sit there and watch her monumental failure? I've got better things to do with my time. Never mind being an object of ridicule at the country club. Never again. Mark my words. That girl will never amount to anything.'"

She swore she'd never tell anyone about that. Not even Darcy knew. She closed her eyes in shame.

"I wanted to believe that my father thought I was out of hearing, but I couldn't rule out the possibility that he wouldn't have cared even if he had known I was listening."

She'd cried herself to sleep that night. But the next morning, she swore she'd be the best at everything she undertook from then on. With or without her father's support. And she'd never let a man make her cry again.

After that, every triumph, every A+, every volleyball match or basketball game won, every debate won, bolstered her self-esteem. And with every win, the exhilaration of the hunt, and the thrill of the kill fed her soul. But nothing she did ever won not only her father's love, but his respect.

"Thank God for Darcy's parents," she continued. "They were there to cheer me on as if I were their own child. I'm sure their love and support was the only thing that kept me from becoming a serial killer."

Their loyalty to her, and to one another, taught her how important it was to have a few very close friends in her life. But the lack of her parents' support taught her if she wanted to succeed in anything, she'd have to do it on her own. And that was what she'd done.

She'd never been in love. Never let herself fall. And she didn't need a psychoanalyst to tell her why she craved attention from men, primarily those with no depth. And why she went from sexual fling to sexual fling, without regard for developing any kind of long-term relationship. Until now. Until Nathan.

"I watched my father stop at nothing to win. To stomp out their competitors, to intimidate their suppliers, to win the Navy's bids. But I didn't want to win that way." She looked Nathan straight in the eye, and continued. "I'd no more sleep with someone to win their business, than I would stab a competitor in the back."

———

As Nathan gazed into her eyes, witnessed the pain he saw there, he wanted to slit his own throat for causing her even more pain. He reached out for her hand and, taking it in his, brought it to his lips. "I'm sorry. I should never have jumped to that conclusion."

"I suppose it was a valid conclusion to jump to."

"No. There's no excuse."

This explained so much. The next time he saw Milton he'd be hard-pressed not to kick him in the teeth. Or better yet, the nuts.

"And now you know the whole sordid story of the dysfunctional Armstrong father-daughter relationship."

"Sugar, the only dysfunction there applies to your father. Come here." He gestured to his lap. Once she'd settled there, he took her face in his hands. "Despite it all, or maybe because of it all, you turned into a strong, independent, sexy woman who's not afraid to carve her own path. For that, you should be proud."

———

As they cleared away the dishes, Nathan's phone rang. Glancing at the screen, he frowned. The number was unknown to him but the area code was his sister's.

Seeing his frown, Laura asked, "Everything okay?"

"I don't know. I'll tell you in a minute. Hello." Nathan dropped back into his chair.

"Is this Nathan Maxwell?"

"Yes."

"Nathan, you probably don't remember me, but we were in high school together. I'm Nadine Hendrix."

"I remember you, Nadine."

"I'm a nurse now at Darla General Hospital, and, well, your sister is here."

Nathan stood up, startling Laura, who placed her hand on his chest, an expression of alarm on her face.

"Is she okay? What happened? Was there an accident?"

"No. She came in with acute right flank pain and vomiting. She's being evaluated now, but at this point it's hard to know whether it's appendicitis or possibly kidney stones until we do more tests. She wanted me to call you."

Nathan glanced at his watch and paced away. Too late to get a flight out tonight. "Dammit, I probably can't get there until tomorrow. Tell her, tell her I love her and to hang in there. I'll be there soon."

He hung up and turned to Laura. "I have to go. I have to get a flight out first thing in the morning."

"Nathan, what's wrong?"

"Amanda's in the hospital, and they're not sure what's wrong."

With the pitch only a week away, he sure as hell didn't need to be flying off to Georgia, but it couldn't be helped. He'd call Hawk first thing. He was a family man. He'd understand. He hoped.

Nathan stared out the window. "I can't lose her. She's all I have left."

Nathan's gruff voice tugged at Laura's heart. She was no good at times like this. She never knew what to say or what to do. Taking his face in her hands, she spun him to face her.

"Everything will be okay. You're not going to lose her." Pressing her mouth to his in a tender kiss, she was shocked by the depth of emotions she felt for him. "Let's book our flights."

"Our?"

"Of course. I'm not going to let you go alone. You're too upset." She walked away before he could see how much his distress affected her.

"But, you've got the pitch."

"So do you."

"But she's *my* family. Why would you do that?"

"What are friends for?" She turned back. "Wait—you do have Internet on the farm, right?"

He chuckled. "Yes."

"Then we're good."

———

Laura gazed out her car window at the North Georgia hill country. Hard to imagine the polished, urbane Nathan Maxwell growing up here.

They'd flown into Hartsfield International Airport in Atlanta, where they'd rented a car and headed northeast for almost two hours into the mountains of North Georgia, almost to the North Carolina border. Nathan had been quiet most of the trip, only pointing out items of interest here and there. Worried about his sister, no doubt.

He'd called the hospital and was told she'd been discharged, but that was all they could tell him given the privacy laws. So they were headed straight to the house, where he'd called several times and not gotten an answer.

She placed a hand over his, and when he looked her way, she said, "Everything will be all right."

His mouth lifted a little at the corner, then, taking her

hand, he brought it to his lips. The sweetness of the gesture set butterflies to fluttering in her belly.

"Just another half hour." He turned his attention back to the road.

She wasn't sure if the ETA was for her benefit or his.

A little while later, Laura sat up and took notice when they entered a small town. As they passed under the one stoplight, she spotted a tidy square off to the left with a red-brick courthouse, a grocery store on one corner, a gas station on another. A dilapidated bar sat across the square from the grocer. A farm supply and hardware store, pickup trucks parked out front, rounded out the occupied buildings. The rest appeared to be empty, their darkened windows a sad reminder of how small towns were often left behind even in times of economic prosperity.

"This is the booming town of Darla, Georgia, elevation eighteen hundred eighty-five feet, population at last count six hundred fifty-two. It's about to get a bit bigger. A major retailer is building a regional distribution center not far from town."

"That's good, right?"

"That remains to be seen."

Just past the town square, they came upon a school, Samuel Jefferson Middle and High School.

"Named for the town's first mayor," Nathan supplied.

Laura twisted to look back at the red-brick building, white columns adorning the front. "Is that where you went to school?"

"Eighth grade through twelfth."

"Did you play any sports?"

"A little junior varsity baseball. Pitcher. But I really didn't have time for it. Farm took up all my time, especially after my grandmother got sick." His voice carried no disappointment, as if to his mind, it was just what you did. Gave up something you loved to take care of your family.

"Were you any good?"

"Managed to bean your purse snatcher in the back of the head with my phone at twenty paces."

"Right." She shivered at the memory of that day. And the long, lonely night that followed.

They turned right onto a bumpy dirt road where trees closed in on either side. "The farmhouse is up here on the left."

Pulling into the dirt driveway, Nathan stopped the car in front of a white clapboard house nestled into the hillside behind it. Off to the side sat an old pickup truck in a color formerly known as blue. A slightly sagging front porch resembled like a lopsided grin, while the windows gazed out across the fields on the other side of the road. Red-brick chimneys flanked the house. The tin roof had seen better days, and the house could use a coat of paint.

On the left, about thirty yards from the house, was a tiny barn and what appeared to be a chicken coop that looked nothing like Martha Stewart's. On the right grew an enormous oak tree, a tire swing hanging from one of the sturdy lower branches.

"My great grandfather built this house in the early 1900s. It replaced the original home from the early 1800s."

Laura sat back and took it all in. This is where Nathan grew up. She could picture him swinging in the tire swing, tossing a baseball in the front yard, riding his bike down the long country road. "So your family has lived here for generations?"

"Yep. Come on."

Nathan strode up to the house, threw open the unlocked front door, his long legs eating up the distance while Laura picked her way across the lawn in her signature stilettos.

"Amanda?" Nathan called. When he didn't get an answer, he yelled louder. "Amanda!"

Still no answer.

"Dammit." He charged up the stairs.

Laura heard him opening doors before he clambered back down the stairs.

"Where the hell is she?"

A screen door slammed in the back of the house.

"Amanda?"

"Nathan? Is that you?"

A tall, rangy young woman came around the corner. Her Wrangler jeans molded to lean, muscular legs, and a faded red T-shirt showed off biceps Laura would kill for. On her feet, no-nonsense work boots. Her hair, a lighter, sun-kissed version of Nathan's, hung in a braid draped across her shoulder.

"What are you doing here?" Amanda asked, clearly surprised by his appearance.

"What do you mean?" He scrubbed his hands through his hair "The hospital called me last night. Said you were in the ER with acute pain. You-you told Nadine Hendrix to call me."

Amanda laughed. "I did?"

"Yes. You did. I told Nadine to tell you I was on my way."

Amanda shook her head. "They gave me some really good drugs. I don't remember any of it."

"What the hell are you doing home? And out of bed?"

"I passed a kidney stone last night, or rather in the wee hours of the morning. Other than a mild backache today, I'm fine. And let me tell you, after that experience, I'm really looking forward to giving birth some day."

"Jesus!" He hauled his sister in for a hug. "You scared ten years off me."

"I'm sorry." She withdrew, and glanced at Laura. "Aren't you going to introduce me?"

"Oh, yes. Laura, this is my sister, Amanda. Amanda, this is Laura Armstrong."

Amanda's frank appraisal of Laura began at her ponytail and ended at her Manolo-enclosed feet.

Where Nathan's eyes were the color of whiskey, Amanda's were the color of coffee, dark and rich. She had the most exquisite skin. Not a stitch of makeup, not even lipgloss or blush. Clearly, she wore lots of sunscreen.

Feeling like she'd just failed inspection, Laura held out her hand to Amanda who looked at it a moment, then latching on to her wrist, hauled Laura in for an unexpected hug. She eyed Nathan over his sister's shoulder. He wore a perplexed look, topped off with a grin.

Releasing Laura, Amanda stepped back. "You didn't tell me you had a girlfriend! 'Bout damn time!"

R elieved about his sister, Nathan choked back a laugh at Laura's discomfiture, as she sputtered and stammered to clarify that they were just friends. Offering no assistance in that department, Nathan reached out for Laura's hand, grasping tighter as she tried to tug free.

"Well, I'm glad you're here, anyway," Amanda said. "This calls for a celebration. I've got a pot of fresh black-eyed peas on the stove, a pecan pie in the fridge, and the makings for cornbread in the cupboard. All we need is some fried chicken to go with it. I'll just go pick out a chicken. Be back in a few. Meanwhile, Laura, make yourself at home."

Amanda headed toward the back of the house and shortly the screen door slammed again.

"Is she going to do what I think she's going to do?" Laura's face went pale, as she lifted her hand to her throat.

"I don't know. What do you think she's going to do?" Nathan asked, holding back his amusement.

"Is she—" She swallowed. "Is she going to . . . kill a chicken? For dinner?" The last part came out in a squeak.

"You haven't lived until you've had farm-fresh chicken."

Laura covered her mouth. "Super."

CHAPTER TWENTY

After retrieving the bags from the car, they reentered the house, the cool dim interior a contrast to the bright sunshine. The screen door slammed behind them, and after all the excitement, Laura was finally able to observe her surroundings.

To the right of the front door was a tidy living room, with a love-worn sofa and chairs centered around a fireplace, the same red brick as the chimneys. Beside the fireplace stood a bookcase loaded with books, *chotchkies*, and framed photos. Hand-woven rugs scattered over the warm pine floor like so many fall leaves.

To the left of the hall was an office, where an ancient roll-top desk stood guard at the front window. The top was open to reveal stacks of papers, a *Farmer's Almanac*—did people really still use those things?—and other office paraphernalia stuffed into the nooks and crannies. More bookcases lined the walls with books on farming and animal husbandry.

"The bedrooms are upstairs." Nathan led the way up a steep staircase, carrying their suitcases, to a second floor with four doors opening off the hallway. "There's only one bathroom, so we'll all have to share."

"Oh."

"The Ritz it ain't," Nathan said with some chagrin. "You'll be in my grandmother's room." He headed down the hall to a door on the end.

"I'll be—" Laura stopped. "We're not sharing a room?"

"I thought it best if we didn't. It might make Amanda uncomfortable. She's always been shy."

"All right," she muttered. If he called that forthright welcome Amanda had given her shy, she'd hate to see his definition of boisterous.

He ushered her into a cozy room with a beautiful old spool bed, covered in a faded wedding ring quilt. Homemade curtains hung in the windows overlooking the hills behind the house. A chest of drawers stood next to the tiny fireplace, framed black-and-white and daguerreotype photos perched along the top.

Setting her Vuitton bag on the bed, he pulled her toward him. "Thank you for coming. It means a lot to me."

Laura shrugged. "What are friends for?"

"Is that what we are? Friends?" His hands rested on her hips, gazed into her eyes, and the familiarity of his touch warmed her from the inside out.

"Friends with benefits," she clarified with a teasing smile. A frown crossed his features. "What?"

He shook his head. "Nothing. I'll let you get unpacked and meet you downstairs."

Nathan left, giving her the opportunity to check out her accommodations—a.k.a. snoop. The photos intrigued her. Nathan's ancestors perhaps?

She picked up one of a beautiful young woman, hair in a Gibson Girl style, ringlets framing her oval face, a slight smile touching her lips. His great-great grandmother? There was another of a woman standing in front of a late-1940's-style automobile, spectators on her feet, a perky hat on her head. His grandmother maybe? A photo of a young brunette woman with eighties big hair, cut sweatshirt hanging off her shoulder—the only color photo on the chest —captured her attention next.

Carrying the photo over to the window, she held it up to the light. Nathan's mother. No question. He had her eyes, her hair color. Her smile. Who was this woman? What had happened to her? And had she given Nathan the love and affection he deserved? She hoped so.

Laura returned the photo to its place, wondering why it mattered so much to her.

———

Nathan heard Laura's footsteps upstairs treading on the familiar creaky floorboards of his grandmother's room, as he poured over the notices from the mortgage company, the certified letters from the developer and their attorneys, the bills.

Combing his hands through his hair, he sank to the chair in front of the desk. The developer's offers were fair. They could pay off the mortgages, take the remaining money and never look back. Maybe Amanda could find a smaller farm for sale, start new.

But that wasn't the point. This was the only real home Amanda had ever known. The safe, stable environment she deserved. And she loved it. Every creaky floorboard, every drafty corner, every plant, tree, and rock on the property. She got her strength from this farm.

His sister had been painfully shy when they'd first

arrived, but she'd come out of her shell when she tended the farm animals. She had a special knack for soothing them, communicating with them. And she had a green thumb to boot. When she was nine, Gram had given her a small plot to plant her very own vegetable garden, and damned if it hadn't thrived under her care.

As he grew older, and Gram grew more frail, he took on more and more responsibility for the farm, including the bookkeeping, while his sister took on the planting and animal care. The high school football coach had salivated over Nathan's muscular build, gained throwing around bales of hay and bags of chicken feed, not to mention his speed in the forty. The baseball coach wanted him, too. His curveball had been a thing of beauty. But after his sophomore year, things like sports and other after-school activities just weren't in the cards for him.

As Amanda hit her teens, she began to draw the attention of the young men in the town, and Nathan gained a reputation as her protector. He wouldn't let his baby sister make the same mistakes as his mother. She would go to college and earn her degree in agricultural science. It had been her dream to take over the farm, reclaiming the leased acres and cultivating them herself.

Over the years, his grandmother leased out more and more of the property for grazing and cultivation, but Amanda had come home with that degree, and as the leases expired, she'd taken over their cultivation, adding new crops like organic soybeans and sorghum grain. She'd also added beef cattle to the land.

No. This land was hers. She'd nurtured it, sweated over it. By George, she would keep it.

———

Hoping to satisfy her curiosity, Laura crept down the hall, uttering a curse when a board groaned beneath her feet, and headed in what she hoped was the direction of Nathan's room. Sticking her head in the only other open door off the hallway, she hit pay dirt.

The small room held what looked like a double bed, no headboard, covered with a blue chenille bedspread. His clothes, some jeans, a few T-shirts, his boxers, were in neat piles on top. A battered chest-of-drawers stood in the corner next to the room's only window. A colorful throw rug lay on the floor at the foot of the bed.

Hmm. She didn't know what she'd expected. Posters of his favorite sports heroes, maybe? A centerfold of Phoebe Cates? But his walls were bare except for a few paint-by-number landscapes.

What had he been like as a little boy? A troublemaker? A good student? A protector, as evidenced by his concern over his sister? He'd already told her about baseball, so he must have been a good athlete. But what else had he been?

Shaking her head, she left his room. Since when did the inner-workings of people's lives interest her?

———

Laura could feel her arteries hardening just looking at the food laid out before her. A bowl of what appeared to be otherwise healthy black-eyed peas, surrounded by pieces of fatback. Crispy fried chicken, of the freshly wrung variety. Roasted corn-on-the-cob swimming in butter. Corn-bread made with bacon grease. Pecan pie in a crust so flaky it could only have been made with lard. And a big pitcher of sweet iced tea to wash it all down. The one healthy concession, a plate of fresh-sliced tomatoes and cucumbers.

Laura felt Nathan's eyes on her as she took a seat at the big table in the middle of a kitchen that looked like it hadn't changed since the 1950's.

Amanda chattered on about this cow or that laying hen, Nathan asking questions every so often. Amanda took Laura's plate and heaped it full with peas, tomatoes, cucumbers, and cornbread.

"White meat or dark?" Amanda asked.

"Hmm?"

"Would you like a breast, a drumstick, a thigh? I also fried up the gizzard and the neck."

Laura could feel the blood drain from her face. Gizzards? Necks? *What the hell?* If she didn't select something fast, the next thing she knew Amanda would be offering her the feet. "Oh, breast is fine. Thank you."

She waited, eyeing the food, while Nathan and Amanda helped themselves. Her eyes widened when she saw Nathan put the gizzard on his plate. *Blech. Note to self: do not kiss Nathan again until he brushes his teeth. With bleach.*

She took her first tentative bite of the chicken, trying to forget it didn't come from her local meat market. *Wow!* Okay. She took another bite. "Mmm." Did she just groan out loud?

"Good, huh?" Amanda chirped. "My grandmother's recipe. She always made the best fried chicken."

Nathan's face split into a big, silly grin, as he shoveled a forkful of fat-laden black-eyed peas into his mouth.

They ate in silence for a few minutes, and Laura found herself licking her fingers. Miss Manners—a.k.a. her mother

—would be horrified. The thought made her smirk, as she stuck another finger in her mouth.

———

Nathan looked across the table at Laura, as she sucked a finger into her mouth. Aside from the erotic thoughts that sprang to mind, seeing the perfectly poised, well-mannered Laura Armstrong licking her fingers made him smile.

If someone had told him the day he met Laura that she'd be sitting at the table in his grandmother's kitchen he'd have told them they were nuts. Or on drugs.

Covering a laugh, his gaze traveled to his sister. He never really noticed before he left, how much she'd changed. And even more since he'd been gone. She'd been confident in her farming and animal husbandry skills, but now, she displayed a strength and courage he never thought he'd see from his otherwise shy sister.

Having these two women here in, for all intents and purposes, his childhood home, made him feel complete for the first time in a very long time.

Hating to ruin the warmth of the occasion, he knew they had to discuss the elephant in the room. Saving the farm. "After dinner, Amanda and I need to go over some farm business. I hope you don't mind."

"Oh, I've got work to do," Laura said, throwing him a meaningful glance.

Ah, yes, the pitch. He hadn't forgotten that he also had work to do there. It would be a late night.

"I'll clean up," Laura offered.

"No," Amanda interjected. "Gram would have our

hides if we let a guest clean up the kitchen. It won't take long. Besides, I know where everything goes."

Nathan stared at Laura, his mouth agape. He'd be willing to bet she'd never cleaned anything in her life, much less the kitchen. He doubted she even knew how. Which made him appreciate the offer that much more.

———

Powering on her laptop, Laura settled again at the kitchen table to catch up on emails. Her team was putting in weekend hours, making revisions to the pitch, polishing the presentation, fine-tuning the numbers. Which left her feeling guilty over her absence.

Reviewing the documents in her inbox would go a long way to assuaging some of that guilt.

Opening the draft proposal, she got down to business.

Before long, she could hear Nathan's and Amanda's voices drifting in from the office, just on the other side of the kitchen. Trying not to eavesdrop, she focused on the campaign's objectives, tweaking them to a laser-sharp focus.

"Even if we pay off the mortgages, the house needs a new roof, the barn is practically falling down around poor Midnight. There's a leak right over his stall, and the septic tank's been backing up."

"Amanda," Laura heard Nathan's patient voice, "one thing at a time. First and foremost, pay off the mortgages, or at the very least get caught up." He sighed. "If we lose the farm, none of the other problems matter."

Laura's ears perked up.

"You're right. I'm sorry."

"So where do we stand on the mortgages? Since we're not technically in default—"

"Yet."

"Yet. The ten thousand I sent you appeased the mortgage company, right?"

The mortgages Nathan was talking about that day in Santa Margherita Ligure?

"For now, but I'm always teetering on the brink, with the developers breathing down my neck, ready to pounce like a hungry mountain lion."

"I've reviewed the farm's books, and you made a profit on the cattle you sold, as well as the organic soybeans."

"Transitioning the farm operations to organic is lowering the production costs, and with the increase in returns per acre, I can reach my overall economic goal with half the acres. This gives me grazing land for more cattle. I can do this, Nathan. I can make the farm profitable. I just need to get out from under the banks. And fend off the developers."

Laura heard the determination in Amanda's voice, and knew it well. She'd heard it in her own voice many times.

"I know you can," Nathan continued. "And the bonus I'll get when Hawk Media gets the cruise line account will allow you to do just that. Get out from under the banks. And as for the developers, once the mortgages are paid off, they'll have significantly less leverage."

Laura sat back in her chair and frowned, her work all but forgotten. Nathan counted on the account to pay off the mortgages? That made her reasons for wanting the account seem petty in comparison.

"I'll pay you back. It might take me years, but I'll pay you back every cent."

"No." Nathan's voice was emphatic. "I'm part of the reason we're in this mess. I didn't need to go to Duke—"

"Nathan, we both earned our education from the

money Gram borrowed from the banks. At the very least, I'm paying you back half."

"We'll talk about it. First, I've got to score that account. And to that end, I've got work to do."

"I'm off to bed, then. Don't stay up too late."

"Amanda, I know you're tough. Just like Gram. But I want you to take it easy the next few days. I can handle things. I haven't forgotten how, you know."

"I feel fine."

"I mean it, butterbean." Nathan interjected.

Butterbean? Laura thought with a soft laugh.

"I'm glad you're home. I've missed you."

"I've missed you, too."

A moment of silence, then Amanda said softly, "Gram would have been so proud of you, Nathan. I love you."

Unbidden, tears stung Laura's eyes and filled her throat. What must it be like to have someone love you like that? Especially your own family.

"She would have been proud of you, too."

She heard Nathan's boots scraping on the hardwood floor. Blinking back the tears, Laura focused her attention on the draft proposal, in case he came into the kitchen, but she didn't see the words on the screen.

CHAPTER TWENTY-ONE

Lying in bed wearing nothing but his boxers, his arms behind his head, Nathan stared up at the ceiling of his childhood bedroom. Well past midnight, and he didn't expect to fall asleep anytime soon.

Thoughts skipped across his mind, like a flat rock across a smooth pond. He thought about the first night he'd spent in this house, less than twenty-four hours after his mother's death. His scared little sister had tiptoed into his room, and asked if she could sleep with him. He'd cradled her in his arms until the first rays of sun broke through the fog of a hill country morning.

He thought of Amanda now. All grown up, no longer that scared little girl. He thought about how much she'd done on her own. And how much he wanted to help her.

Which circled his thoughts back to the pitch. He'd been pleased with the overall proposal, but he'd made some revisions to the presentation, fine-tuning the scope of work, along with the road map for achieving the campaign's objectives.

Nathan recalled his grandmother's admonition: *Always do the right thing no matter how hard it is.*

Problem was, Nathan didn't know what the right thing was anymore.

Surely, saving the farm for his sister was the right thing to do. But so was pursuing his developing relationship with Laura. And he owed Hawk the truth about his relationship with her. But that confession could result in him being removed from the account. Which brought him back to his sister and the farm.

Too many competing interests.

His wayward thoughts then skittered to the woman sleeping in his grandmother's bed just down the hall. The woman whose bed he'd shared. The woman who now stood in his way. And the woman who occupied his thoughts more than he cared to admit. He was fast on his way to falling in love with Laura.

Heaving a sigh, he scrubbed his hands over his face.

Rising, he crept down the hall, careful to miss the noisy floorboards he remembered so well growing up. Cracking open her door, he was surprised to see her still awake, a magazine across her lap.

She lifted a brow. "Don't you knock?"

God she looked gorgeous. Propped against the pillows, her hair draped over her shoulders, a lacy little nightgown peeking out from under the covers. "I thought you'd be asleep."

"So, you're what? A Peeping Tom?"

He chuckled. "You're right. Sorry. I'll just—"

She tossed the magazine and covers aside and crawled to the foot of the bed, kneeling there. "You don't have to go." Her lace nightie taunted him with the parts it covered. And the parts it didn't.

"I don't?" God knew he didn't want to go. He wanted to slip those silky straps from her shoulders and run his hands up her body.

"No, you don't." She reached out a hand to him and he walked to the side of the bed. Lifting her arms, she encircled his neck and pulled him in for a kiss that quickly took a turn for the steamy. Rising up onto her knees, she pressed that lace-clad body to his bare chest, her lips never leaving his.

He leaned into her, pushing her back on the bed, as he lowered himself between her legs. The sound of her breathy moans just the thing to take his mind off the farm, the account, and the bonus.

"God, how I need you," Nathan whispered. He stared into her wide eyes, his hands caressing her face. "Does that bother you? That I need you?"

She broke the eye contact. Tried to turn her head, but he wouldn't let her.

"I don't know," she said. "Depends on how you need me."

"I need you like this." Giving her an out, he tugged the straps off her shoulders, baring her breasts.

"Then, no." She sighed. "That doesn't bother me at all."

———

Waiting for her heart rate to normalize, Laura's mind returned to the conversation she'd overheard earlier. Should she say something? Confess that she heard everything? Not yet.

"Were you born here, in this house?" Her question was met with silence. Just when she'd thought he'd dosed off, he answered.

"What happened to your rule about no personal questions?"

"First, I'm right in the middle of your personal life. I think that ship already sailed. Second, I spilled my guts last night. Now it's your turn."

"Right." He lay perfectly still next to her, his arm wrapped around her. "I was born in Atlanta to a single mom."

"What about your father?"

"I don't know who my father is."

Laura digested that information for a minute.

"And Amanda?"

"Amanda was also born in Atlanta. The child of another mystery man."

Laura sat up and turned to face him, propping up on her elbow.

"How did you come to live here?"

"It's a long sordid story. You should go to sleep." He made to rise, but she held on to his arm.

"Don't go. Stay. Tell me."

———

"My mother was eighteen when I was born."

"Is that your mother's photograph on the chest-of-drawers?"

"Yes. She left home when she learned she was pregnant, and alienated herself from her own mother. She never gave my grandmother the chance. I guess she was just too ashamed, so . . . she just left." He sighed.

"She went to Atlanta?"

"Yes. She worked as a waitress, a bar tender, a maid, anything that would earn her money to feed herself and put a roof over her head. Once I was born, however, she had to cut back on the number of jobs she held in order to take care of me."

In the dim light from the moon, she could see the grim set of his mouth.

"This resulted in less . . . desirable living accommodations. We finally moved to Edgewood, a slum in Southeast Atlanta, ironically situated on the edge of Inman Park, an affluent neighborhood. By the time I was three, Amanda had come along. And by the time I was seven, I was taking care of her while my mother went to work."

"Is that what you meant when you said you didn't grow up in a great neighborhood?"

"You remember that?" he asked into the dark.

"Of course."

Silence reigned for a few breaths. He shifted his position so that he faced her. "I knew when my mother turned to prostitution to support us.

"Oh, Nathan." She laid a hand over his chest, her own heart aching for him.

"She'd leave after Amanda and I had gone to bed and not return until the early hours before dawn. I woke one night to get a drink of water and found our neighbor, Mrs. Sammons, sleeping on the couch. That became a regular occurrence."

"Life was difficult at best. I had to protect myself and my sister from the criminal elements that haunted the neighborhood schools, streets, and housing project where we lived. Watching our mother struggle for every dollar she earned, I swore that if we were able to get out of that situation, neither me nor my sister would ever live hand-to-mouth again."

"Even with all the struggles, I made sure Amanda went

to school, did her homework. She excelled in school, lousy as they were. My fourth grade teacher, Ms. Sylvester, took both of us under her wing. Brought us books from the library to read, and with the streets too dangerous for Amanda, reading became a favorite past time."

He traced the outline of her face with his fingertips. "My sister and I stood as a solid unit against the hunger and desperation of life."

"Where is your mother now?"

"She died of cervical cancer when I was ten."

"I'm so sorry." She didn't know what else to say. She could see that ten-year-old boy, a seven-year-old sister by his side, wondering where he would go, how he would live. "What was her name?"

"Holly."

"Where did you and your sister go?"

"A grandmother we never knew we had showed up at the hospital the day our mother died. Gram, as she told us to call her, took care of the funeral arrangements, packed up our meager belongings, and along with our mother's body in the hearse behind, drove here."

"We learned about country-living, feeding the animals, collecting the eggs, milking the cow, and tending the garden. Went to the small school. Away from the dangers of the city, we thrived. I put on muscle working on the farm, while time spent outdoors put color in Amanda's cheeks."

"Even so, she remained timid and shy. Kept to herself mostly. The only time she really came out of her shell was when she was with the animals. It was like she spoke their language, and they hers. It was clearly in her blood."

Remembering Nathan referring to his grandmother the first time they met on that sidewalk in Manhattan, which in the dark of the room seemed a lifetime and a world away, she said, "And your grandmother, you loved her, didn't you?"

"My grandmother taught me what love was, taught me to love, and what it felt like to be loved."

"You don't think your mother loved you?" It broke her heart to think Nathan's mother didn't love him.

"I don't know. I often wonder if she was ashamed of me. Of Amanda. I'd like to think she loved us. That she just didn't have time to show us. She'd been too busy trying to keep a roof over our head and food on the table."

"I think that alone proves she loved you." Laura took his face in her hands, stared into his eyes. Into his soul. She'd never felt so close to someone in her life. She kissed him. Not with passion, the only kissing she'd ever known, but with compassion. "Your grandmother would be so proud of you. And so would your mother."

———

Following her nose the next morning, Laura found Nathan in the kitchen, standing at the stove, a dish-towel thrown over his shoulder. The scent and sizzle of bacon set Laura's mouth to watering, and her arteries to clogging.

The bacon wasn't the only thing making her mouth water. Wearing well-worn jeans, a blue T-shirt, and a day's growth of stubble on his face, Nathan was as appetizing as any meal. Her stomach did a delightful little somersault at the thought of that stubble scraping across tender flesh.

"Good morning, sleepyhead. Coffee's in the pot, cream's in the fridge. Help yourself." He flipped the bacon, before picking up his coffee mug and taking a pull.

"I've already been up and out taking care of the

morning chores. Feeding the chickens, gathering the eggs, checking on the hogs."

"Hogs?" She eyed the bacon with some trepidation.

Nathan glanced over and chuckled at her expression.

Scooping up the bacon, he laid it on a platter covered with a paper towel. "Put this on the table." He handed Laura the dish then bent over and took another platter heaped with pancakes out of the oven where they were warming.

Just as Laura and Nathan placed the food on the table, Amanda entered, followed by the now-familiar sound of the screen door slamming behind her.

She strode over to the sink to wash up. "I see you haven't lost your skills living in the big city."

"You know what they say, you can take the man out of the country, but you can't take the country out of the man," he quipped, as he approached the table.

They spent a few minutes digging into the breakfast.

"Sleep well?" Amanda asked, eyeing both Nathan and Laura.

"Absolutely. You?" Nathan asked.

"I did. But, Laura, you must have had a restless night."

Laura froze, her fork halfway between her plate and her mouth, as she shot a glance at Nathan. "No. I slept fine. Why?" Really good, actually. Especially after the last round of sex in the wee hours of the morning.

Amanda's eyes settled on Nathan. "Well, the walls of this old house are thin, and Nathan you remember how Gram's bed always creaked and groaned when she had a fitful night?"

Nathan set his fork on his plate, his face turning a deep red.

Amanda snickered. "Honestly, Nathan. Why are you

two sleeping in separate rooms?" She glanced between them. "Or should I say *pretending* to sleep in separate rooms? I'm a big girl, and you of all people should know I see enough sex on the farm that I'd have no issues when it came to you and your girlfriend."

"I'm not—" Laura interjected.

"So, if you'd prefer to go *incognito*"—Amanda slathered butter on her pancakes—"perhaps you should both stay in your room. Your bed doesn't make as much noise," she said, pointing at Nathan.

At that moment, Laura fell in love with Amanda.

———

"I'm going to have to hit the gym twice a day when we get back to New York. Between last-night's dinner and this-morning's breakfast, I've probably consumed my weekly calorie allotment in two meals. How does your sister keep her girlish figure eating all that fat?"

Nathan took Laura's hand as they walked back to the barn and the chicken coop. "You forget. She doesn't ride a Herman Miller desk chair all day. She probably burns more calories before lunch, than we do all day."

"And I thought you said Amanda was shy. She doesn't strike me as shy at all. But rather . . . forthright."

He looked back at the house where'd they'd left Amanda poring over an article on organic fertilizer.

"Yeah. That's . . . well, I don't know what that is. She's never been so . . . demonstrative with people outside the family."

"Maybe standing on her own two feet. Taking care of this farm. Gives a person confidence."

"I guess."

They stood for a moment watching the fuzzy yellow chicks and white laying-hens scratching and pecking for feed.

"Don't tell me if one of these chickens is going to be tonight's dinner."

Nathan chuckled. "I saw a roast in the refrigerator. I think pot roast is on tonight's menu."

Laura snorted. "Let me guess, one of the cows?"

"Of course."

Laura glanced over in horror at the cows grazing placidly in the field across the road. "I was only kidding."

"You do realize the filet mignon you order in restaurants comes from cows?"

"Out of sight, out of mind."

Shaking his head, he took her hand. "Come on. I'll show you some cute animals we don't eat."

They entered the dim interior of the barn. He inhaled the sweet scent of hay combined with the pungent odor of manure, and memories flooded in. Making out with Angela Simmons. The first calf his sister raised for 4-H. The blue ribbon she'd hung outside the stall. Helping to bring another calf into the world.

He watched as Laura picked her way through the barn in her ridiculous heels. "Don't you have any other shoes with you?"

"No. Why?"

"Those aren't very practical."

"They're boots, aren't they?"

Nathan snorted. "What size are you?"

"Seven."

"Same size as Amanda. You can borrow a pair of hers."

Leading Laura to the corner, he knelt down in front of a mother cat and four little kittens in a variety of colors.

Laura knelt down next to him. "Awww." She lifted her gaze to his. "How old are they?"

"Look to be about four weeks old." He reached down, scooped up an orange one with a white star on its forehead. It mewed for its mother. He rubbed the furry little head against his cheek.

Handing Laura the kitten, she cradled it in her hand and gently stroked between its ears with her finger. "It's so tiny," she murmured.

Gazing at the wonder on her face, he asked, "Did you have pets growing up?"

"No. My mother said they'd make a mess in the house."

"And you never wanted one when you grew up, moved out?"

She rubbed her cheek across the kitten's silky fur. "Never really thought about it. Having a pet doesn't really fit my lifestyle, and in case you haven't noticed, I'm not exactly the nurturing type." She returned the kitten to its littermates.

Laura was wrong. She was the nurturing type. She just did it differently. "After lunch I need to drive into town, pick up some supplies to repair a section of the barn roof. Care to ride along?"

"Okay. But I think I can skip the lunch part, so why don't we go now?"

"Well, if it ain't Nathan Maxwell, Darla's little darlin'."

Standing in the aisle of the local farm supply and hardware store, Laura turned to see a man who appeared to be a good decade older than Nathan. His face creased with lines from too much time in the sun, possibly smoke from the cigarettes he reeked of. He swiveled his gaze to Laura and licking his lips, took in her snug capris, her form-fitting halter top, her skyscraper heels.

Ick. She needed another shower after that look.

Always the gentleman, Nathan nodded at the man, "Ricky," then made to step around him, but Ricky blocked his path.

"I heard your crazy grandmother mortgaged the farm to send you and your sister to school, and that you're about to lose it to the bank. I also heard tell that you've turned down the developer's offer to buy it."

"Not your concern, Ricky. Now, if you'll excuse me . . ."

"Well, now I don't have much excuse for you. Once a bastard, always a bastard. Thought you were too good for the likes of Darla. As if having a whore for a mother makes you any better than the rest of us."

Laura sucked in a breath, itching to kick ol' Ricky in the nuts.

Nathan froze, his hands fisted at his side.

"All that fancy education can't make a silk purse out of a sow's ear," Ricky goaded.

"Don't make me open up a can of whoop ass. Apparently the ass-kicking I gave you in sixth grade didn't stick." Nathan's casual delivery couldn't hide the tension in his body.

Ricky got up in Nathan's face. "You want an ass-kicking, Maxwell? I'll give you an ass-kicking."

Nathan shoved Laura behind him. "I'm not here to teach you manners, Ricky. I don't have that much time."

Laura snickered, and Nathan threw her a look. "Now step aside."

A staring contest ensued, which ended with Nathan as the victor. Ricky stepped aside, apparently realizing discretion was the better part of valor.

She heard Nathan release his breath and they proceeded down the aisle.

"Who the hell was that loser?"

"Ricky Wilder, town bully."

"Did he bully you?"

"Can we talk about this later?"

"Sure."

Nathan took the can of silicone roof sealant out of the cart and placed it on the checkout counter, followed by a couple bags of roofing screws, and a paint roller and extension.

"Nathan? Nathan Maxwell? Well, I'll be." The older

gentleman behind the counter wore a broad grin. "What brings you back to Darla? You here visiting your sister?"

"Mr. Reddish." Nathan put his hand out. "Good to see you."

"Really sorry to hear about your grandmother. Pat was always a ray of sunshine."

"Thank you, Mr. Reddish."

"Heard you moved up to New York City. Still in the advertising business?"

"Yes."

Laura chimed in loud enough for Ricky to hear, "He's Vice President of Business Development for an ad agency. I'm Laura, by the way. Nathan's girlfriend." She could feel Nathan's perplexed stare, but she continued. "Yeah, Nathan's in charge of million-dollar ad campaigns and oversees the strategic vision for accounts. You probably remember his team's Jack Daniels campaign."

Nathan's confusion turned to shock.

"Was that yours?" Mr. Reddish asked Nathan, something akin to pride on his face. "I loved those ads. Did you get to meet Sam Elliot? I just love that guy."

"Yeah, he was great."

Ricky had sidled up behind them, so Laura turned to him. "I'm sorry, Ricky, is it? We haven't been introduced. I'm Laura. I didn't catch what you do."

At Ricky's grimace, Mr. Reddish supplied, "He's between jobs."

"I see. Well, good luck with that." She turned back to the counter as Mr. Reddish rang up the supplies, effectively dismissing Ricky.

"It sure was good to see you, Nathan. Don't be a stranger. And give my best to that beautiful sister of yours." He handed Nathan the receipt.

As they walked toward the door, Laura faced Ricky once more. "By the way, Ricky"—she cocked a hip, indicating her body with her hand—"not even in your wildest dreams."

Nathan grabbed her arm and towed her out the door.

———

"Don't poke the beast," Nathan said as he placed his free hand on the small of her back and directed her to the rental car. He popped the trunk and taking the bag from her, placed it next to the sealant can before closing the lid.

Walking around to the passenger door, he opened it for Laura.

"Maxwell!" Ricky stood not far from the car.

"Oh, for crissake!" Nathan muttered. "What now, Ricky?"

"I just wanted to tell your girlfriend that if she wants a real fuck to give me a call. Number's still in the book."

That's it. Seeing red, Nathan strode over to Ricky, and mid-stride drew back his fist before slamming it into Ricky's face. Ricky's knees wobbled once, twice, then he went down hard on his ass before collapsing to his back.

Nathan leaned over Ricky's prone body, blood trickling from his nose. "Apparently one ass-kicking wasn't enough for you."

He walked back to the car. "Get in," he told Laura.

She climbed in and shut the door. "Your hand! Does it hurt?"

"Like a mother." He threw the car into 'reverse' and pulled out onto the main drag. He wasn't lying. His hand throbbed like a son-of-bitch.

"Why did you do that? Punch him?"

"He insulted you. I wasn't going to let him get away with that."

Clasping her hands gently around his injured one, she brought it to her lips, where she gingerly pressed a kiss to his bruised knuckles. "Thank you." She gazed at him with genuine gratitude. And maybe something more.

"I'd do it again, if only to have you look at me like that."

Her expression warmed his heart and eased the throbbing in his hand. A little.

"Open up a can of whoop ass?" Laura asked, her brow lifted.

He snorted. "Yeah. That was a little juvenile."

"And oddly sexy."

He shook his head and laughed.

When they'd almost reached the turn off to the farm, Nathan asked, "How did you know my agency in Atlanta created the Jack Daniel's campaign?"

She shrugged. "I did some research. Needed to know who my competition was."

He couldn't fault her for that. He'd done the same thing.

"And why did you tell Mr. Reddish that you were my girlfriend?"

"Because Ricky was listening," she said, as if the reason were obvious.

"Is that the only reason?"

"Of course. What other reason would I have?"

Ain't that a pisser. His grandmother used to say, 'Don't ask the question if you won't like the answer.'

"Heard tell you decked Ricky Wilder in front of Mack's Farm Supply and Hardware," Amanda said, as she slathered butter on a biscuit so light and fluffy it could float right off the plate.

Nathan flexed his hand. "Yeah, and I've got the sore hand to prove it."

"Apparently, Mr. Reddish left him lying in the parking lot, and when Ricky whined about it, Mr. Reddish said he must have done something to deserve it." Amanda snorted.

"And how'd you come to know all this if you haven't left the house?"

"Bonnie Zucker called me right after it happened."

"Leave it to Bonnie, still the eyes and ears of Darla." Nathan shoveled a forkful of mashed potatoes and gravy into his mouth.

Laura watched the exchange, noticing that Nathan's accent had become heavier in the short time he'd been home. It made her insides tingle.

"I picked up the supplies to repair the barn roof. I'll get on that first thing tomorrow morning."

"I'm sorry you're working so hard." Amanda said, a note of sadness in her voice. "I didn't intend—"

"Oh, stop. I don't mind. In fact, it feels pretty good to put this body to some use."

And what a body it was, Laura thought.

Seeing an opening, she went for it. "I have a confession to make," she blurted out. Both Amanda and Nathan stopped mid-chew and stared at her. "I overheard your conversation last night—about the farm. I didn't mean to, but as you said, the walls are pretty thin."

Nathan put his fork down and looked away. She knew

that he remembered what he'd said about the bonus and the Imperial account.

"Anyway, I've got an investment account, and I'd like to invest in the farm." She ran on before either could stop her. "With the popularity of organic produce, grass-fed beef, and free-range chickens, I think the farm could be hugely successful. You could make contact with some *chichi* restaurants in Atlanta and Charlotte, and I could help you with that. I've got contacts with some top restaurants in the area that my agency handles."

"No," came Nathan's quiet reply.

"But, I'd consider it a business deal."

"No," he said once more. He shoved his plate away and crossed his arms on the table.

Amanda filled the awkward silence. "Laura, you're really sweet to offer, but this is something we have to do on our own. Gram did so much for us, and we want to return the favor by keeping the farm in the family." She shot a glance at Nathan as he rose from the table, taking his plate to the sink.

"I'll clean up," he said, as he turned on the faucet. "Amanda, I need a word with Laura."

Amanda slid Laura a look, then made a face that said, *Sorry*.

———

"**D**o you think I want your money? That that's why I'm with you?" he asked, his back still to Laura.

"No. Of course not."

"That I'd even take your money?"

"You wouldn't be taking it." She placed a stack of dishes

on the counter next to the sink and stood there. So close. "It would be an investment."

Even as pissed as he was, her scent could drive him mad.

"And I suppose you heard. That the Imperial account is more than just another account to me," he said.

"Yes."

"Are you doing this to relieve any guilt you might have if Giddings-Rose gets the account?"

He felt her bristle. Turning to face her, he saw the blue sparks in her eyes.

"I offered because I wanted to help. And because it made good business sense." She swiveled to walk away, but he snagged her arm, pulled her back.

"I'm sorry." He gazed into her eyes, watched as the fire banked, and with it the tension in her body eased.

She sighed. "Look. I want to help. If you won't let me invest in the farm, at least let me put you in touch with a friend who's handled these types of issues before."

"Who is it?"

"My best friend's husband, Josh. They live in New York."

"The one you work with for the gala?"

She narrowed her eyes at him. "How'd you know that?"

"I Googled it."

"You Googled it, why?"

"Curiosity." He shrugged. "Why did you Google me?"

"Didn't your grandmother ever tell you curiosity killed the cat?"

"But satisfaction brought it back." Grinning, he hauled her in for a hug. Placing his hands over her mighty fine ass, he gave it a squeeze, then grabbing her shoulders he pushed her back and looked down into her eyes. "Thank you. For caring. For offering to help. I really appreciate it. But no money." He kissed her nose. "So, when can we meet Josh?"

———

As Laura walked down the stairs, she frowned at the boots on her feet. Amanda's. She had on a pair of well-worn jeans and a T-shirt, also Amanda's, all of which Nathan had left on the bed for her. *Hint, hint.*

Being more curvaceous than Amanda, the shirt was a little snug over her breasts, and the jeans, well, they hugged her, er, curves.

Inhaling the mouthwatering aroma of fresh-brewed coffee, Laura headed for the kitchen. Empty. No bacon frying, no pancakes on the griddle. *What's up with that?*

Hmm, but a tantalizing smell wafted from the oven. Taking a peek, she gasped when she saw cinnamon buns the size of saucers. "I'll never make it out of here without gaining ten pounds."

Placing one on a plate, she poured herself a cup of coffee and sat at the table. Pinching off a bite of the bun, she stuck it into her mouth. "Mmmm." Closing her eyes, she savored the gooey frosting, the spicy cinnamon, the flaky pastry. The hell with the farm. Amanda should open a restaurant. New York would go crazy over her Southern delights.

After devouring the entire bun, she went off in search of other humans. Hearing hammering coming from the direction of the barn, she remembered Nathan intended to repair the barn roof. She came around the corner, and there he stood on the roof, in all his shirt-less glory, sweat sluicing down those hard abs, jeans slung low. She licked her lips. "Glory be," she said, then realized she'd uttered one of Amanda's favorite phrases.

Nathan waved at her, then disappeared over the side. A minute later, he came around the corner of the barn toward her holding what looked like a bag of chips. "Mornin', sugar." He leaned in for a sweaty kiss.

Laura pressed her finger into his bare . . . hard . . . chest, holding him off. "Not until you've had a shower."

"You didn't mind my sweat on you last night."

"That was different."

Nathan chuckled, making her innards do a little dance. He held out the bag. "Pork rind?"

"Pork what?" She peered into the bag to find it full of something akin to Styrofoam puffs.

"Pork rinds. They're a Southern delicacy."

"Um. Maybe later." *Like* much *later*.

"How's it going?" she asked, shielding her eyes from the morning sun and looking up at the barn roof.

"It's going okay. Did you eat breakfast?"

"You mean those five-thousand-calorie cinnamon buns? Yes, I did."

"And?"

"And, they were almost better than sex." At his lifted brow, she continued, "I said almost."

"Good to know who, or should I say what, my competition is."

"Where's Amanda?"

"In the barn grooming Midnight."

"I thought she was supposed to be resting."

"You tell her. She won't listen to me."

Laura headed in that direction, and Nathan called out to her. "What?"

"You're adorable in those clothes." He tilted his head.

"What your ass does for those Wranglers ought to be illegal."

"It is. In all fifty states," she said as she sashayed off.

Nathan's laughter followed her into the barn.

———

Laura found Amanda with the horse, a currycomb in her hand as she groomed it. The horse nickered Laura's presence.

"Do you need help on the roof?" Amanda asked without turning from her task.

"No."

Amanda laughed. "I thought you were Nathan."

"Aren't you supposed to be resting?" Laura asked as she picked up a mane and tail comb from the bench outside the stall.

"Did Nathan send you in here to remind me?"

"No. Okay, yes." Laura began working through the horse's mane. At Amanda's questioning glance, Laura supplied, "I used to take riding lessons, taking care of your horse was part of the deal."

They worked in silence for a few beats.

"Nathan worries about you," Laura continued.

"And I worry about him." Discarding the currycomb, she picked up a hoof pick, walked around Midnight and lifted his hind hoof. "That's what family does."

Unless you're part of the Armstrong family, Laura thought.

"Don't hurt him."

It took Laura a moment to realize Amanda wasn't talking about the horse.

"You see," Amanda continued, as she cleaned

Midnight's hoof, "when Nathan loves, he loves with his whole heart. It's the only way he knows how."

"Oh, he's not . . . I mean we're not . . . we're just friends." Laura untangled a knot in the mane quicker than she untangled the knot in her tongue.

"Friends with benefits?"

"Yeah, something like that."

Amanda moved to the horse's other leg, then picked up his hoof. "You're the first woman Nathan's brought home."

Laura didn't know how to respond to that, so she continued running the comb through the mane.

"He's got a lot of love to give, especially to the woman lucky enough to capture his heart." She came around the other side of the horse and stood directly across from Laura, stroking Midnight's nose. "I think you're that woman."

CHAPTER TWENTY-THREE

"Come take a walk with me." Nathan held out his hand to her. They'd just finished another artery-clogging, but delicious dinner of baked ham—Nathan's favorite—butterbeans—Amanda's favorite—fresh corn-on-the-cob—her new favorite—biscuits, and homemade peach cobbler. A walk sounded good.

"Where to?"

Nathan shrugged. "Around."

They strolled hand-in-hand down the dirt road, past the cow pasture on one side, a small, wooded area on the other. Birds flitted across the road, a cow lowed in the field, and other than the sound of the wind in the trees and their feet scuffing along the dirt road, it was peaceful, silent. So different from the noise of the city.

She'd slept like a rock out here in the country. Between the fresh air, the quiet, and Nathan's skillful sex, she'd never felt more rested.

Rounding a bend in the road, they came to a small area surrounded by a wrought-iron fence, headstones dotting the enclosure. An ancient oak provided shade to the eternal occupants.

"My family cemetery." Nathan unlatched the gate, which swung open with a rusty groan.

Some headstones had shifted over the decades, tilting at odd angles, others were straight but weathered, their engravings barely visible. One looked new. Nathan stopped in front of it.

The headstone read: Dorothy Patricia Parham-Maxwell.

Beneath that:

Beloved grandmother, cherished mother, loving wife.

The date of death just six months earlier.

"My grandmother," Nathan said. "I haven't seen the headstone since it was installed." He knelt down, plucked a couple of weeds growing on the slight rise above the grave, brushed the dirt off his hands.

Laura stepped up behind him, wrapped her arms around his waist, and rested her head on his strong back. His hands covered hers as he stood staring down at the headstone.

Laura spied another headstone, newer than the rest, directly across from where Nathan's grandmother was buried. Releasing him, she walked over.

HOLLY RENEE MAXWELL

HOME AT LAST

Nathan's mother.

"My grandmother brought her back here to be buried."

She nodded, unsure what to say. She and Nathan moved down the line of graves, stopping to read the names. Generations who were born and died on this farm.

Nathan stopped in front of a headstone so dark, she

could barely make out the engraving. "Turns out I was named for my great-grandfather, and Amanda, my great-grandmother. All those years I felt rootless, adrift in the world, thinking my only family was my sister and my mostly absent mother. And all along I had family roots so deep on these one hundred thirty acres, my sister is a member of the Daughters of the American Revolution."

She could hear the pride in his voice. Pride in a rich ancestry.

"So, what's this history you have with Ricky?"

He just shook his head.

"Come on. You can't expect me to just let the incident in the hardware store go."

He drew her over to a stone bench beneath the oak tree, propped his elbows on his knees and hung his head. Picking up a stick, he began to draw circles with it in a patch of dirt.

"Not long after Amanda and I came to live with our grandmother and started a new school, we were confronted by a group of boys who cornered us on the way home one day. Ricky was their leader.

He heaved out a breath. "Ricky called my mother a whore, said she screwed men for money, and that Amanda and I were bastards who didn't even know who our fathers were. The rest of the kids laughed."

Laura sucked in a breath, her heart breaking for Nathan and sweet Amanda. "What did you do?"

"Other than pulling Amanda behind me, I did nothing. What had Ricky said that wasn't true?"

He dropped the stick, and his hands fisted. "But then they said my mom died of AIDS, asked if I had AIDS. When I didn't answer, Ricky said, 'AIDS got your tongue?' and laughed at his own joke. By that time a small crowd had gathered, some of the kids egging Ricky and his gang on, others just waiting for the fight."

Laura sat tense next to him, barely breathing with the anxiety she felt for him.

"I didn't spend ten years on the streets of Atlanta and not learn a thing or two. I told Amanda to run along. I wanted her far from the fray once it started. When she finally turned to go, Ricky yelled, 'Hey, little girl, you gonna be a whore just like your mother?'"

Laura sucked in a breath. Closed her eyes.

"Well, that did it. I kicked Ricky in the knees, and when he went down screaming, I threw a right hook and caught one of the other boys on the chin. Before he could throw another punch, Ricky was on me. After that everything happened so fast, that I don't remember, but in the end, I had a black eye, a cut above my left eyebrow, and a fat lip, but the other kids were much worse for wear, including Ricky. They might talk big, but they couldn't fight worth a shit. They'd never make it in inner-city Atlanta."

Nathan finally turned to look at her. "Ricky's parting shot was that I'd never be anything but a whore's bastard."

The pain she saw in his face wrenched her heart. Raising her hands, she cupped his face, gazed into his eyes, and said, "I should have kicked Ricky in the nuts when I had the chance."

Nathan barked out a laugh, the corners of his eyes crinkling, eyes sparkling. Mission accomplished.

———

Nathan stretched out his long frame in one of the room's chairs, feet propped up on an ottoman, a beer on the side table, as he watched the Braves baseball game.

After a hot morning spent on the roof of the barn, he deserved a quiet evening. He wasn't opposed to manual labor, he'd done it most of his life, but it sure made him appreciate his cushy office job.

Laura and Amanda sat close on the sofa, their heads bent close over a photo album across their laps.

"Here's Nathan in his baseball uniform."

Laura snickered. "You were so skinny."

"Hey! I filled out when I got older."

"I'll say."

Nathan felt Laura's eyes on him. He took a tug on his beer, turning to look at her and winked.

"Is this you?" Laura asked

"Yes!" Nathan hissed out, doing a fist pump as the Braves drove in two runs.

Amanda giggled. "Yep. That's me with the first vegetables I harvested from my garden. I'd forgotten about that photo. God, I was skinny."

"And that's your grandmother?"

"With one of her many blue ribbons for her award-winning blackberry pie. Mmm. Remember that pie, Nathan?"

"Sure do."

"Try as I might, I just can't get it like hers. Not too sweet, not too tart, and a crust to die for." She closed the photo album and turned her body to face Laura. "What about you? What's your family like?" Amanda asked.

Nathan's ears perked up, but he kept his eyes on the TV.

"Oh, well, let's just say my grandmother doesn't make award-winning pies."

"You're so lucky to still have your grandmother."

Laura drew a pillow across her lap, hugging it to her.

The body language not lost on him, Nathan frowned, remembering her grandmother's treatment of her for going on the cruise and missing her birthday.

"Yeah." Laura's lack of enthusiasm went unnoticed by Amanda.

"How about brothers and sisters?"

"I have a younger brother, but we don't really get along."

"Yeah, some siblings are like that, I guess. I know we get on each other's nerves sometimes, but Nathan and I get along pretty good. And your parents, what do they do?"

After Laura explained that her father owned one of the world's largest shipbuilding companies, Amanda asked, "So you grew up in New York?"

"Yes, well, outside the city. I grew up in Westchester County, about an hour north."

"Must have been something growing up the daughter of one of the world's richest men."

"Oh, it was something." She gave Amanda a wan smile and caught Nathan's eye. Her expression said, *Help.*

———

"**A**manda? Any of that peach cobbler left?"

For once, Laura was happy he read her so well. After that conversation with Amanda in the barn earlier, and then Nathan's story in the cemetery, Laura felt off balance. Out of sorts. And tales of her family woes were not high on her list of topics she wanted to discuss.

"Good gravy, you must have a bottomless pit. It's in the pie safe."

"Hey! I was up on that roof most the day, butterbean."

"Butterbean. How does someone get a nickname like

butterbean?" Laura asked, seizing on an opportunity to take the conversation in another direction. Away from her. "And you can't tell me it was because of your weight."

"I loved butterbeans. I'd never had them until I got to the farm, and I asked to have them every night for dinner." Amanda offered a good-natured shrug. "Pretty soon Gram and Nathan started calling me butterbean."

"And what about Nathan? Does he have a nickname?"

Amanda snickered.

"Oh, we're not going there." He cast an eye toward Amanda. "Don't even think about it."

"Now you really have to tell me," Laura cajoled.

"Amanda," Nathan warned.

His sister looked between him and Laura.

"Come on," Laura said. "I'll protect you."

"I'm not scared of him. I've got too much on him."

Nathan had risen to stand over her, causing her to descend into a case of the giggles.

"It's"—more giggles—"It's hambone." She rolled on the sofa, clutching her stomach, as gales of laughter filled the room.

Laura snorted, then erupted into laughter herself. "Hambone?" She gazed up at Nathan. "Why?"

"Because when Gram baked a ham," Amanda said between chortles, "he'd gnaw the bone clean, he loved ham so much."

Laura laughed again. The nickname tickled her funny bone, but it also tugged at her heart. The thought of two children who'd been living on the edge for so long, finally getting their fill made her thankful for Dorothy Patricia Parham-Maxwell.

———

After an uneventful flight home, he and Laura drove straight to Darcy and Josh's house Monday evening so Nathan could meet with Josh and talk over the best way to handle the bank and the developers.

A tall, clean-cut man in slacks and a dress shirt answered the door.

"Dracula," Laura nodded in greeting.

"Medusa," Josh returned.

"Why did God make snakes before lawyers?" Laura asked.

"To practice," Josh answered.

Nathan lifted a questioning brow at the woman who'd just joined them—the one he'd seen in the photo in Laura's apartment.

"Don't ask," she said, as she shook her head. "You must be Nathan." She stuck out her hand.

"Yes," Nathan replied as he took her dainty hand in his. "Laura tells me you're a writer. Romances, right?" Nathan asked.

"Yes," Darcy said with some reticence.

"What?"

"I'm waiting for the derisive comment."

"I don't have a derisive comment."

"Oh. Sorry. I get a little defensive."

"Why should you apologize for doing what you love?"

"Why, indeed?" Her smile lit up the room, and Nathan liked her instantly.

———

After Laura introduced Nathan and Josh, Darcy said, "You boys talk business, we're going to talk baby stuff."

Laura grimaced. "We are?"

"Yes." Darcy hooked her arm through Laura's and hauled her off to the kitchen. For someone so petite, Darcy sure was strong.

"So that's Sexy Southern Guy, a.k.a. The Liar?" Darcy whispered as soon as they were in the kitchen.

"I thought we were talking baby stuff."

"We are, but first things first. Is it him?"

"Yes."

"I didn't know you were, you know, back together." Darcy gave Laura a non-too-gentle shove. "You don't call. You don't write. How am I supposed to keep up with things?"

"We were never together-together. It was just a ship-board fling."

"And this is what? A New York City fling?"

"Maybe."

"Well he's certainly gorgeous. And, love the accent. It's so Rhett Butler."

"Hello? That's what I tried to tell you."

"What about the competition? The Imperial account?"

"We've agreed not to discuss anything to do with the Imperial account, and may the best woman, or man, win."

"Well, that's very adult of you."

"What does that mean?"

"It means that in Laura's World, everything usually takes a backseat to work. You must really like him if you're willing to let bygones be bygones and not let work interfere."

Laura shrugged. "He's gorgeous and he's great in bed. What's not to like?"

"Well, I *like* him. He didn't make a snide comment

about my profession. That speaks volumes. At least to me it does."

"I'll be sure to keep that in mind," Laura answered. She placed her hand on Darcy's still-flat belly. "How's my godchild treating you?"

"The little peanut is giving me morning sickness, but by noon it's over and done, and then I'm fit as a fiddle."

They spent a half hour catching up with one another, giving Josh and Nathan time to discuss the farm and then returned to the living room where the two men were wrapping up.

"I'll call Elizabeth first thing tomorrow morning and put her in touch with you and Amanda. She's great."

The two men shook hands.

"I can't thank you enough," Nathan said as he wrapped his arm around Laura's waist and gazed down at her. "And I can't thank you enough for introducing me to Josh." He pressed a kiss to her forehead, and she felt the heat creep into her face. Unaccustomed to such intimacy and tenderness, and in front of her friends, the gesture left her feeling awkward.

"Hey," Darcy said, relieving her from further embarrassment, "we're having a party for some of Josh's clients next Friday. We'd love it if you and Nathan would join us."

"Um . . ." Laura hedged, desperately trying to come up with an excuse.

"Oh come on, it'll be fun. Seven o'clock."

Laura released a long-suffering sigh, then looked up at Nathan. "You game?"

"Sure. Why not?"

"Fine."

CHAPTER TWENTY-FOUR

I nstead of dropping her off at the front of her building, Nathan insisted on bringing her luggage up.

In the elevator, he asked, "Why don't you like Josh?"

Laura drew back in surprise. "Who said I didn't like him?"

Nathan barked out a laugh. "Okay, then."

Once she'd opened her door, he set her bags inside, then stepping into her, he ran his hands down her arms before clasping her hands with his. "Thank you."

"For what?"

"For coming with me. For being there for me. For being so nice to Amanda. She really likes you, you know?"

"You're welcome. And I really like her, too."

"The next two days are going to be pure insanity for both of us, so I don't suppose we'll see one another."

"No. Probably not." She already felt lonely.

"So, goodnight." He leaned down and gently kissed her mouth. Pulling back, he gazed into her eyes. "Get some sleep, and start fresh tomorrow." He pressed another gentle kiss to her lips and left.

After the door closed with a quiet click, she leaned against it and sighed like a love-struck teenager.

———

The word insanity didn't begin to cover Laura's Tuesday. It was after nine p.m. before she walked through the doors of her apartment building. Nothing like a fourteen-hour day to make you appreciate a ten-day Mediterranean cruise.

Ignoring the lights, she walked through her dark apartment straight to the bedroom and a nice hot shower. Before she could even slip out of her shoes, her buzzer sounded. "Oh, good gravy! Who could that be?"

"Yes?" Whoever it was would hear the annoyance in her voice.

"It's Nathan. Can I come up?"

Nathan? What was he doing here?

"Everything okay?" she asked.

"Yeah. I just . . . I need to talk to you."

"Come on up."

She walked back through the living room, flipped on some lights, and opened her door.

The usually cool and calm Nathan looked harried as he stepped off the elevator, tie loose, hair mussed as if he'd been running his fingers through it.

He strode up to her, cupped her face in his hands and drew her in for a kiss so soul-searing she felt it all the way to her toes. Wrapping her hands around his wrists, she met his kiss with everything she had. Only one night apart and she craved him like a dieter craves a gallon of ice cream.

He finally broke the kiss. "This is going to complicate

matters even more than they already are, but . . ." He took a deep breath. "I'm in love with you."

She took an automatic step back. "No you're not." Her heart jackhammered in her chest.

"'Fraid so."

"You don't even know me." She took another step back.

He didn't try to close the space she'd created between them. He just stood in the same spot. "Oh, but I do." He spoke softly, his sexy Southern drawl sending tingles along her spine. "I know that you walk around with this cool, I don't give-a-fuck cloak around you, but underneath is a woman who cares deeply for her friends."

"I know that you have a reputation for being a hard-nosed business woman, but that you also use your incredible talent to help a worthwhile cause. I know that you're loyal, that you have a strong work ethic, and that you appreciate beautiful craftsmanship in everything from stilettos to cinnamon buns. That you have the grace and poise of a princess, but you lick your fingers when you eat fried chicken."

She couldn't take her eyes off his face. How could he see these things? Things not even her family could see?

"But I also know that you have a difficult, contentious relationship with your father, and despite that you're successful, generous, and steadfast. That in your apartment you have no photos of your family, but that the photos you do have are of the people you love. And who love you. And I know that when your grandmother disinherited you, it wasn't the loss of the money that upset you."

"Why are you doing this now?" she whispered. Tears stung her eyes.

She looked down, but he reached out, lifted her chin to his gaze. "Because I know you think you have something to prove. To your father. To the world. To yourself. But you have nothing to prove to me. And I wanted you to know that."

She tore away from his grasp as the tears blurred her vision. Nathan stepped back. "I want you to know that win or lose the Imperial account, I'll still love you, and I'll still be proud of you. Good luck tomorrow."

He skimmed a finger along her cheekbone, then turned and left.

———

What the hell was she supposed to do with that? She angrily swiped at the tears that ran down her cheeks. Laura Armstrong did not cry. She didn't become a puddle of mush because some guy confessed his love for her.

Laura Armstrong stood on her own two feet. She ate her competition for lunch. And she lived her job. It had been everything to her for so long. Her family, her significant other, her child. It was who she was. She'd had no room in her life for a man, a commitment, love.

Her shoulders sagged beneath the weight of her sudden revelation. Because the truth was, there was nothing in her life *but* room.

For the first time in her life, she was scared. Scared she'd come to rely on Nathan. Something she swore she'd never do. But also scared that she'd be alone. Left behind. With nothing but her career accomplishments to keep her company.

She always thought the next account she'd landed, the next promotion she'd achieved, would be the one to bring her happiness. That her life would be complete when she'd achieved her Life Plan.

But that wasn't enough anymore. The joy in her job wasn't fading, but something else was taking precedence.

Dammit to hell. Frustrated, she headed for the shower. She couldn't think about this now. She had an account to land.

———

Late Wednesday morning, the Giddings-Rose offices were a hive of activity with the pitch less than two hours away, and the team making last minute changes to the proposal, which they still had to print and bind. All hands were on deck, standing by to jump in and assist with compiling the final pitch packet. With their offices only blocks from Imperial's, they could tweak and perfect right up to the last minute.

Laura paced from creative, with their giant desktop Macs, to research with their spreadsheets, back to creative, all the while relaying questions, ideas, changes. She lived for this! The exhilaration, the adrenaline rush. The hunt. And hopefully, the kill.

Setting aside her worries for Nathan, whose team was presenting at that moment, she focused with laser-like attention on their pitch.

"There's alcohol at the end of this day," she shouted to her team.

Long nights and weekends worth of work would be boiled down into a one-hour pitch. Confident in their approach, Laura only sought to fine-tune the message.

Dante called her over to show her the latest revisions to the app graphics.

"Yes. Just maybe move this"—she pointed to an icon on the screen—"here." She watched a minute as he worked his magic. "Perfect."

Striding down the hall, she popped her head into Katie's office. "Do we have the final numbers for the demographics page?"

"In three seconds . . . here." She handed Laura a printout. Laura then walked back down the hall to creative.

"Who's working on the demographics page?"

Raoul shot up his hand. "Me."

Handing off the printout to him, Laura paced over to Celeste, who was putting the finishing touches on the cover page with the pitch tagline, 'Imperial Cruise Lines, Where unparalleled freedom meets incomparable luxury.'

"We almost there?" Laura asked.

"You tell me." Celeste leaned back so Laura could get a look at the screen.

"That's it! Let's print this baby."

Shouts and clapping exploded around the office.

———

Glancing around the table as he concluded his presentation, Nathan felt good. Damn good, in fact. The presentation had gone very well, with lots of discussion, lots of questions, which showed his audience had been paying attention.

Jack and his father sat among other members of the board, taking notes, casting glances at one another. They'd seemed very intrigued by the Braniff Airways-inspired campaign, and with the name for the new line Hawk Media had proposed: Halcyon Cruises.

"Ladies and gentleman," Nathan concluded, "thank

you for your time and your attention. I appreciated the interaction and the opportunity to present to you today."

"Thank you, Nathan. We'll have our decision to you in about a week," Jackson said, receiving nods from the other board members. "Great job."

Nathan looked over at Hawk, and received a subtle nod of approval. Releasing a calming breath, he gathered his documents as his audience stood and left the room for a much-needed fifteen-minute break before Giddings-Rose presented. He knew Laura would be outside with her team, feeling the same jitters as he'd had over an hour ago.

Hawk clapped him on the shoulder as they left the room. He leaned in and whispered, "You nailed it."

Nathan's smile of relief froze when he saw Laura standing with her team. She appeared every inch the polished professional in a navy suit and creamy blouse that managed to appear both conservative and sexy at the same time. A pair of snakeskin stilettos graced her feet.

She must have felt his eyes on her, because she glanced up. She lifted her brows as if to ask, 'How'd it go?'

He replied with a short nod.

As he and Hawk proceeded to the elevator bank, he gave himself a mental headshake. Who would have ever thought that he'd be wishing his competition good luck?

———

As the board members filed back in for the Giddings-Rose pitch, Laura had Celeste place a proposal at each seat.

Jack came into the room, nodded her way, his father behind him. *This was it*, she thought. This was the account that would earn her a VP position. The next step in her Life Plan was coming together.

When she took her phone out of her purse to turn it off, she saw a text from Nathan.

I KNOW YOU AND YOUR TEAM WILL GO OUT AFTERWARD TO BLOW OFF SOME STEAM, BUT GIVE ME A CALL LATER. WE'LL BLOW OFF SOME STEAM OF OUR OWN.

She thought about his confession last night and she wondered, Could Nathan be part of my Life Plan?

———

That Friday evening, Nathan escorted Laura up the sidewalk to Darcy's house for a party she had no desire to attend, but Nathan seemed set on going.

"We only have to stay an hour," she said, as they climbed the steps to the front door.

"Whatever you want."

Laura opened the door and entered.

"Don't you knock?" Nathan asked.

"Please. It's Darcy."

She stepped into the foyer, Nathan right behind her, and glanced around for Darcy. She saw her talking to Gloria, her agent. To her left stood Josh talking with his in-laws. Darcy's brother, Brandon handed a plate of food to his partner. Millie stood in the shadows as was her want. She'd yet to see anyone who might be one of Josh's clients.

Just as confusion began to set in, all the guests turned in her direction and yelled, "Surprise!"

"What the—"

Nathan's hands grasped her hips as he stepped up behind her and whispered, "Happy Birthday, sugar."

That was when she saw Katie, Celeste, and Curt from the office.

The next few minutes were utter chaos with hugs from Darcy and her parents and siblings. Even Gloria gave her a pat on the back.

She blinked back tears, wondering when she'd gotten so sappy.

Josh followed suit with a kiss to her cheek. "Maleficent."

"Prince Humperdinck."

"Wait." Josh held up his hand. "How many account executives does it take to change a light bulb?"

Laura blinked in confusion.

"How many would you like?" Josh replied.

Laura shook her head. "I don't get it."

"Were you surprised?" Darcy asked as she pressed a glass of champagne into her hand.

Gratefully she took the bubbly and threw it back, hoping to calm her nerves. "My birthday isn't until Wednesday."

"I know. But who wants to celebrate on a Wednesday?"

"No one, that's who. Let's party!"

―――――

Nathan watched as Darcy and Laura entered the living room. Laura didn't realize how many people loved her. Him included.

Though her parents were noticeably absent.

The night he'd met with Josh, Josh had enlisted his help to get Laura to her birthday party. Nathan was more than happy to join the conspiracy.

True to form, when he'd picked Laura up, she'd knocked his socks off. Dressed in a dark-blue drapey jumpsuit that brought out the blue in her eyes and left lots of luscious skin bare, her hair flowing down her back. Her designer fragrance wreaking havoc on his libido. He already anticipated getting her out of the jumpsuit and into bed.

Josh approached. "Thanks for joining in the conspiracy. Darcy was stressed trying to figure out how to get Laura here, and with the baby, she doesn't need the stress."

"No problem. When is she due?" Nathan asked.

"April."

"Congratulations."

"Thanks. We're both very excited."

"Josh, are Laura's parents coming?"

A grimace passed over Josh's features. "No. They, uh, had a previous engagement."

"I see."

"Do you?" Josh turned to Nathan. "Do you see that she deserves so much better than she thinks she does? That she's worth what it takes to dig beneath that prickly exterior and see her for who she is?"

Nathan considered Josh's astute observation before answering, "Yes. I do."

———

The party was in full swing when the doorbell rang. Standing closest to the door, Laura opened it to find Jack and another hot hunk standing on the stoop.

"Jack! What are you doing here?"

"Sorry we're late, but I didn't want to miss the party."

Stepping inside, he pressed a kiss to Laura's cheek, and glanced behind him at his friend.

"Laura, this is my friend, Novak Hunter. Novak, Laura Armstrong."

As she shook Novak's hand, she got the distinct impression he was more than just a friend.

She shot a glance at Jack, who gave her an imperceptible nod.

Happy for Jack, she led the couple into the room and began the introductions.

"Jack," Nathan said, "I didn't expect to see you here."

"Well, I just stopped by for a few minutes to wish my girl here happy birthday."

"I see."

Laura looked up in time to see the frown on Nathan's face, and she had to smile. Clearly, Nathan was still jealous of Jack and what he thought was their affair.

"Nathan, this is Novak. Jack's friend."

"Novak." Nathan nodded. "Can I talk to you a minute?" he asked, lips tight.

"Sure. Please excuse us."

Nathan steered her into a tidy office. "Why is he here?"

"Since I didn't send out the invitations, I can only surmise that Josh or Darcy invited him." Her voice had gone cool. Jealousy was one thing, rudeness another.

"I thought you weren't seeing him anymore?"

"I'm not." She sighed. "I never was, actually."

"What does that mean?"

"It means, Nathan, that Jack and I were never having an affair."

"What? Why did you leave me to believe you were?"

"First, you jumped to your own conclusions that night at the fundraiser. Then I did it just to piss you off. But then . . ." Laura hesitated.

"But then?" Nathan prodded.

"But then I did it to protect Jack."

"What do you mean, 'to protect Jack?'"

"Jack's and my family have been friends for a long time, but beyond that, I consider Jack my friend."

"And?"

She blew out a breath and seemed to be wrestling with something. "Nathan, that man out there, Novak, isn't just Jack's friend." At Nathan's continued confusion, she clarified, "You know, his partner. His lover."

She watched as comprehension dawned, and his brows shot up. "No, way."

"Yes, way. Jack is gay."

"Well, I'll be damned. Why didn't you tell me?"

"It wasn't my secret to share."

"Woman. You are something else." Enfolding her in his arms, he pressed a kiss to the top of her head. "Loyal to the bone."

CHAPTER TWENTY-FIVE

As soon as Nathan and Laura got back to her apartment, she stepped out of her heels. "You are a sneak," she said, as she waggled her finger in his face. "How long have you known about this party?"

"Since the night Josh and I first met. He enlisted my help to get you there," he said with a grin.

Laura shook her head, as he wrapped his arms around her waist and kissed her nose.

"I like your friends."

"Yeah, me, too."

He swayed with her in his arms, "And you know what, they really like you. In fact, they love you, you know that?"

"Pfft."

"And so do I."

She grew still in his arms, so he withdrew, and reaching into his pocket pulled out a box.

"This is for you. I bought it in Florence, but we had . . . well, you know."

Her heart jackhammered in her chest.

He reached out for her hand and, turning her palm up, placed the box there. "Open it."

Laura looked from the box to his face, her breath shallow.

Lifting the lid, she saw a pair of delicate silver earrings, set with sapphires.

"They reminded me of your eyes," he whispered, as he pressed his forehead to hers.

"Oh, Nathan, they're beautiful." She brushed a finger over them as if they were the most fragile thing she'd ever seen. No one had ever given her such a thoughtful gift. Ever.

"I'm glad you like them."

"I don't like them, I love them." She encircled his neck, drew his mouth down to hers.

———

"Laura Armstrong," she said into the phone. She sat at her desk on Wednesday morning, her birthday, going over emails.

"Ms. Armstrong, this is Melinda, Mr. Jack Jeffries' assistant."

Laura's heart plummeted like an elevator with a broken cable. "Yes," she could barely get the word out around the knot in her throat.

"It's short notice, but he would like to know if you're free for lunch today."

"Yes." She didn't look at her calendar. She'd make it work.

"Perfect. He'll meet you at Fred's at noon."

"Did we get the account?"

"I really can't say."

"Right. Thank you." She hung up the phone, and pressed her hand to her stomach to still the butterflies that had suddenly taken flight. Her face split into a grin so wide it hurt.

Then she sat back with a groan. "Oh, God." If Giddings-Rose got the account, that meant Hawk Media didn't. Which meant no bonus for Nathan. What would Nathan do about Amanda and the farm? And her?

———

Nathan strode down the hall to Hawk's office, entering without knocking. "This is it."

Hawk glanced up from his computer, a questioning look on his face.

"Imperial just called. Mr. Jeffries wants the team down there at two o'clock for a meeting."

Hawk came around the corner of his desk, clapped Nathan on the back. "Good job, man. Good job."

"Thanks." The relief was palpable. The bonus was his, and the farm was Amanda's, free and clear.

As he walked back down the hall to his office, Nathan's elation took a hit and his steps slowed. "Holy hell," he muttered. Laura wouldn't get her VP position.

———

Laura followed the hostess to Jack's table. Taking a deep breath, she plastered a smile on her face to cover her nerves. Jack rose, greeted her warmly with a kiss to her cheek.

After she took her seat, Jack told the hostess he'd signal when they were ready to order. Seeking to quell her already bouncing leg, Laura pressed her hand to knee, but something about his expression gave her pause.

"Laura, I won't keep you on pins and needles. I know how much the Imperial account means to you."

Dread filled her, leaving a bad taste in her mouth.

Jack took a deep breath. "Imperial decided to go with Hawk Media."

Nothing like ripping the Band-Aid off. "I see." She would. Not. Cry.

"I wanted to be the one to tell you. In person. As your friend, I owe you that much." He reached out and covered her hand with his.

She pulled away. His gesture of kindness only made it that much more difficult not to cry. "Thank you." She cleared her throat of the tears building there.

"I'm sorry. The board thought that Hawk Media's ideas were innovative, but maintained the spirit that is Imperial."

She couldn't bear the sympathy in his eyes.

"I appreciate you telling me." She sat silent for a couple of beats. "But dammit!" Looking away, she swallowed her anger and frustration.

"I hope we can remain friends," Jack said, his voice soft and sincere.

"Don't be ridiculous, Jack. Of course we can remain friends." She took a sip of water, hoping it would clear her throat before she continued. "Hawk Media is an excellent agency. I'm happy for Nathan." And she was. Truly happy for him. And Amanda. She'd be able to keep the farm. "Does he know yet?"

"No. We're meeting the team at two o'clock, so I'd appreciate it if you'd keep this under your hat until then."

"Naturally." Well, this was some thirtieth birthday present.

"Shall we order?" Jack asked, breaking into her thoughts.

"I don't think so. I hope you understand."

He nodded. "Of course."

She rose from the table, reached her hand out for Jack to shake. Instead, he brought her hand to his lips and kissed the top. "I always knew you were a class act, Laura Armstrong."

Squaring her shoulders, she made her way through the crowded restaurant. Stunned, she barely responded to the maître d' as he wished her a good afternoon. She stepped out into the July heat, ignoring the doorman's offer to hail a cab for her. She'd rather walk.

Thinking of Nathan's concern that her relationship with Jack made the winning agency a foregone conclusion, she laughed. A harsh bark that drew the unwelcome attention of another pedestrian.

Her father came to mind. She wondered if he had influenced the decision.

What the hell was she going to do now?

First, she'd wait until two as Jack had asked, then she'd put on her big-girl panties and tell her team and her boss the news and congratulate Nathan.

Then, she'd lick her wounds and re-evaluate.

———

"Good afternoon." Jackson's mellow voice drew everyone's attention as he entered the room. Jack stood next to his father, who nodded at him.

Jack took a seat at the head of the table and folded his hands in front of him. "I realize this is rather unorthodox, but I prefer to give such news in person."

"First, I speak for myself and the board when I say both agencies gave excellent pitches."

Ah, the consolation speech, Nathan thought with a sigh. Well, Laura would get her promotion. She deserved it.

"The ideas presented were fresh, innovative, cutting edge even." Jack continued after a brief pause, "Both agencies have a solid reputation for getting the job done, or we wouldn't have given you the opportunity to pitch. That being said, this has been a very difficult decision on the one hand, and a very easy one on the other."

Nathan held back a groan, wishing Jack would just get to the point, which was that Nathan could kiss his bonus goodbye. And he'd have to figure out some other way to get the farm back on its feet.

"After much discussion among the board members, Imperial has elected to go with Hawk Media."

Nathan jerked his head up. *What?* His breath left in a rush.

Did Laura know? he wondered. And if so, how was she handling it? For his part, he was experiencing a discordant concoction of excitement and misery.

"Each agency had very different, and very intriguing approaches to refreshing Imperial's brand, but the board thought Hawk understood the Imperial philosophy better. We especially liked that you weren't proposing to throw the baby out with the bath water. Imperial will still cater to the clients who brought us to the dance, but we'll add a new line, a new clientele, to take us into the future of cruising. In fact, with the help of Hawk Media, we'll redefine the cruise industry."

"So, congratulations to you"—he nodded to Nathan— "and your entire team. We look forward to working with you."

CHAPTER TWENTY-SIX

Hawk and Nathan shared the company car back to the office.

"Great job, Nathan. Congratulations for landing our biggest account to date."

"Thanks. It feels good."

"Now, you want to tell me how your relationship with Laura is going?"

"How'd you—" Nathan choked out.

"Because I've seen Laura Armstrong, and if I were single and in your shoes, I wouldn't give her up."

Son-of-a-bitch.

Nathan's phone buzzed with an incoming text.

"Go ahead. I'm sure it's important." Hawk took out his own phone and called his wife to tell her the news.

Nathan read the text . . . from Laura. It said, simply: Congratulations. And his euphoria took a nose dive.

Sunday evening, Laura sat on the back porch of her family's vacation home in the Hamptons, watching dusk turn to dark, a glass of Kentucky bourbon at her elbow.

She'd spent the last two days walking the beach, the nights watching the stars, and reassessing. Her life, her career, her future.

Her relationship with her father aside, everything she'd set her mind to, she'd achieved. Defeat was a new experience for her, and she didn't like it. It left a bitter taste in her mouth and a hollow feeling in her stomach.

Taking a sip of the bourbon, she let it burn its way down her throat and into her belly. Holding up the glass to the waning light, she thought of Nathan and wondered what he and his team had done to celebrate.

She'd ignored his countless text messages and phone calls. Didn't listen to his voice messages.

A guilty pang pierced her heart. A good sport would have celebrated with him. But she hadn't felt like being a good sport. She'd felt like sulking.

To assuage her guilt, even if only a *soupçon*, she lifted her glass in a silent toast to him, then sighed.

What would her father say about her defeat?

Then it struck her. Nothing. He would have said nothing even if she'd won the account and secured her promotion. It didn't matter to him, one way or the other. It would *never* matter to him. She could become President of the United States and he'd still think of her as a monumental failure. The little girl who'd publicly humiliated her father.

For some reason, the realization that she'd never change her father's mind was freeing.

Why had she lived her life trying to please him? Trying

to prove something to him? She had nothing to prove to anyone. Not even herself. Nathan had said so himself.

Nathan.

She drew her legs up under her, took another sip of bourbon. If she were completely honest with herself, the time she'd spent with Nathan had been the happiest time in her life. What did achieving the next step in Laura's Life Plan mean, if she had no one with whom to share it? No one with whom to celebrate the achievements? And no one with whom to lament the failures?

And now? The hollowness in her stomach moved to her chest. She missed Nathan. She remembered burrowing into him on the cruise after she'd learned her grandmother had disinherited her. How he'd helped the passenger who fell, and how he'd chased off her attacker in Pompeii. How he'd made her laugh. And how he'd made her shiver when he whispered his sweet southern nothings in her ear.

Groaning, she tossed back the rest of the bourbon. She was a *schmuck*. Nathan had worked hard and had achieved something that would not only enhance his reputation in the advertising world, but that would save his family farm and his sister's livelihood, and all she'd done to show her pride was congratulate him in a text message.

She'd have to see what she could do to fix that.

———

Nathan looked up as his assistant approached his desk carrying a large gift basket.

"Who's that from?"

"I don't know. You'll need to open the card." She handed him a small envelope and then stuck around the end of the desk, clearly curious.

Nathan lifted a brow at her, but she simply smiled in return. *Fine.* He slipped his letter opener beneath the flap and withdrew the card.

I'm so proud of you ! Can you forgive me for being a selfish bitch? If so, I'd love to celebrate with you later. Alone. Bring the Champagne.

Sitting back in his chair, Nathan didn't know what to think. His text and voice messages had been ignored. He'd figured Laura had decided she couldn't maintain their relationship after losing the account to him.

He understood her disappointment. He'd been disappointed for her. But dammit. To completely ignore him. He'd been worried sick about her. And hurt.

"*Somebody* has excellent taste," Cassie said, as she poked around the basket. "*Krug Clos du Mesnil* Champagne, Belgian chocolates, and . . . pork rinds?"

"Yes. Thanks for the inventory."

"What are pork rinds?"

"A Southern delicacy." He tore through the cellophane wrapping the basket, grabbed the bottle of champagne, and rounded his desk. "I'm taking the afternoon."

———

"Someone's here to see you," Sanjita said.

Laura glanced up. "Okay." She shrugged at Katie's confused expression.

Sanjita stepped aside and Nathan strode in, looking so good she could climb him like a tree. God, how she'd missed him. "Nathan! What are you doing here?"

"You haven't returned my text messages or calls, so I

came over to talk to you in person." He nodded a greeting to Katie.

"I'll just . . . go . . . analyze some demographics," Katie said, a grin on her face as she left the room.

"Think you can break away from your day for a few minutes?"

She lifted a brow. "What have you got in mind? I could be wrong, but I think HR frowns upon office quickies."

Nathan laughed, the sound music to her ears.

He took her hand and led her in the direction of her sofa, raising her expectations for that quickie.

She waited expectantly for him to make his move. Kiss her . . . something. Instead, he just stared.

"You hurt me," he said, his voice gruff with emotion.

She drew back. Not what she'd expected. She gazed into his warm, golden eyes and with all the remorse she felt, she said, "I'm so sorry."

"I was also worried about you."

"You were?"

"Of course. I didn't know where you were, what state of mind you were in, nothing. Even Darcy didn't know where you were."

"You called Darcy?" That explained the panicky text message from Darcy.

"I didn't know who else to call."

"Again, I'm sorry."

He nodded. "Don't ever do it again."

Ever? That sounded so . . . long term. "No. I won't."

"Good." He took a deep breath then knelt in front of her, taking her hands in his.

Thinking he had something naughty in mind, she released a nervous laugh. When he hesitated, a little warning bell went off in her head.

"Marry me, Laura."

"Mar—" She snatched her hands from his grasp, threw them up in exasperation. "Are you crazy?"

"Yes. Crazy in love with you."

"In case you haven't noticed, I'm not the marrying kind." She stood, tried to turn away from him, but he rose, placing his hands on her shoulders.

"Why do you think it's so impossible that someone could love you? Want to marry you?"

"You know the answer to that. I came from a family that didn't feel love, much less express it." She swallowed around the knot in her throat. "I don't know how to do this," she whispered. "What more proof do you need than my recent behavior? Don't you see? I'm not equipped for love, let alone a commitment."

"You're wrong. You may not have had the greatest role models when it came to love, but you know *how* to love. You do it every day with those close to you. It comes so naturally to you that you don't even notice you're doing it."

She shook her head, tears blurring her vision. Love? Did she love him?

"I love you, Laura. I want to spend the rest of my life showing you just how much."

"I'm scared."

"Me, too. I've never done this before. But I want to take the plunge with you." He smiled as he took her hand in his, brought it to his lips. "Marry me."

"Say yes!" Katie blurted out.

Laura turned to see the doorway to her office crowded with people, Katie front and center.

Katie's entreaty was followed by a chorus of similar encouragements.

"Come on, marry him," Sanjita chimed in.

"Yeah, come on," Havi goaded.

"What are you waiting for?" Katie added.

"Are you going to leave me hanging here? In front of all these people?" Nathan asked as he looked down at her.

She swiped at the tears on her cheeks, the butterflies in her stomach beating a rapid staccato. "Yes. I mean, no. I mean, I'm not going to leave you hanging." She drew in a breath, released it on a shaky sigh. "Yes, I'll marry you."

Nathan pulled her in for what Darcy would have called the Perfect Kiss, filled with tenderness, lust, and love. Retreating just inches from his mouth, Laura stared into his eyes. The quivering in her belly settled as she finally said the words she never thought she'd say. "I love you."

Looked like Laura's Life Plan had just changed. For the better.

EPILOGUE

I t was only fitting that she and Nathan were married on the *Nave dei Sogni*, their Ship of Dreams. As his gift to his two favorite advertising executives, Jackson had provided the ship exclusively for their wedding and honeymoon, during a week the ship would normally have been out of service.

As the ship churned through the dark November Mediterranean waters, she and Nathan spoke their vows in front of the ship's captain in a short, intimate ceremony.

After saying their 'I do's' they joined the revelers in the main dining room for toasts and roasts.

Everyone who meant the most to her and Nathan had made the trip. Even Katie finally got her chance to sail on the 'floating Four Seasons on crack.'

Laura noticed that Gloria had already made friends with Sergio the bartender, while Darcy sipped her club soda with lime. Laura admitted to being worried about her friend being seasick on the ship, but Darcy looked like the picture of health, her baby bump visible beneath her teal bridesmaid's gown.

Josh and Millie stuck to her like glue, jumping to attention at any twinge of discomfort on her face.

Nathan's sister Amanda stood talking with Darcy's brother and sister, while Jack and Novak huddled together near the food, heads bent in conversation. She couldn't be happier for Jack. It seemed he'd finally found that special someone.

Just as she'd found hers. She gazed down at the simple platinum band she now wore on her left ring finger. The diamonds could come later. Paying off the mortgages on the farm the first priority.

Speak of the devil. Her Sexy Southern Gentleman made his way across the room, his eyes on hers, a soft smile lifting the corners of his mouth.

Taking her hand, he led her out on the dance floor for their first dance as husband and wife. Laura thought such traditions foolish, but Darcy insisted.

"Sugar, have I told you how beautiful you look?"

"Only a half dozen times." Laura laughed. "But don't let that stop you from telling me again. You look pretty hot yourself." Simple, elegant black tuxedo, satin shawl collar, black tie. Oh yes. He looked *damned* hot. Rhett Butler, eat your heart out.

"Thank you, Mrs. Maxwell."

They swayed to the music for a few beats.

"I'm okay if you want to hyphenate your name, you know," Nathan offered.

She drew back. "No. This may sound strange, but I feel more at home with you and Amanda than I ever felt with my own family. I'm proud to take your name."

His chest swelled, and his throat tightened as he gazed down at Laura. *His wife.* Just when he thought he couldn't get any happier.

When she'd glided down the aisle, all poise and grace, his heart had skipped a beat, maybe two. She looked sophisticated and sexy, elegant and breathtaking, all at once. Her white lace dress hugged her curves in all the right places. She'd flashed him the sardonic smile he remembered so well on that day only seven months earlier when he'd rescued her from her predicament.

When he'd seen that she wore those same red shoes beneath her wedding gown, he'd chuckled to himself.

In seven months he'd met and married the woman of his dreams, landed the account of his dreams, and paid off the mortgage on the farm. Amanda was now free and clear of any debt, and could focus her energies on making the farm profitable.

Someone tapped Nathan on the shoulder. Hawk. "May I cut in?"

Nathan stepped back, allowing Hawk to dance with his wife.

"Congratulations, Laura," Hawk said as he led her around the dance floor.

"Thank you."

"I just wanted to tell you how much the folks at Hawk Media have enjoyed working with you these last few months. I have to be honest, I was skeptical at first. I didn't know how this little joint venture would work, but you allayed those fears with your professionalism."

Hawk Media had hired Giddings-Rose to handle some of the media buying and to oversee the development of her idea for the Concierge Tours App.

"If we're being honest, I'd have to say the same thing. I thought there might be some resentment between the two agencies, but we've really melded over the last few months."

"This could the beginning of a beautiful relationship," Hawk said. "Not unlike your's and Nathan's."

Laura drew back. "Well, aren't you the romantic."

The music ended. Taking her hand and placing it in the crook of his arm, he escorted her to where Nathan stood watching them.

"I was just telling your wife how impressed I've been with her work and professionalism," Hawk said, as he returned her to Nathan's care.

"If you're so impressed with her, why doesn't she work for you?" Nathan asked Hawk.

"That's a good question." Hawk turned to Laura, "Why don't you work for me?"

"Because I'd want your job," Laura returned, without missing a beat.

Hawk's eyes widened, then he chuckled. "Enough said."

———

Gloria tottered around the wedding guests, proud of her latest accomplishment. And she thought getting Darcy hitched had been difficult. Queen of the Booty Calls proved to be nearly impossible.

She snorted as she passed Milton. At least his nose wasn't stuck in his phone, but only because there was no signal.

Her gaze roamed the room's shadows where she knew Millie would be hiding. Spotting her not far from where

Darcy stood with her brother, she shook her head. At least Darcy had managed to get her in a dress that wasn't brown.

No rest for the weary. Throwing back her gin and tonic, she approached Darcy.

"I've been thinking."

Darcy absentmindedly rubbed her protruding belly. "About what?"

"Well, you'll be needing a nursery for my great-godchild, and I'd like to make that my gift."

Darcy's eyes widened as she gazed at Gloria. "Your gift?"

"Yeah. You know, remodel that guest room down the hall from the master bedroom. Paint, window-coverings, maybe some built-in bookcases or something."

"But—"

"No buts. Just accept my gift."

"O-Okay."

"I have just the guy to do the work."

"Sure. Give him my number, and have him give me a call when we get back. What's his name?"

"Ian. Ian Brand."

Her work done for the night, Gloria headed off to the bar for another drink. Matchmaking was thirsty work. "Hey, sweetcakes," she called to Sergio, "how about another Bombay Sapphire gin and tonic?"

Turning back to the room, her eyes lit on Millie. "Hang on, girlie, your time is coming."

REVIEWS

Did you enjoy this book? Please let other potential readers know.

Reviews are the most powerful tool in an author's toll box when it comes to gaining new readers–more powerful even than the most expensive ads. Honest reviews help bring them to the attention of other readers.

If you enjoyed this book, I would be grateful if you could take a few minutes to leave an honest review on the retailer's website. Even a short review can help.

Thank you!

DREAMS OF HER OWN

EXCERPT FROM BOOK 3 OF THE DREAMS COME TRUE SERIES

If the Guinness Book of World Records had a category for the world's most boring life, Millie Stephens knew she would hold the record.

Bundled up in her brown wool coat against the chill of a New York fall, she hurried down the Brooklyn sidewalk to the pharmacy to pick up a prescription for her boss.

As personal assistant for best-selling romance author, Darcy Butler-Ryan, Millie kept her calendar, edited her manuscripts, handled her social media, and through her agent, Gloria Madison, scheduled her public appearances, among other duties. Since Darcy had become pregnant, Millie had also taken it upon herself to run errands and generally oversee Darcy's health and well-being.

Thus, the trip to the pharmacy for Darcy's anti-nausea medication.

She consulted the day's to-do list to see what other errands were on it. Lists were her life. They provided organization, structure, and a sense of accomplishment. She loved ticking things off her list so much that if she accomplished something that wasn't on the list, she'd write it down just so she could have the pleasure of marking it off.

She had a list for everything. Errands. Tasks. Books to be read. Special dates to remember. If something needed doing, she had a list for it, all appropriately categorized, of course. Shoving her errand list into her coat pocket, she stopped at the corner and waited for the pedestrian signal. As soon as the light changed, she stepped out into the pedestrian crosswalk, anxious to get to the pharmacy and out of the cold. She glanced to her left and froze, as a delivery truck barreled down the street as if the red light meant nothing. And as if she truly were invisible.

Fear stole her ability to move and she scrunched her eyes closed hoping death would at least be quick. She strived for invisibility, but now she'd give anything to stand out.

Next thing she knew she was yanked from behind and hauled up against a hard object, bands of steel around her waist, her feet dangling in the air.

"Are you okay?" a gruff male voice asked, his breath warm in her ear.

She nodded, unsure if she could do any more than that.

"I'm going to set you back on your feet. Do you think you can stand?"

Nodding again, she realized the hard object at her back was a man's chest, and the steel bands were his arms. She slid down his body and felt the sidewalk beneath her feet. A wave of dizziness washed over her.

"Breathe," her rescuer encouraged. He turned her to face him, his hands on her shoulders, and she gazed up and into eyes the color of a winter-gray sky, earnest with concern. His already tousled brown hair ruffled in the wind whipping around the corner, and his chin bore the stubble so many women were fond of.

She inhaled deeply, drawing in the scent of something spicy and leathery. "Better?"

She nodded, still speechless.

"You should always wait after the signal changes before you cross a street. I've got an appointment. You're sure you're okay?"

She nodded.

"Be more careful next time," the stranger in the leather jacket said before he turned to walk away.

Millie managed to put one foot in front of the other for another block before coming to a bus stop and collapsing onto the bench. Her legs shook, her hands quivered, and she struggled to take in a deep breath. All she could think about was how your life was supposed to flash before your eyes when confronted with a near-death experience, and hers . . . didn't. Instead it was like a film projector that had run out of film – just a blank screen.

What did that mean?

It meant, Millicent Grace Stephens, that your life has been so boring that the highlight reel was nonexistent. Her thirtieth birthday was right around the corner, and what had she accomplished with her life?

Not much, that's what.

Sure, she had a bachelor's in literature, summa cum laude, with a focus on the Middle Ages from Sarah Lawrence College. She had a job she loved. And she could support herself. Other than that, she might as well have become a nun for all the excitement her life held.

She recalled the hard strength of her rescuer's chest against her back. The rough and tumble look of him. She'd bet her first edition autographed copy of Edith Wharton's

Age of Innocence, that his life wasn't boring. That if he had a near-death experience he'd have a highlight reel worthy of an action movie.

Rising on still-wobbly legs, she drew in a long, slow breath, and resumed her errand in an I-almost-died daze.

ABOUT THE AUTHOR

Rebecca Heflin is a bestselling, award-winning author who has dreamed of writing romantic fiction since she was fifteen and her older sister sneaked a copy of Kathleen Woodiwiss' Shanna to her and told her to read it.

Never quite sure what she wanted to be when she grew up, Rebecca didn't attend college until age 30, and earned her bachelor's in literature, before going on to complete her law degree.

Ever the late bloomer, Rebecca finally turned her attention to fulfilling her dream of writing, and published her first novel at age 48. When not passionately pursuing her dream, Rebecca is busy with her day-job at a major state university.

She and her husband are also co-founders of a non-profit organization, which raises money to help cancer patients and their families.

Rebecca's pen name is an abbreviated version of her great-great grandmother's name: Sarah Anne Rebecca Heflin

Apple Smith. Whew! And you wonder why she shortened it.

Rebecca writes women's fiction and contemporary romance, and she is a member of Romance Writers of America (RWA), Florida Romance Writers, RWA Contemporary Romance, and Florida Writers Association. Rebecca and her mountain-climbing husband live at sea level in sunny Florida.

Sign up for Rebecca's monthly newsletter, Rebecca's Readers, for all the latest news on upcoming releases, appearances, and contests.

ALSO BY REBECCA HEFLIN

THE PROMISE OF CHANGE

RESCUING LACEY

DREAMS COME TRUE SERIES

DREAMS OF PERFECTION, BOOK 1

DREAMS OF HER OWN, BOOK 3

STERLING UNIVERSITY SERIES

ROMANCING DR. LOVE, BOOK 1

WINNING DR. WENTWORTH, BOOK 2

EDUCATING DR. MAYFIELD, BOOK 3

SEASONS OF NORTHRIDGE SERIES

A SEASON TO DANCE, BOOK 1

A SEASON TO LOVE, BOOK 2